The Turncoat's Gambit

The Turncoat's Gambit

Andrea Cremer

PHILOMEL BOOKS

PHILOMEL BOOKS

an imprint of Penguin Random House LLC
375 Hudson Street, New York, NY 10014

Copyright © 2016 by Seven Crows Inc.
Map illustration © 2014 by Rodica Prato.
Penguin supports copyright. Copyright fuels creativity, encourages diverse voices, promotes free speech, and creates a vibrant culture. Thank you for buying an authorized edition of this book and for complying with copyright laws by not reproducing, scanning, or distributing any part of it in any form without permission. You are supporting writers and allowing Penguin to continue to publish books for every reader.

Philomel Books is a registered trademark of Penguin Random House LLC.

Library of Congress Cataloging-in-Publication Data
Names: Cremer, Andrea R., author. | Title: The turncoat's gambit / Andrea Cremer. | Description: New York, NY: Philomel Books, [2016] | Sequel to: The conjurer's riddle. | Summary: "In an alternate nineteenth-century America, Charlotte is on the run from both the empire and the revolution. Now she must figure out whom she trusts, once and for all"—Provided by publisher. | Identifiers: LCCN 2016003127 | ISBN 9780399164255 (hardback) | Subjects: | CYAC: Science fiction. | Adventure and adventurers—Fiction. | Voyages and travels—Fiction. | Classification: LCC PZ7.C86385 Tu 2016 | DDC [Fic]—dc23 | LC record available at https://lccn.loc.gov/2016003127

Printed in the United States of America.
ISBN 9780399164255
1 3 5 7 9 10 8 6 4 2

Edited by Jill Santopolo.   Design by Semadar Megged.
Text set in 11.75-point Sabon MT Std.

In honor of John Santopolo

British
Territory

Disputed
Western
Territory

Mexican
Territory

Pacific
Ocean

Indian
Territory

Mississippi
Trade
Zone

Amherst Province

Cornwallis Province

Arnold Province

French
Territory

Spanish Territory

Atlantic
Ocean

Disputed British/French
Caribbean

In a revolution, as in a novel,
the most difficult part to invent is the end.

Alexis de Tocqueville

COMMODORE COE WINTER unbuttoned his stiff officer's jacket while his mind soured on the knowledge that he'd misjudged a situation and that his mistake would be costly. Perhaps too costly. He shrugged the jacket from his shoulders and would have tossed the garment onto the bed, but then thought better of it. With a measure of care, Coe laid the jacket over the back of a chair. In the Floating City, whether at the House of Winter or his officer's quarters on the Military Platform, a valet would have collected any of Coe's cast-off clothing, making sure to clean, fold, and press all pieces of the commodore's wardrobe so they would be ready when needed again.

The spare room Coe occupied in the Daedalus Tower offered no such luxuries. Coe's quarters bore no ornamentation. A serviceable but plain desk sat opposite an equally serviceable and equally plain bed. The room had no windows, and the reek of iron seeped into all things in any way permeable. More than once, Coe had had to stop himself from crinkling his nose while in New Orleans when he realized the stagnant, metallic odor clung to his clothing, accompanying him wherever he went.

For a commanding officer of the Imperial Air Force, being cooped up in an iron fortress proved a particularly agonizing torment. Necessity had brought Commodore Winter to New Orleans, but not a day passed without Coe wishing his fate might somehow have kept him in the Floating City or at least aboard one of the great Imperial warships that patrolled the skies.

Only a little while longer, and things will change. Coe hardly found comfort in the thought, considering that his own folly had without a doubt prolonged his stay in the French colonial city. But nothing could change that now. It was time to move forward, adjusting his strategy in accordance with recent, unfortunate developments.

Coe didn't relish relating this latest information to his superiors, but there was no helping that either. He went to the desk and bent over a long narrow strip of paper. Taking up a pen, Coe dipped the metal nib into an inkwell and set to writing his message, in cipher, of course.

2.

NEVER BEFORE HAD Charlotte experienced a terror of heights, but as the *Perseus* forsook the waves for the clouds, she wondered if she might not succumb to such a fear. The ship continued its ascent, leaping into the heavens as the churning seas below grew distant. Charlotte glanced at Jack and took comfort in seeing his face was a mask of astonishment that matched her own. He was still holding her, and Charlotte thought to move away and make an attempt to get her bearings but instead grabbed his shirtsleeve when a long, loud metallic groan made the deck shudder beneath them, as if some massive beast had been roused from slumber and now moved restlessly belowdeck. The sound and its accompanying vibrations continued, taking on a steady rhythm that transformed the startling noise into something familiar.

"Engines," Charlotte breathed.

Jack stirred beside her. "I've heard tales of pirate ships that could take flight to outrun the Imperial Navy, but by Hephaestus, I never believed it."

"The *Perseus* is only one of less than a dozen that have such a capability. And you should be glad it wasn't just a tall tale." Linnet moved into a crouch, grasping the deck rail. "Else we'd be drowning at the base of that maelstrom."

Charlotte became more at ease with the knowledge that an engine churned beneath her, even more so when the *Perseus* began to level off, gliding alongside low, bulbous clouds that swirled in shades of silver, gray, and white.

Linnet stood, and Charlotte scrambled to her feet, accidentally knocking Jack aside in her hurry to right herself.

"Well, then," Jack said, "the moment our lives aren't in danger, you're rid of me."

"That's not—" Charlotte began, but saw the mirth in his eyes; her lips went thin. "Do you really think now is the time for jesting?"

"It's always a good time for jesting," Jack replied. "If we worried about whether or not the time was right, we'd spend all our time dour and serious. Hardly a way to live."

Charlotte looked to Linnet, expecting Jack's sister to have an appropriate retort. Linnet's attention, however, had been drawn to the ship's aft, where the captain was shouting orders at his crew, all of whom wore harnesses hooked onto lengths of rope knotted to the ship's sides. This arrangement allowed the sailors to attend their tasks without risking what would doubtless be a fatal plunge from the deck.

With his men busy securing the water-vessel-turned-airship, Lachance shifted his attention to the trio of passengers near the *Perseus*'s prow. The pirate captain took the deck in long, swift strides. He had eyes only for Linnet, not bothering to spare even a glance at Charlotte or Jack.

"Are you unharmed, Linnet?" he asked.

The way Jean-Baptiste Lachance spoke Linnet's name—and Charlotte felt rather certain this was the first and only time she'd heard him call Linnet by her given name—made Charlotte shiver. His voice remained quiet, but carried a depth that Charlotte innately knew was something rare and of raw beauty. It made her want to turn away, but she couldn't tear her eyes from the scene. Linnet and this near-stranger, standing face-to-face, having just outrun death.

"Tell me." Lachance reached for Linnet, but stopped his outstretched hand before he touched her.

Linnet's mouth quirked in a strange way, somehow conjuring both regret and delight. With a sigh, she took a step forward and wrapped her arms around Lachance's neck. He went still, waiting for her to move rather than responding to her action. Linnet lifted onto the balls of her feet and put one hand on the base of his neck. She pulled his head down until his face was only a breath's distance from hers. She paused then, looking into his eyes. The corners of his mouth turned up ever so slightly.

Linnet sighed again. "Athene have mercy on me."

She kissed him.

Charlotte did turn away then, pivoting around with cheeks burning as if the couple before her had burst into flames and seared her skin.

Beside her, Jack snickered. "Of course Linnet would fall for a pirate."

Without thinking, Charlotte balled her hand into a fist.

Jack looked at her, his mouth quirked as if expecting her to share in his mockery.

The sound of her fist meeting his jaw was even more satisfying than she'd expected. The blow sent Jack staggering backward several steps.

"I appreciate your defending my honor, kitten." Linnet kept her arms wrapped around Lachance's shoulders, though her face was turned toward Charlotte. "But my brother can't always control his doltishness."

"That should be taken into consideration, I suppose." Charlotte smiled at Linnet.

Jack rubbed his face, glowering at both girls.

"Whatever ill thoughts you're harboring, you must remember that you brought your current sorrows upon yourself." Charlotte tried to keep her tone solemn, but a fit of giggles bubbled up. Soon she was doubled over, eyes watering and laughter stealing her breath.

Linnet stepped away from the pirate captain and encircled Charlotte's waist with one arm, holding her steady.

"All is well now, Charlotte," Linnet murmured, recognizing the increasingly hysteric pitch of Charlotte's gasps. "All is well."

Charlotte leaned into Linnet. The laughter that had taken control of her was a much needed release, purging fear from her body to let relief flood in. When the torrent had passed, Charlotte wiped her eyes as she straightened.

"Thank you." She kissed Linnet's cheek.

Confident that Charlotte was no longer in danger of tipping over, Linnet released the other girl's waist and said, "Of course."

Lachance had been watching them, his expression mostly bemused, but Charlotte saw a hardness behind his gaze.

"Thank you," Charlotte said to the pirate. "You saved our lives. That was incredible."

The iron quality in Lachance's eyes suffused the smile he gave her. "I'm quite happy that we all survived that ordeal. But believe me when I tell you I would have mourned for my ship longer than for you. I may not have mourned you at all, given that some deceit on your part brought disaster upon us."

Charlotte stayed quiet. She couldn't fault Lachance for his anger. They had put him, his crew, and the *Perseus* in terrible danger and hadn't given any warning that such an episode might transpire. Then again, how could Charlotte or Linnet have known? How had the Imperial Navy found them?

"Let her be." Linnet broke the heavy silence. "If you're going to blame someone, blame me. I engaged your services."

Lachance turned his droll smile on Linnet. "Blame is a

waste of time. What I need are answers, and I'll get them from whomever I must. It is very clear that this contract of ours has drawn me into some troublesome business. If you keep the truth from me, I have no way of avoiding another unpleasant encounter with the Empire."

"Agreed," Linnet said. "No more secrets."

She glanced at Charlotte as if anticipating an objection, but Charlotte quickly nodded. Though a pirate, Lachance had proven himself an ally. Allies couldn't be wasted.

"Don't I get a say in this?" Jack muttered.

They ignored him.

"My cabin," Lachance said, and left them.

Linnet began to follow, but Charlotte caught her by the elbow.

"I have to see about Grave and Meg," Charlotte told her. "They've been belowdeck through this whole ordeal."

"Of course," said Linnet. "Come to Lachance's quarters when you can. Bring them both."

Charlotte nodded. She left Linnet's side, but gained Jack as a shadow.

"You're not going to apologize for hitting me, are you?" Jack said.

"An apology is warranted only when one regrets one's actions," Charlotte replied. "I don't regret hitting you."

"I regret that you hit me," Jack said. "My jaw still hurts."

"Then maybe you should apologize for acting like—as Linnet said—a dolt."

They'd reached the stairs that led belowdeck. Charlotte stopped, turning to face Jack.

Jack hooked his thumbs around the fastenings of his suspenders. "It was a joke."

"Somewhat," Charlotte told him.

"I'm sorry?"

"You were making a bit of a jest," Charlotte replied. "But your words were mean-spirited, and you continue to hold an ill will toward Linnet, despite all she's done for us."

Jack's shoulders hunched in anger. "You don't understand. You never could."

"I understand that your father treated your mother poorly." Charlotte kept her voice calm. "I understand that because you love her, you wanted to take away the heartache she felt."

Jack shifted his gaze away from her.

"Linnet did nothing to cause your mother pain," Charlotte continued. "Yet you refuse to stop treating her as though she was the source of all your family's sorrows."

When Jack didn't respond, Charlotte took his hand in a gentle grasp. "I have no right to tell you not to be angry, but I will tell you that you must direct your fury where it belongs—at your father, or the Empire even. But Linnet is your sister and your friend. It's time for you to accept that."

"I can't—" Jack's voice cracked a bit. He drew a long breath. "I'll try."

"Good." Charlotte squeezed his fingers. "I'm glad you're here, Jack."

He finally showed the hint of a smile. "I'm glad Lachance didn't keelhaul me."

"Don't be too relieved," Charlotte replied with a soft laugh. "He still might."

She started down the stairs, and Jack followed.

"You don't need to follow me," Charlotte said, glancing at him.

Jack offered a smile that managed to be sheepish and wolfish at once. Something Charlotte suspected only Jack could pull off.

"I'm not following you," he said. "I just want to be with you. Near you. There hasn't been enough of that."

She hesitated on the stairs, watching him.

"Do you disagree?" he asked. Any tentativeness in his expression had melted.

"No," Charlotte said, enjoying the gentle tingle in her limbs as she answered. "I think you're quite right about that."

"Glad to hear it," Jack said. "After you, my dear Lady Marshall."

He bowed, making Charlotte laugh and shake her head at his antics before she continued belowdeck. They shouldered past sailors busy cleaning up after the rough seas and skies the *Perseus* had endured—a job Charlotte didn't envy, but the pirates scrubbed and swabbed without complaint.

Meg and Grave were seated on one of the lower bunks in their small cabin; they both stood up when Charlotte and Jack entered the room. Meg crossed to Charlotte, catching her in a fierce embrace. She hugged Jack as well.

"Merciful Athene, it's good to see you both," Meg said quietly. "Is Linnet well?"

"Yes," Charlotte said. "Captain *Sang d'Acier* acted true to his name. He saved us with a feat I still have a hard time believing truly happened."

"We *are* airborne, then?" Meg asked. "I felt the ship rise, heard the engines, but I can't imagine . . . I've never seen a sea vessel take to the air."

Charlotte nodded, then looked to Grave, who was still standing in silence alongside the bunk.

"Are you well, Grave?"

"Yes," Grave replied. "I wanted to come to the deck and make sure you were safe, but Meg said we had to stay here. That you would come for us when the time was right. I thought you would want me to listen to her."

"I do," Charlotte said. "It's good that you were in the cabin. The situation above was terribly dangerous. I'll admit I was acting foolishly when I insisted on staying in the open."

"I told you," Jack muttered.

"But that's why I wanted to leave here." Grave frowned. "When you're in danger, I should be with you, to protect you."

Charlotte didn't know what to say. Grave's strength did make him capable of taking on many adversaries, but Charlotte felt it was she who had to protect him. Should she try to make him understand?

"It's good that you care for Charlotte's safety, Grave," Meg interjected.

"Yes," Charlotte added. "Thank you, Grave."

Grave smiled at her, seemingly satisfied by this exchange, which only perplexed Charlotte further.

"You'll have your chance to go above deck now," Charlotte told him. "Lachance wants to see us in his cabin."

Meg lifted an eyebrow. "Do you have any idea of what he'll say?"

Charlotte tried to laugh, but it sounded more like a nervous hiccup. "Anything he says that doesn't involve throwing us off the ship will be good news to me."

"Mmmm." Meg pursed her lips. "It's that kind of meeting."

"I'm afraid so."

Jack piped up. "At least he's in love with Linnet, so he probably won't do anything that terrible to us."

Charlotte cast a sidelong glance at him.

"What?" He spread his hands, showing his innocence. "That's a good thing."

"I hope you're right," Meg said to Jack.

3.

LACHANCE LEANED BACK in his chair, his feet resting on the massive desk in his quarters. He surveyed their small party, his face giving nothing of his mood away.

"An explanation," he said. His gaze rested on Linnet, but Charlotte stepped forward to address the pirate.

"I'm sorry that taking us on as passengers put you and your ship in such terrible danger. I hope you'll believe me when I assure you that the attack on the *Perseus* came as a surprise. We believed our escape route to be secret."

"But when the Empire has knowledge of your whereabouts, an attack wouldn't be surprising?" Lachance asked. He looked at Linnet. "It's unlike you to play at politics, *ma sirène*."

"Far more than politics is at work here, Lachance," Linnet replied.

"We have something the Empire wants," Charlotte told him.

Lachance scratched at the stubble on his jaw. "And yet you were within the heart of the Resistance. It could be said that the City of Masks is the safest place for someone hunted by the Empire."

"What we're protecting," Charlotte said carefully, "is something that doesn't belong to the Empire. But neither does it belong with the Resistance."

Sang d'Acier's eyes narrowed. "And what is it that needs such safekeeping?"

Charlotte balked at the question. She didn't think it wise to lie to the captain, but she was equally reluctant to reveal too much of their story.

"It's me." Apparently Grave didn't share Charlotte's misgivings. He came to stand next to Charlotte.

"You?" Lachance stood up, rounding his desk to take a closer look at Grave. After eyeing the boy for a few moments, Lachance appeared unimpressed. "Why?"

"I'm not like other people," Grave answered plainly. "The Empire and the Resistance want to know how I am and why I am."

"How you are and why you are?" Lachance looked to Charlotte. "Does he always speak this way?"

Charlotte nodded.

"And the Order of Arachne wants to kill me," Grave added.

"What?!" Lachance glared at Linnet.

Then Grave was addressing Charlotte instead of the

pirate. "I understand now that I'm the one who is putting you in danger. I don't want that."

"It's not your fault, Grave," Charlotte said.

"But if I left, you would be safe, wouldn't you?" Grave asked.

"That would be a simple solution," Lachance quipped. "Perhaps there is a reward for turning him in?"

"Be quiet." Linnet's voice had the snap of a whip.

Charlotte considered Grave's words, uncomfortable with the weight of their implication. His eyes were on her, their strange amber tone holding her attention. Within his gaze she saw something she didn't understand. A depth of feeling. A promise. Not love—at least not of the romantic sort—but a profound truth.

Grave spoke again. "I will leave if it will protect you."

With a shake of her head, Charlotte told him, "I don't want you to leave for my sake. Truthfully, Grave, I don't think we'd be safe even without you. The Empire knows we're part of the Resistance, and the Resistance believes we've betrayed them."

"Haven't we?" Jack asked quietly.

Charlotte wasn't ready to answer that question. Her mother's plan to use Grave as a tool of war had prompted Charlotte to flee the city, but Charlotte didn't know that her choice constituted a complete betrayal of the Resistance. She still believed that the Empire should fall. She wanted to fight for that cause, just not the way Coe and her mother envisioned that fight.

Linnet went to the pirate captain's side. "I'll tell you

everything you need to know about Grave, but later. Right now I need to know if you can—no, if you're willing—to keep us safe."

"Safe from the Empire, the Resistance, and the Order of Arachne?" Lachance laughed. "Is that all?"

"At least take us to a haven," Linnet pressed. "Then be on your way and rid of us for good."

Lachance looked at Linnet, a sadness creeping over his features. "I would give you anything you ask, *ma sirène*, but you must understand. I have to consider my men. Their safety."

Meg scoffed at him, entering the fray. "Aren't they pirates? Every day in that life is risk. You're *Sang d'Acier*—already a wanted man."

"Living as a wanted man is easy," Lachance told her. "Being a hunted man is another thing entirely."

"It's not you they're hunting," Meg said.

"It is now." The captain went back to his chair. "The *Perseus* will be a target. I have no choice but to hide my ship and disperse my men until we are no longer considered desirable prey."

Charlotte said quickly, "Then for now we need the same thing. To be hidden."

"We'll find a safe haven," Lachance replied. "But the larger problem remains. You've said you could not have anticipated the Empire's attack, *non*?"

"Of course not," Charlotte said. "We would have warned you."

"Then someone else made it known to the Imperial Navy that you'd be fleeing New Orleans by sea." Lachance smoothed the corners of a map on his desk.

Linnet cursed under her breath.

"I am quite surprised this truth eluded you," Lachance said to Linnet.

"I was careful," Linnet snapped. "You know I'm always careful."

Lachance sat back, folding his arms across his chest. "I have no doubt. That makes the question all the more troubling: who revealed your secret? And why?"

Unbidden, a chill spread over Charlotte's skin. "Obviously some agent of the Empire."

"Perhaps," Lachance replied. "No. My apologies, mademoiselle. Undoubtedly, the Empire is at work here, but that answer alone is too simple."

"He's right." Linnet paced in front of the desk. "I hate that he's right, but he is. There's no lack of Imperial spies in New Orleans, but Ott knows who they are. Whoever tracked us has managed to evade Lord Ott's detection, and that's no mean feat."

"Someone new, then?" Jack asked.

"Possibly . . ." Linnet went quiet for a moment, then said, "But a new face in certain circles often draws the most attention."

The cabin grew tense with a silence that Meg at last broke. "What about an old face?" she said. "A face so familiar no one would dare suspect treachery."

"Who?" Charlotte asked.

Meg glanced at Charlotte but spoke to Linnet. "Have you ever questioned Ott's loyalties? If anyone is in the position to operate as a double agent, it's him."

"No." Linnet stabbed an accusing finger at Meg. "I won't argue that Ott's greatest allegiance is to profit, not the Resistance, but he is not working for the Empire."

"How can you be sure?" Meg asked.

Lachance rose from his chair and walked to Linnet's side. He slid his arm around her waist, and it surprised Charlotte when Linnet didn't push him away.

"Happily, I can affirm the truth *ma belle* speaks," Lachance told Meg. "I claim no great wisdom when it comes to the power of the Empire and those who fight against it. But I do know well the world of shadows that chases beneath these Goliaths. Ott is trusted by pirates, swindlers, speculators, and bandits. This lot will not truck with spies, at least not the official sort of which we now speak. Ott is one of us."

By *us*, Charlotte understood Lachance to mean himself and Linnet. The rest of them he counted among the Resistance, and that was fair enough. But it left Charlotte wondering where she wanted to be counted. To which world would it be best to belong? And did Linnet consider herself allegiant to the underworld Lachance described? Linnet had crossed Ott in order to give aid to Charlotte, but in doing so, Linnet had also crossed the Resistance. What did that mean? Did that make her a treacherous employee, but a loyal friend? Did it matter? Where should one's loyalty lie?

"I hope you're right," Meg said to Lachance. "But the question remains. If not Lord Ott, then who? Who is this double agent?"

Meg cast her gaze about, searching each face in the room. But no one had an answer.

4.

BIRCH STARED AT his workbench, searching for an explanation for his current conundrum. Or rather, conundrums. He'd hoped to resolve the first problem through work. Fixing his mind upon the intricacies of metal, combustibles, gears, and wheels had always served to untangle whatever other mental knots plagued his mind. Once his hands became occupied and his brain focused on the building or dismantling of this or that device, Birch found that some secret part of his consciousness was independently able to work out other troubling issues—sometimes resolving questions or worries he hadn't even realized were straining him.

This particular day, however, Birch had no trouble identifying the source of his consternation. Charlotte was gone, and Grave gone with her. Jack was also missing, though it was unclear whether he'd conspired with

Charlotte and they'd departed New Orleans together, or if Charlotte had fled the city, and Jack—being Jack—was chasing after her. The futility of such an action on Jack's part was up for debate. In Birch's estimation, Jack didn't believe in futility.

Whenever Birch sought answers or explanations, he received only silence or evasion.

Ash's mood had been stormy since his sister disappeared, though Birch suspected that Ash's discontent had as much to do with Meg's miraculous arrival and just as sudden departure as with Charlotte. Birch had hoped that since they'd been reunited in New Orleans, Ash would resume his leadership role. Displaced from the Catacombs, their little group was at loose ends. Yes, they were safe and among allies, but the Daedalus Tower and the Resistance itself presented a strange new environment. Ash had been in the city longer than any of the rest of them. He had the ability to provide guidance, reassurance. Instead, he'd melted into the walls—meeting with his mother, Coe, and other high-ranking figures of the Resistance. That left Birch, Pip, and Scoff to find their own way.

At least Birch had the workshop.

He sighed. Pip, who sat on the stool alongside his, sighed as well. The little sound tugged a smile onto Birch's lips for the first time that day. Pip, after officially declaring herself his apprentice now that they had a proper workshop in which he could teach her, had taken to imitating his every move. And apparently his every gesture and sound as well.

Pip had been a buoy for Birch's spirit in recent days.

She remained cheerful and earnest, despite it being obvious that Charlotte's departure had left the young girl as confused and sad as anyone else. Whatever project Birch elected to work on, Pip threw herself into the role of his assistant with enthusiasm. She had a natural affinity for the machinery, and Birch was impressed by the speed with which she learned and her ability to solve complex mechanical problems. Pip often spotted potential crises before they manifested.

She'll be a fine tinker, Birch thought. *Much less likely to blow things up than I am.*

Birch had never been reluctant to admit that particular shortcoming of his.

"Hello, hello!" Aunt Io bustled up to Birch's assigned worktable. "What wondrous mechanisms are we creating today?"

Pip spun around on her stool and beamed at Aunt Io. "Good morning!"

"Good morning to you, Pip," Aunt Io said.

"We haven't gotten much of a start," Birch said as Aunt Io leaned down to give him a peck on the cheek.

"But I'm sure we'll think of something," Pip said.

Io's cascade of blue hair shimmered when she nodded. "Very good. Very good. There are numerous mundane tasks I could set you to: weapons building and repair, transport maintenance, this and that. But young minds should be encouraged to innovate, I say. I'll keep the taskmasters off you as much as I can."

"Thank you, Aunt Io." Birch was as grateful to have

Aunt Io back in his life as he was for Pip's dogged loyalty. The world of late, which had always been dangerous and unpredictable, had tilted violently toward confusion and chaos. These two women, one very old and one quite young, kept him from feeling that he would fall right off the rapidly approaching edge of the universe into oblivion. Birch knew these were rather grand and stark terms in which to consider one's existence. But as a tinker, he could envision no way of summing up his life: order and disorder, creation and destruction.

Life in the Catacombs had been about creating and protecting. He'd crafted gadgets and machines to keep his fellow exiles safe and secure (though admittedly many of the devices, when operated, had a primary objective of blowing things up—ergo, destruction). Even though the Catacombs were so named, Birch had always thought of the hideout as a cocoon. Mysterious layers that shielded children of the Resistance until they'd grown enough to burst forth into the world, ready to fight for freedom that had been denied to the generations before. When those of age left the Catacombs, others would arrive to be cocooned in safety. The cycle repeated again and again.

Only now the Catacombs were rubble. Its secret corridors and honeycombed walls had been blown apart, never to stand again. And that had been Birch's doing.

Pip alone knew how heavy the decision to destroy the Catacombs weighed on Birch. In daily conversations as they worked side by side, he'd confessed to her that nightmares often jarred him from sleep. Dark dreams in which he overloaded the engines powering the Catacombs, but without enough time to allow for escape. The walls fell around him, on top of him, crushing him for the treachery of sabotaging the haven he'd called home.

The strains of their flight into the wilderness in search of a new haven—New Orleans, hub of the Resistance—had distracted him from too much pondering of his choices at first. And the oddness of new surroundings had held Birch's attention for a bit longer. Now, though, that Charlotte, Grave, Meg, and Jack had escaped again for reasons that eluded Birch and now that he'd fallen into a routine of sleep, meals, and work in the Daedalus Tower, he could feel doubts hovering over his shoulder, poking at him, demanding answers and explanations.

Most exasperating of all the questions: why had he been left behind?

Birch couldn't help but worry that he'd failed Charlotte in some way in the course of the overland journey to this new city. Had his annihilation of the Catacombs signaled to her that he was too impulsive to trust? Were his inventions lacking in originality and purpose?

He sighed again.

This time Pip didn't echo, mesmerized as she was by the flurry of Aunt Io's hands gathering and discarding parts.

"Now, what have we here?" Io held up a whirligig crafted of brass and copper. "Surely we can compose something quite interesting if we begin with this."

She flicked one of the blades of the whirligig, making

it spin wildly. Aunt Io held up the spinning object. "Oh, I could just watch this all day. Couldn't you?"

Pip nodded enthusiastically.

Catching the girl's affirmation in her peripheral vision, Io continued, "But a tinker's place is not to watch nor to observe. We are Makers of Things. We are Inventors of Ideas and Masters of Their Execution."

Pip nodded with so much force Birch worried she might tip forward off her stool.

Aunt Io lightly closed her fingers around the whirling bits of metal.

"What purpose could this serve other than to entertain our eyes?" Io asked. "Not just this object as it is, but we must always consider what it could be."

Now that the whirligig was still, its blurred parts could be examined as separate pieces, components of the whole. Birch's mind began to rearrange those pieces, reassembling them, attaching them to other parts, detaching them. His melancholy had all but vanished, and his hands twitched with eagerness to snatch up tools and get to work. Pip's eyes lit with curiosity as she grinned at Birch's aunt.

Aunt Io set the whirligig on the bench and clapped her hands with pleasure. "Excellent, excellent! I see that hunger in your eyes. This is where Greatness begins."

"Ahem."

Their mechanical communing disrupted, Birch, Pip, and Io turned their backs on the workbench.

Coe, dressed smartly in the navy and red uniform of

a Resistance officer, offered Aunt Io a short, crisp bow. "Pardon the interruption, madam. I'm afraid I have need of your nephew."

Io clucked her tongue. "More Resistance business, I suppose. Ah well, what the leadership deems important I must defer to. Away with you, Birch. I'll focus my teaching on your wee apprentice today."

"Really?" Pip grinned, making it clear she'd expected Io would depart if Birch was no longer in the workshop.

"Of course, my dear!" Io tugged one of Pip's green pigtails. "We women must band together whenever men start huffing about their important business. That's usually when they get themselves into trouble and we have to save them."

Pip laughed, then blushed and gave Birch a guilt-touched smile. Birch smiled back, masking his disappointment. Important or not, Birch doubted he'd enjoy whatever Coe had to discuss, especially when he'd just shaken his foul morning mood at the promise of some quality tinkering.

"I won't attempt to argue with an authority such as yourself," Coe said to Io. "A good morning to you both."

He bowed again, then looked at Birch. "If you'll come with me."

Birch took off his work apron and goggles, hanging them on one of the hooks at the end of the workbench. He followed Coe out of the workshop and into the long corridor of the Daedalus Tower. Despite his regrets about the Catacombs, one of the things Birch had come to appreciate about his new environs was that even outside the tinkers' shop, the scent of metal suffused the air. The sensory reminder that a new project was never far off helped take the edge off any homesickness for the New York Wildlands.

Coe led Birch up a staircase to a part of the Tower where he'd never been. Birch knew that the area they approached housed the quarters and meeting rooms of the Resistance officers. How any of that might be relevant to Birch escaped him. Not only was he a new arrival, but he was a tinker—not a soldier and certainly no military strategist.

Nevertheless, when Coe opened a heavy door and said, "After you," Birch quickly went inside, curious about what awaited him.

"Good morning, Birch." Caroline Marshall wore a military uniform similar to Coe's, and her dark hair had been pulled into a severe plait.

"Thank you for coming." Ashley's smile was too grim for Birch's liking.

"It's a pleasure to see you again," Birch said to Caroline.

Like Ash, Caroline wore a smile that was polite but stiff. "I apologize for stealing you away from the workshop. It has been reported to me that you spend every day with our tinkers."

Birch nodded. "It feels closest to home, I suppose."

Caroline's answering laugh was brittle, and Birch felt rather uncomfortable. "Home or not, the Resistance recognizes those who put their skills to use. Your presence in the workshop signals your value to our cause."

It seemed the reports sent to Caroline Marshall had failed to mention Aunt Io's insistence that Birch undertake projects of his own liking, rather than those with the most utility for the Resistance.

"Ashley speaks highly of you," Caroline said. "Of your loyalty to him and Charlotte and your bravery. Your actions saved the lives of precious children."

"Thank you," Birch said, supposing it was quite a good thing that the leaders of the Resistance weren't upset about the destruction of the Catacombs, even if he remained ambivalent about his choice.

"For these reasons, we've asked you to join us." Coe gestured to a chair beside Ashley.

Taking a seat alongside Caroline so that the two officers sat opposite Ash and Birch, Coe continued. "We have a troubling matter to discuss. You likely already know what it is."

When Coe waited expectantly, Birch said, "You mean Charlotte leaving?"

"Not just Charlotte," Caroline said. "My daughter took Grave with her."

"Jack has allied himself with this foolish escapade as well," Coe added.

"And Meg." Ash said her name under his breath. Neither Coe nor Caroline acknowledged him.

Birch didn't know who to direct his question to, so he asked the room. "Do you know why she left?"

The two officers exchanged a long look.

"I'm afraid Charlotte has received some misleading

information," Caroline answered. "She came to believe Grave was no longer safe in New Orleans."

"But where would he be safer?" Birch blurted out.

Coe nodded, his smile pleased. "Exactly. The Daedalus Tower is without question the best place for Grave—and Charlotte—to be, which is why we are concerned that Charlotte has been purposefully led astray. Without the protection of the Resistance, Charlotte has rendered Grave vulnerable to the Empire. Resourceful as she may be, it is only a matter of time before they are captured."

Birch's hands felt numb. Why would Charlotte do such a thing? It made no sense.

Observing the fear that had gripped Birch, Caroline said, "We are all afraid for them. Our highest priority is to find them and bring them to safety." She paused, folding her hands as she rested her elbows on the table. "And to expose the turncoat who is responsible for Charlotte's ill-advised departure."

"Turncoat?" Birch looked to Ashley for an explanation.

"We don't know who it is," Ash said quietly.

Coe tugged at the collar of his jacket and cleared his throat. "But we have our suspicions."

Birch didn't think he wanted the answer, but he still asked, "Who?"

"I'm sorry to say I believe this is the work of my brother," Coe replied.

"Jack?" Birch's voice cracked. "But he lived with us. He *knows* us."

"And that puts him in an excellent position to manipulate you," Caroline said. "After considerable discussion, I'm inclined to agree with Coe. Jack has had motive and opportunity to lure Charlotte away from us. At first I thought he simply chased after her for personal reasons, but it may be that more sinister goals motivated him."

Birch stood up so quickly his chair tipped over, landing on the floor with a clatter. "What motive? Jack is one of us."

"I believed he was," Coe said, standing so he could rest his hand on Birch's shoulder. "And I wish the pieces hadn't fallen into place, revealing the likelihood of his treachery."

"What pieces?" Birch asked.

Coe shook his head, sighing. "My brother always felt he had to live in my shadow. I was older, of course, but I also received accolades he was denied. My rank, my appointments. Our father is a hard man. He gives little praise, and he had more generous words to spare for me than for Jack. When we became involved with the Resistance and Jack volunteered to seek out allies away from the city, I thought he would find the independence and confidence he'd always lacked. For a time, I think he did. But it wasn't enough."

"You don't know that." Ash fixed a hard glare on Coe. "You weren't with us in the Catacombs. Jack was happy."

"I'm sure a part of him was," Coe replied. "And you're right. I wasn't there. I'd remind you, however, that you weren't there for our childhood. I know my brother. It pains me to suggest that he's working against us, but I have to accept that possibility."

Ash didn't respond.

Birch's discomfort was only increasing. "Why now? What would make Jack turn on us?"

"Because he knows we've reached a tipping point," Caroline answered. "The French have agreed to ally with us in an offensive campaign against the Empire with the aim of driving them into the sea. Forcing them from this continent for good. Jack knows this, and if he brings our strategies to the Empire, he'll be the greatest war hero of our time. Greater than Benedict Arnold."

"It would be the kind of acclaim he's always wanted," added Coe.

Their words were dissonant in Birch's head. He wanted nothing more than to be rid of them and out of this room.

Ash made a sound like a snarl. "That's not true."

"Ashley." Caroline spoke in a soothing tone. "We've spoken about this."

"It's not Jack," Ash told them. "There's no way he's a turncoat. No matter what you believe about the things he wants, he would not betray us to the Empire."

"If not Jack, then who?" Coe asked.

Ash closed his eyes, his brow knitting as if in pain. "Meg."

5.

HARLOTTE HAD ANTICIPATED nothing less than a hazardous and unpleasant return to the sea when Captain *Sang d'Acier* deemed the time and place ideal for the change. To her surprise, the ship's transition proved much less frightening than when it had launched into the sky. The *Perseus* made its descent gradually, floating down through cloud banks until sea foam at the crest of the waves lapped at the ship's keel. When their captain shouted his order, the crew sprung into action. Levers were pulled, ropes guided and tied off, and flying gear stowed while the equipment required for sailing was reclaimed from stowage.

When the *Perseus* settled into the water, it felt like sinking into the cushions of an overstuffed settee. Sailors scrambled up masts to remove the harpoons and cables that had served as ribbing for the sails during their flight and set to work patching each puncture site. Though the deck was crowded with gruff pirates bustling from task to task, Charlotte couldn't tear herself away. She took care not to be a hindrance to the workers, but watched the ship's transformation as closely as she could, mesmerized by the quick, skillful turnaround.

The late-afternoon sun blazed at the ship when it took to the waters once more, scattering diamonds across the tips of each ocean swell. As soon as Charlotte determined she wouldn't cause too much of a disruption, she made her way to the stern.

When she neared the tall brass ship's wheel, Lachance greeted her. "How do you fare, mademoiselle?"

"I'm well, thank you," Charlotte answered. "I'll confess I much prefer returning to the water to leaving it."

Lachance laughed, a sound both smoky and sweet. "With the benefit of time and a fair wind, this ship can be as graceful as any dancer and as gentle as a mother lulling her babe to sleep. Taking to the air required haste, I'm afraid."

"Haste for which I remain grateful," Charlotte said.

In the distance, off the port side of the ship, Charlotte could spy the dense green of a coast—the reason she'd sought out Lachance.

"Where have we landed?" she asked.

Lachance nodded toward the shoreline. "Spanish Florida. Once we cleared the Bahamas, I took us down."

Linnet appeared on the stern, still rubbing sleep from her eyes.

"Did you rest well, *ma sirène*?" Lachance asked with an

unapologetically wicked smile. "I trust you found my bed to your liking."

"I was going to compliment you on your landing," Linnet replied. "But since you've shown no manners of your own, I won't bother. How are you, Charlotte?"

"Fine," Charlotte said quickly.

There hadn't been an opportunity for them to speak in private since escaping the Cerberus patrol, and she was full of questions for Linnet. Shortly after the *Perseus* had climbed into the skies and out of its enemies' reach, Charlotte had spent a few hours belowdeck in a bunk. When she'd awakened, Meg was still asleep in the opposite bunk and Grave was sitting in a hammock strung between the far posts of the bed. He was awake, of course, but completely still and utterly silent. Charlotte had invited Grave to join her in the fresh air, but to her surprise, he had declined, insisting he preferred the cabin to the deck.

"The ocean," Grave had said. "I don't like to look at it."

Once on the deck, Charlotte found her only company to be the pirates. She'd assumed Jack and Linnet had found napping places of their own below, but now it seemed Linnet's place of respite had been in the captain's cabin.

"I was just asking Captain Lachance about our landing site," Charlotte added, trying to fill the awkward moment with words unrelated to Linnet and the pirate captain's odd relationship.

"Spanish Florida," Linnet said. She didn't look at the

coast, but kept glaring at Lachance. "The Royal Navy won't patrol this coastline."

"Then Spanish Florida is a safe place for us to stay?" Charlotte asked.

This time Lachance's laugh had a sharp edge. "No. We will sail along their coast, but our destination is north of the Spanish border."

"You're taking us back into Imperial territory?" Charlotte couldn't fathom what wisdom there could be in this decision. "Why not the French islands?"

"The Spanish resent visitors," Lachance told her. "Even those who trade with them know that their visits will be brief or they risk being thrown into prison. Spain guards its remaining territory like a jealous lover. Any outsiders are suspect, viewed as potential conspirators in league with the French or the English. They forget that the French and English are too busy tangling with one another to care about Florida. Yet, their lunacy only grows. You'll soon see how it has been made manifest."

Letting that somewhat cryptic description pass for the time being, Charlotte instead asked, "Surely the French islands, then."

Lachance flashed her an indulgent smile. "The allure of *les îles* I do not deny. Do you know the reason pirates flood the islands?"

Charlotte shook her head.

"While they are within reach of the law," Lachance told her, "it is a long reach. Many things can evade the sight of authorities. Many things can happen without consequence—at least not 'official' consequence."

"Wouldn't that help us?" Charlotte replied.

Linnet answered, "At first glance it might seem that way. But the lawlessness of the Caribbean could work against us. If word of the Empire's hunt for the *Perseus* gets out, which it undoubtedly will, people of all sorts will be looking for us. Pirates, spies, bounty hunters. All of them will expect us to hide out in the islands."

"So you're taking us somewhere you think they won't expect us to hide?" Charlotte asked.

Lachance nodded.

"If it works, it's brilliant," Linnet told Charlotte. "If it doesn't, well, at least it was a clever idea."

"*Merci, ma sirène.*"

Charlotte frowned at being left out of this exchange. "Where?"

"Beaufort Inlet," Linnet said. "Cornwallis Province." She began to laugh under her breath. Lachance was grinning at her.

"And why is that clever?"

Linnet put her arm around Charlotte's waist. "Oh, kitten, you have not spent enough time with pirates."

"I haven't spent any time with pirates," Charlotte snapped in frustration. Then she glanced at Lachance with chagrin. "Before now, I mean."

"A tragedy," Lachance replied.

"Beaufort Inlet is notorious among pirates," Linnet told

Charlotte. "For it was there that Captain Edward Thatch ran aground."

Lachance removed his hat with a flourish and then bowed his head.

Charlotte's brow furrowed. "Edward Thatch?"

"You'd likely know him by the name of Blackbeard," Linnet said.

"Oh!" Charlotte had heard tales of Blackbeard, but she'd always thought of him as a creature out of folklore and not a real person.

"It would not be an exaggeration to say Blackbeard was, and still is, revered for holding the laws of the sea above the laws of men," Lachance told Charlotte. "His demise raised a keening among pirates that would have drowned out the fiercest gale."

Linnet moved away from Charlotte to snatch Lachance's hat from his hand and plop it back atop his head. "The second bit of what you said is definitely an exaggeration."

"Have you ever heard pirates keen?" Lachance straightened his hat. He returned his attention to Charlotte. "When the *Queen Anne's Revenge* struck that shoal, it was the beginning of the end of Blackbeard's reign."

"Pirates believe that to sail into Beaufort Inlet is to invite certain doom," Linnet said. "No captain will go near it."

Charlotte looked at Lachance. "But you will?"

He shrugged. "I have never been superstitious."

"It is unlikely that anyone would look for us there," Linnet said. "And the Royal Navy pays little attention to the Outer and Inner Banks of the Cornwallis Province. Charleston boasts the height of colonial leisure, and the islands up and down the coast are home to fishing towns. In no way is the region a locus of power. Quiet and isolated. That's what we want."

Charlotte agreed with the rationale of this plan, but she wondered what it would mean for her life. From the moment she'd decided to flee New Orleans, Charlotte's mind had focused on the present alone. Now the future loomed in a gray fog of uncertainty. When the *Perseus* left them on the Cornwallis coast, what then? Would they hide among the fishing men and women indefinitely, cut off from the rest of the world? Would she be able to tolerate such a life?

Suddenly disconsolate, Charlotte stayed quiet. She'd made her choices. How could she voice these doubts? Especially when they sounded so selfish.

"Aha!" Lachance's abrupt exclamation made Charlotte jump. "There it is!"

"It's bigger than the last time I saw it," Linnet observed in a flat tone. "I wonder if they're almost finished."

"It has no head," Lachance replied with a dismissive wave of his hand. "It cannot be near completion if there is no head."

Linnet cupped her hand against her forehead to shade her eyes. "That's true. It does need a head."

The object of their scrutiny stood at a great distance from the shoreline. That fact, along with how high it rose above the surrounding trees, revealed that it was overwhelmingly massive.

"That's the Doomsday Machine," Charlotte murmured.

"Yes. Spain's hope is that once completed, it will deter England and France from invading if those two empires should ever turn their enmity from each other and toward Iberia," Linnet said.

"Can it really do what they claim?" Charlotte asked.

Linnet shook her head. "I have no idea. I don't think anyone knows, probably not even the Spanish. But I hope we never find out."

The Doomsday Machine was a colossus made in the image of Hephaestus himself. Currently headless, the god of forges grasped a hammer in each hand, and according to Spanish claims, if activated, these hammers would break the very crust of the earth, sending ripples of destruction along the eastern seaboard and not ceasing until Florida was severed from the rest of North America.

As the *Perseus* sailed northward, the Doomsday Machine remained in view. The absence of its head served only to make the colossus's presence more unsettling. Charlotte agreed with Linnet, hoping never to learn if such a machine could accomplish its task.

6.

THE *PERSEUS* DROPPED anchor shortly after passing Shackleford Banks while night shrouded the coast. When Charlotte joined Meg on the deck, the air was cool and thick with salt. A steady breeze ruffled the ship's sails, restored to their original positions as the *Perseus* slid through dark waves. Heavy clouds hid the moon, but the sky and sea were illuminated at intervals by the sweeping beam of Cape Lookout's lighthouse.

Charlotte was more at ease under the cover of night, but she noticed Meg's tight grip on the ship rail.

"Do you disagree with the captain's decision to leave us here?" Charlotte asked.

Meg relaxed slightly, smiling at Charlotte. "It's not that, Lottie. I'm just weary and a bit heartsick."

"About Ashley?" Charlotte was surprised that Meg would make such an admission.

"That's part of it," Meg said. "But mostly I wish I didn't have to make difficult decisions. Decisions that always seem to take me away from those dearest to me."

Charlotte looked at Meg in alarm. "You're leaving us?"

"I don't know yet." Meg took Charlotte's hand. "We'll talk of it when we're ashore." Squeezing Charlotte's fingers, Meg said, "But I have decided that this time I won't make the decision alone. All of us will be affected, so all of us should be involved in making the choice."

While it was better than waking up to find Meg gone, Charlotte's chest seized up with fear and sadness at the thought of her leaving them for a second time.

The crew of the *Perseus* lowered one of the ship's small boats into the water. Sailors climbed down the rope ladder to fill the boat with bundles that Charlotte assumed were provisions Lachance was giving them.

"Let's go," said Meg.

Lachance and Linnet were waiting beside the rope ladder, while Jack and Grave had just emerged from below and were crossing the deck to join them. Meg descended first, followed by Jack, then Grave.

"Charlotte." Captain Lachance offered his hand and assisted her over the rail.

The thick rope of the ladder bumped against the side of the ship as Charlotte climbed down. When she reached the bottom rung, Charlotte turned toward the boat, but a pair of hands was already clasping her waist and lifting her aboard. When her feet touched wooden planks, she quickly turned to find Jack looking down at her.

Charlotte was about to scold him, but his hands were still holding her lightly, their warmth countering the damp breeze off the sea. Without saying anything, Charlotte carefully pulled away from him and took a seat beside Grave. Her heart was still skittering about, and her expression must have been strained, for Grave said, "I don't like being this close to the water either."

Charlotte offered him a little smile. "We'll be ashore soon enough."

Grave smiled back.

Jack sat on the other side of Charlotte while Meg, Linnet, and Lachance sat opposite. Charlotte hadn't expected the pirate captain to accompany them in the small boat, but then again, he might have been reluctant to say his goodbyes to Linnet aboard the ship and was using this excursion to the shore to prolong his time with her.

Four of Lachance's men rowed them across the inlet and between the small islands closer to the shoreline. In the darkness, Charlotte couldn't make out any signs of a town or settlement until they were almost to the beach. Houses, shacks, and huts of clapboard formed clusters along the coast. A few larger buildings huddled around a long fishing pier where boats rocked quietly while their owners slept.

The sailors hopped out to haul the small craft onto the sand, their splashes in the surf alarmingly loud. When they were ashore, Charlotte encouraged Grave to hurry out of the boat. She immediately followed him, avoiding any offers of assistance from Jack—she had no desire to act the helpless maid in front of pirates . . . or ever.

Lachance's men unloaded the supplies. The captain took them aside, speaking quietly. When he'd finished, the men returned to the small boat, pushed it into the water, and scrambled aboard.

Lachance sauntered over to them.

Linnet pointed at the sailors rowing away. "Where are they going?"

"Back to the ship, of course," said Lachance.

She poked him in the chest. "Why, then, are you still here?"

Lachance lavished his most radiant smile on her, which only made Linnet scowl.

"The interests I currently wish to pursue are here," Lachance said.

"Your interests?" Charlotte had never heard Linnet screech, but it seemed she was on the verge of doing so. "Your *interests?*"

"Now, now, *ma sirène*, assuming I meant you. Such vanity." Lachance pushed her finger away. "I have a business venture here, and it's been some time since I've stopped in for a visit."

Wrestling her emotions into submission, Linnet said flatly, "You hate being ashore."

"I do," Lachance replied. "But a man cannot flee his fate."

"In this case, I think maybe he should," Jack whispered to Charlotte. "He'll live longer."

Charlotte covered her mouth to hide her laugh.

Linnet stepped closer to Lachance, her voice low. "I fulfilled the terms of the contract. This is not what we agreed on."

"And I encountered many surprises on our journey that I had not agreed to," Lachance said. "The tables have simply turned, Linnet."

After casting a last look at the boat rowing away, Linnet said, "At least tell me you know of a place we can stay."

"Do not fear, *ma belle*," Lachance replied. "I would not dare disappoint you."

He scooped up two bundles of supplies, but rather than heading toward the seaside buildings, Lachance began to walk inland. Jack and Grave grabbed the remaining bundles, and the rest of them followed the pirate.

The beach gave way to a grassy dune that pitched steeply upward. When they'd scrambled over it, Charlotte spotted what appeared to be a proper town a short distance away. Their destination proved to be a tavern, the Weir, that sat on a corner of the town square.

Lachance took them around the building. Linnet raised an eyebrow at him when the pirate produced a key to unlock the back door.

"As I said," Lachance told her. "A business venture."

The door opened into a small corridor. To their right, a staircase led to the second story of the tavern. Ahead, Charlotte could make out objects and furnishings that indicated a kitchen, and to their left was a larder. A light appeared at the stop of the stairs, outlining the shape of a man.

"S-s-sir!" A jerk of the man's hand caused the lantern to waggle from side to side, making dizzying shadows run up and down the walls. "I had no word of your impending arrival."

"An unplanned visit, Thomas." Lachance took off his hat. "But not one meant to cause you trouble. My friends and I need food and beds."

"Yes! Yes! Right away." The man scrambled down the stairs to take the hat from the captain. "I'll wake Matilde, and she'll make preparations in the kitchen."

Thomas glanced around at their group. "How many rooms, sir? In addition to your suite, I mean."

"We three ladies can share a room," Linnet answered before Lachance could speak. "And a second should suffice for these two gentlemen." She indicated Jack and Grave.

"No trouble at all." Thomas bowed awkwardly and hurried back up the stairs.

"You own this place?" Jack asked Lachance.

The pirate nodded. "I use it when I need to move currency . . . through more traditional channels. Though its existence is a secret I guard closely. Not even my men know of it."

"Speaking of your men," Linnet interjected. "What are they going to do? Just stay in the inlet with the ship?"

"I'll explain when we have a place to sit and food to eat," Lachance said.

After a series of thumps above them, a plump woman appeared on the staircase. She had a girl of about ten or eleven in tow; the child was still rubbing sleep from her eyes.

"Ah, Matilde." Lachance planted kisses on each of the woman's cheeks. "My apologies for rousing you at such an hour."

"Wouldn't have it any other way, sir." Matilde guffawed as her cheeks went rosy. "You remember our daughter, Jeannette."

Jeannette yawned.

"Manners!" Matilde said, appalled. "Captain Lachance puts a roof over our heads, child."

Her mother's tone startled Jeannette into wakefulness. Eyes wide, she quickly curtsied to Lachance. "I'm sorry, sir."

Lachance patted the top of her head. "No need for apologies, *ma petite.*"

Jeannette blushed and curtsied again.

Soon mother and daughter had a fire roaring in the stove, and the clattering of pots and pans filled the background as the surprise guests gathered around a table. The main room of the tavern was simple but pleasant, with a long bar and wood furniture that gleamed in shades of honey. Thomas set a jug of cider and cups before them. Lachance filled the cups, and once they'd been passed around, he lifted his.

"To narrow escapes and unexpected adventures."

Charlotte wasn't certain those were things she wanted to toast, but they all raised their cups.

Lachance gulped his cider down in a few swallows.

"Now, my friends," he said, refilling his cup, "there are decisions to be made."

He waved his hand at the spacious room. "This place is refuge enough for a time. But I prefer action to repose."

"What are you up to, Lachance?" Linnet asked.

"There is a problem that must be solved," he answered. "I will help you solve it."

Charlotte could think of any number of problems they currently faced. She didn't know which one the captain meant.

"You cannot brook a traitor in your ranks," Lachance said. "The turncoat must be found."

Linnet's finger traced the rim of her cup. "You're right. But why would you help us?"

"This knave is troubling to me as well," Lachance replied. "And not just because he tried to wreck my ship. I pay a good sum to certain authorities to ensure the Empire doesn't go out of its way to hunt the *Perseus*. Whoever is hunting you ignored those payments."

Charlotte didn't know whether to laugh or be offended. "You want to help find the turncoat because he . . . or she . . . is ignoring your bribes."

Lachance grimaced. "Bribes are a serious matter. If a respectable payoff no longer holds sway, the world has become a dangerous place."

Jack gave a derisive snort, but Linnet nodded. "Ott would say the same."

"You think that whoever orchestrated this chase is

working outside the usual channels of authority?" Meg's brow furrowed. "Or thinks himself above them?"

"Yes." Lachance reached over to fill the glass Linnet had just emptied. "My men are now on their way to Nassau. While ruled by the Empire in name, the Bahamas are in truth controlled by entrepreneurs like myself."

"It's a pirate haven." Jack snatched the jug out of Lachance's hands. "Everyone knows that."

Lachance shrugged. "However you name the place, it offers a harbor where the *Perseus* can safely dock. The Empire's henchmen can then search the ship to their hearts' delight. Once they realize the cargo they seek is not on the ship, my crew will be free of their harassment. When the time is right, I'll return to them. Until then, it is my purpose to ferret out whoever has caused me such grievances."

"And how do you plan to find this person?" Jack asked.

"By going to the Floating City," Lachance said. "Where I'm certain my gold still buys information."

Charlotte threw an anxious glance toward Grave. "I thought you brought us here to be hidden. Taking Grave to the Floating City would be madness!"

"You will not be coming with us," Lachance told her.

Charlotte went quiet. She didn't want to go New York, but she cared not for the idea of being left behind.

Linnet had picked up on something else. "Us?"

"You have better access to the keys that might unlock this secret than I, *ma sirène*." Lachance lifted her hand and brushed his lips across her fingertips before she could snatch them away.

Linnet didn't reply, looking instead at Charlotte and then back at the pirate.

"He's right, Linnet," Meg said. "You need to get word to Ott about what's happening. He needs to be made aware of the danger in our midst. And if anyone can find a way to trip up this saboteur, it is Ott."

After taking a long draft of her cider, Linnet said, "Yes. I'll go with you."

"I'll be going as well," Meg added.

Linnet startled, knocking over her glass. Lachance leaned forward, assessing Meg.

"There's a danger to Grave other than the Empire." Meg said, and calmly returned Lachance's piercing gaze. "I believe I can put an end to that threat."

"The Order of Arachne?" Charlotte straightened in alarm. "You can't go back to the Temple!"

Meg put her hand over Charlotte's. "Don't be afraid, Lottie. The Sisters will be swayed by the insights of Nicodemus, the conjurer. I'm sure of it. They must be made to understand that Grave's presence in this world is not evil. If I don't go to the Temple, he will never be safe."

When Charlotte's face remained stricken, Meg added, "I'll not go alone. My mother will accompany me. Though she's not of their fold, the Sisters respect my mother's spiritual gifts. Her support will lend credence to my message."

"I have no qualms about your traveling with us," Lachance said. "In truth, the fewer of us who remain, the safer Grave will be. This is a small settlement. Three travelers visiting the Weir will garner little gossip. Double that number—adding the risk that I could be recognized—and word of your presence could easily spread, inviting trouble."

Charlotte grasped the reasoning of this strategy, but it meant she would have only Grave and Jack as companions. Given Grave's unusual character, she was likely to rely on Jack for conversation. She wasn't sure she was ready to rely on Jack for anything. They hadn't been alone since Jack appeared on the *Perseus*. So many things between them remained unsettled—what would it be like when the others left?

She glanced at Jack and found him staring into his cup, which made her suspect his mind had turned to the same thoughts occupying hers. Feeling her gaze, Jack lifted his eyes. Charlotte didn't look away; she couldn't bring herself to. Not with the sudden crackling warmth upon her skin. She'd done what she could to avoid Jack in New Orleans, but perhaps now was the time to stop evading him and to face the truths hidden in her own heart.

7

ASHLEY MARSHALL HAD faced many hardships throughout his eighteen years, but until now he'd never felt miserable. As someone who prided himself on having a stalwart character, Ash didn't want to acknowledge his misery. Yet after the morning he'd had, he could no longer deny his sorry state: dejected, betrayed, lonely. Miserable.

And he wasn't about to stand for it.

Scoff, Birch, and Pip looked at Ash expectantly. After all, he'd summoned them to this obscure corner of the city. It was Scoff's corner, actually, at least for the moment. Surmising that Scoff might suffer from boredom or lack of purpose due to the absence of an apothecary in the Daedalus Tower, the ever-resourceful Aunt Io had secured a shed in the Garden quadrant, where he could continue his experiments.

When Scoff had profusely thanked Io, she'd told him, "I'd be dishonoring my dear Albion if I didn't do all I could to help young talent continue the work he so loved. I do hope you won't turn yourself into a bird. Your friends would surely miss you. Though I'm sure Albion would love the company. And you'd be a fine bird."

Scoff went a bit gray in the face, but managed to smile and nod.

If Aunt Io's remarks had unnerved Scoff, such fears weren't in evidence in his new, makeshift laboratory. Gardening equipment had been shoved into one corner, making room for glass jars and bottles in an array of shapes and sizes, mortars and pestles of stone and brass, weights and scales, and a pile of pouches from which emanated an amalgam of unidentifiable odors.

"You've done an impressive job of procuring all the necessities for your work, Scoff," Ash remarked.

"Incredible, isn't it?" Scoff said. "Another gift from Io."

"She purchased all this for you?" Ash surveyed the room again. While the furniture appeared used, it was still of a high enough quality to be costly.

Scoff rapped his knuckles on the tiered mahogany cabinet with dozens of small rectangular drawers that were no doubt awaiting contents of the pungent pouches. "No. It belonged to her friend Albion. He had no family, so when he . . . disappeared, Io became the beneficiary of his estate. She had all of his things stored away, and she told me I could use whatever I'd like."

"How serendipitous." After a quick search for anything

that looked like a diary or collection of notes, Ash asked, "You didn't, um, borrow any of his formulas, did you?"

Scoff looked a bit guilty. "Only to study."

"I'll just repeat what Io said," Ash told him. "Don't turn yourself into a bird."

"But if you do by accident, I promise to feed you," Pip added. "And keep cats away."

"I'm sure Scoff won't turn into a bird or anything else," said Birch. Scoff threw him a grateful, if abashed, smile. "Now, Ash, why are we here?"

Ash loosened the top button of his collar. What he was about to do bordered on treachery, and he hadn't become fully comfortable with that fact yet.

"This morning Birch and I were summoned to a meeting with my mother and Coe Winter." Ash noted the way Birch's eyebrows lifted, but went on. "This meeting served to inform us that Coe and my mother believe Charlotte left New Orleans because she was misled."

"Misled how?" Scoff asked. He'd begun organizing his ingredients as he listened, sorting the large pile into smaller piles.

"They think someone close to us is working against the Resistance," Ash said.

"A spy?" Pip's eyes widened.

Ash nodded toward Birch. "That's what we were told."

"Do they know who it is?" Scoff had stopped halfway between his table and the cabinet.

"They have suspicions about the identity of the spy," Ash said. "And that's why I wanted us to meet. The people under scrutiny are our friends—and I would argue that we know them better than anyone in the Resistance does."

"I agree," Birch added quietly.

The tension in Ash's chest and shoulders eased; it was a relief to have Birch's support.

"They're inclined to think it's Jack." Ash spoke quickly, before anyone could react. "But I believe it's more likely Meg."

Birch remained silent, but Scoff drew in a sharp, whistling breath, and Pip huffed.

Ashley let his words settle among them.

"If this is true, no matter who the spy is, Charlotte is in danger," he said. "And we need to help her."

"You don't think that Commander Marshall wants to find and help Charlotte?" Birch's tone didn't suggest he objected, but that he was surprised by Ashley's plan.

Ash put his hands in his pockets and rocked back on his heels. What was driving him to search for Charlotte covertly wasn't logic, it was instinct.

"I do think she wants to help."

Scoff moved to his cabinet and opened a drawer. "But you don't think that's enough?"

"I don't know how to describe it," Ash replied. He did, actually—it was like a moth had become trapped between his heart and his stomach.

Birch spoke quietly. "You don't know if you fully trust them."

Ash wouldn't have admitted such a thing, even to

himself, but as soon as Birch had said the words, Ash knew he agreed.

"I was uneasy at this morning's meeting," Birch said. "I can't offer up anything in particular to justify that feeling, only that I had the sense I wasn't being given all the facts. That important information was purposefully being withheld."

Ash was nodding.

"Do you think Coe and the Commander already know why Charlotte left?" Scoff asked.

"I think that's a strong possibility," said Birch.

Ash added, "Then the next question is: why don't they want to share that knowledge with us?"

"Because it's something that would hurt Charlotte." Pip had climbed onto a stool beside the worktable.

Blowing out a long sigh, Ash said, "I can't believe Jack or Meg would willingly put Charlotte in harm's way."

"Of course they wouldn't," Pip said.

"None of us wants to believe that of our friends," Birch said. "But the evidence points—"

"What evidence?" Pip asked, her arms akimbo and her expression challenging. Words tumbled out of her mouth. "Coe and Commander Marshall say it's Jack. But all Coe and Jack do is fight. I don't think Coe has anything good to say about Jack, but who do we know better? Jack or Coe? Why, Jack of course! Why would you listen to Coe without taking into account all that Jack's done for us?"

Pip had to pause to draw breath before continuing her tirade. She turned her blazing eyes on Ash. "And you. I know you're our leader, but you're being silly now. I mean about Meg. She hurt your feelings when she stayed in the city, so you want to be able to blame her for something. Meg took care of *all* of us. She would never hurt *any* of us. You already know that. You need to stop being angry and remember who she is."

Scoff, Birch, and Ash all stared, mouths agape, at their younger counterpart.

Pip sat up straighter and folded her arms across her chest. "You know I'm right."

Ash had to turn away because his eyes suddenly stung with tears.

Scoff cleared his throat, shuffling his feet at the uncomfortable exchange.

Pip took note and stared him down as well. "I don't care if you think I'm being rude. We don't have time to waste . . . I mean Charlotte doesn't have time. We need to help her."

Squaring his shoulders, Ash turned to face her. "You're right, Pip. Of course you're right."

Pip had looked ready to argue with him, so his reply caught her off guard. "I am?"

Ash laughed quietly. "Yes. You are."

"I agree," Birch said. "Helping Charlotte is what we must be focused on."

Scoff picked up a lead weight from his scale, rolling it around in his hand. "I don't mean to be contrary. But how are we supposed to help her? We have no idea where she is."

Pip, who'd been basking in Ash and Birch's approval, looked crestfallen. "I—I don't know."

Ash sighed, shoving his hands into his pockets. "It is a problem."

"I think we do know," Birch countered. Moses crawled from his shoulder to the top of his head, perching like a strange little hat. It gave the strange appearance that the bat was affirming Birch's statement. "We're simply dancing around the answer."

"What do you mean?" Scoff asked.

"We've been worried about who provoked Charlotte's sudden departure," Birch said. "But we need to find out why she left. If she'd determined there was a spy among us, why wouldn't she have identified the turncoat? Something else made her flee."

"Flee with Grave," Birch added.

Ash said softly, "And Meg."

Pip glared at him, but Ash lifted his hands to pacify her.

"I'm not going back to my accusation that Meg is the spy," Ash said. "But it can't be a coincidence that Charlotte left almost immediately after Meg arrived in New Orleans."

"You think Meg knew something that made Charlotte leave the city?" Scoff asked.

Pip was nodding. "Yes! That makes much more sense than Meg working against us. She came to help Charlotte."

Birch eyed Ashley. "She didn't . . . say anything to you. I mean . . . you two were alone, weren't you?"

"No." Ash's neck reddened. "I asked why she'd come to New Orleans. She told me Grave was in danger, but she wouldn't specify what the danger was."

"That's all?" Pip frowned. "All she said was that Grave's in danger?"

The rosy hue crept into Ash's cheeks. "We had other things that—"

"Don't worry about it, mate," Scoff cut in.

"Scoff is right," Birch said, waving off the objection an openmouthed Pip seemed about to make. "That doesn't matter now."

"But I do think it suggests that whatever danger Meg was talking about is the reason Charlotte left," Scoff said.

Ash asked, "So what do we do?"

"We wait. We watch. We listen." When Birch spoke, Moses flapped his wings. The tiny metallic clicking from the movement was like miniature applause. "Until we find out what's really going on here."

Ash and Scoff nodded.

"I want to do something else," Pip said.

The three young men looked at her.

"No one talks to me because they think I'm too little to be important," she said.

Her companions exchanged looks. Ash shrugged. It seemed foolish to attempt to pacify Pip when she spoke the truth.

"You watch and listen," Pip continued. "But I'm going to follow Aunt Io's advice."

Birch tilted his head, regarding her curiously. "What advice?" Moses chirped for emphasis.

"To find inspiration," Pip told him. "And to make something."

She began to smile. "I've been thinking about Charlotte and a quick escape. And I had an idea about pinwheels . . ."

8

THE RECEDING TIDE swirled around Charlotte's ankles, rising to nip at her calves. She'd gathered her skirts, folded over the hem, and tucked the fabric into her wide belt so it ballooned around her knees but didn't drag in the surf. A bucket hung from her arm as she bent to dig in the wet sand.

Four days had passed since Lachance, Linnet, and Meg left the Weir. For two of those days, Charlotte had kept mostly to her room—with Meg and Linnet gone, the room was Charlotte's alone while Grave and Jack shared a second room. They took their meals with Thomas, Matilde, and Jeannette, eating in the kitchen so as to avoid inquiring looks or troublesome questions from the local taverngoers. By the third day, Charlotte couldn't stand feeling useless, so she pestered Matilde for tasks. Refusing offers to help in the kitchen, Matilde at last relented and sent Charlotte out with Jeannette to harvest clams on the shore.

Jeannette showed Charlotte how to look for bubbles in the sand, indicating a clam had burrowed beneath that spot. Digging for the small shellfish proved to be not only a fine distraction, but also a delightful way to pass the time. The girls splashed through the surf, giggling while the sun watched over them and a breeze soothed away any chance of the day growing too hot. They watched fishing boats and skiffs row and sail away from the docks to try their luck in the channel among its tangle of islands. Charlotte's mind and body eased in the fresh air while she enjoyed the accomplishment of gathering a bounty for the kitchen. Not to mention the delectable preparation Matilde served for the evening meal: clams steamed with wine and herbs. Charlotte went to bed that night with a full belly and a spirit more buoyant than she'd known in weeks.

The next morning Charlotte found Jeannette waiting for her with buckets in hand, and together they returned to the sea. At midmorning, Jack and Grave appeared on the crest of the sand dune. Grave lingered on the grassy ridge, while Jack pulled off his boots and came down to the shore.

"Jeannette! Your mother wants you back at the tavern."

Jeannette gave a little whining sigh as she trudged out of the water. She thrust her bucket into Jack's hands before retrieving her shoes and scrambling up the beach. Jack rolled up his pant legs and waded toward Charlotte.

He looked into the bucket and its little pile of clams. "I think this means I'm supposed to help you."

"I can teach you what Jeannette taught me," Charlotte told him. "But I'm still learning how to do this myself."

"What is there to teach?" Jack asked. "It's just digging, isn't it?"

With a sharp smile, Charlotte answered, "Why don't you find out?"

She turned away and resumed her hunt for air bubbles in the sand. Jack splashed around nearby in search of his own bounty. Less than an hour had passed when Jack approached Charlotte, his bucket tipped toward her to reveal the pittance of shellfish he'd added to Jeannette's collection.

"I surrender," Jack said. "Have pity on me and share your wisdom, mademoiselle."

Charlotte laughed and showed Jack her nearly full bucket. "I'll show you how to find them, but first I should take these to Matilde."

She started toward the beach and heard Jack sloshing after her. When she reached the edge of the water, Jack set his bucket in the sand and snatched Charlotte's bucket from her hand. He ran up the dune to where Grave was sitting. Jack said something Charlotte couldn't hear and then handed the bucket to Grave, who stood up and disappeared down the other side of the dune.

Jack, hands in his pockets and smiling broadly, ambled back to Charlotte.

"What was that?" Charlotte asked, picking up the bucket where Jack had left it.

"I thought it would be a good idea to send Grave on that errand," Jack said. "Give him something to do."

Charlotte frowned. "And?"

"And . . ." Jack's grin faded. "I wanted to talk to you."

Suddenly Charlotte could feel her blood jumping through her veins.

"I—" Jack took a step closer. "How are you?"

"Well enough," Charlotte said, wishing her breath weren't coming so unevenly; she had to gasp before she could speak.

Jack moved closer still. "I worry, you know."

"I'm fine," Charlotte told him, though her hands were trembling.

Tipping his face toward the sun, Jack drew a long breath. "Do you think Thomas and Matilde are happy?"

Charlotte regarded him, puzzled. "Why would you ask?"

"I think they are." Jack turned his head toward the islands. "Look at this place. It's quiet. Beautiful."

Following his gaze over the waters, Charlotte watched a flock of seabirds swoop and skim along the surface. She could see the outlines of boats in the distance.

"I wonder what it would be like," Jack spoke softly. "They don't seem bothered by the Empire. It's remote enough that they go about their business without interference. The politics, the fighting. None of it affects them."

"That we know of," Charlotte added. The fishing shacks, the docks, and the village on the other side of the dunes did feel like a world apart from the tumult they'd left behind. But was it always this way? Were there parts of the Empire that were untainted by its abuses and corruptions?

"What if we could stay?" Jack asked. "Forget the war and make a new life. Together."

Charlotte had no words to reply. She'd never indulged in dreams of escaping the life she'd been born to. Before New Orleans, her commitment to the Resistance had been unwavering. But with the wind whispering in her hair and Jack's eyes drinking in her face, she began to want things she'd been denied.

Jack reached for her hands.

She startled at his touch, not because it was unwelcome but because the light caress of his fingers sent a jolt through her whole body. The bucket dropped from her hand, toppling on the beach. Clams spilled into the sand.

Charlotte cursed under her breath and moved to retrieve the bucket, but Jack caught her wrist.

"Leave it."

His other hand slipped around her waist to press into the small of her back. Jack released Charlotte's wrist and touched her cheek. His thumb traced the outline of her lips. She couldn't speak; she could hardly breathe.

"Charlotte."

She closed her eyes when he spoke her name and felt his lips brush against hers. Her mouth opened, tasting him and the salt of the sea air. She put her hands against his chest, then slid them up to grasp the collar of his shirt. She pulled him closer, tight against her.

Charlotte hadn't realized how much she'd wanted this, how carefully she'd shut away this longing. Now she wanted to drown in it. In him.

"Oy!" The harsh shout cut through the haze of Charlotte's desire. "Is that a mermaid giving away kisses?"

A chorus of whoops filled the air.

When Charlotte pulled away, she saw that Jack was looking down the beach toward the fishing settlement. She turned to see a gaggle of young men jostling each other as they made their way along the shore. As they came closer, it appeared they were hired hands, most likely from one of the larger fishing vessels that had anchored a short distance from the docks.

"Don't be shy, lovely mermaid!" Charlotte's heckler was one of the taller men among the roustabouts. He walked with the swagger of a leader. The others were watching him, laughing and grinning.

Jack spoke quietly, keeping his eyes on the approaching gang. "You should go back to the Weir. Hurry."

But it was too late. The men had formed a line between the dune and the sea. As they came forward, the sailors at each end closed ranks to trap Charlotte and Jack in a half circle.

Charlotte assessed the band of youths with increasing alarm. Their faces were ruddy, eyes overbright from drink.

"Go back to your captain," Charlotte said. She straightened in an attempt to make herself imposing. "I'm no mermaid and have no business with you."

The leader eyed Charlotte, then shouted to his companions. "Whaddya say, boys? Ain't she a mermaid? She's a lady in the water, after all."

"Aye, Robbins," one of the men answered. "She must be a mermaid."

Affirmations and chuckling rumbled through the rest of the group.

Jack stepped between Charlotte and the men. "We don't want any trouble."

"Trouble?" Robbins smiled at Jack, revealing a number of missing teeth. "Why would we cause trouble? We're all friends here."

"Good," Jack said. He took Charlotte's hand, leading her sideways to bypass the crescent moon of sailors. "We'll take our leave, then."

Robbins whistled through the gap in his teeth, and the men moved forward to block Jack.

"Why would you go when we've only just met?" Robbins said. "Tell you what. If you ain't feeling neighborly then, we won't keep you, but the mermaid ain't leaving till she gives us a kiss."

The sailors hollered their approval. Charlotte looked them over. They weren't armed for combat, but they did have the tools of fishermen: wooden clubs for stunning fish and long knives for gutting them. Neither she nor Jack had any weapons—or if Jack did, she couldn't see them.

Robbins sent an arc of tobacco spit into the sand. "What's it going to be, friend?"

Without warning, Jack launched himself at Robbins. The attack caught the sailor by surprise, and Jack knocked him down. The pair rolled along the beach. Jack gained the advantage, pinning Robbins in the sand. He began to rain punches down on Robbins's face.

"Run, Charlotte!" Jack shouted as he struck the sailor again.

Freed of their initial shock, the other men rallied to Robbins's aid. They charged at Jack.

As much as Charlotte abhorred the idea of leaving Jack with these brutes, she knew she had no chance unarmed against almost half a dozen men. Jack's best chance was for her to get help. Charlotte scrambled out of the surf and ran toward the dune.

"The lass is running!" She heard the call close behind her.

Someone slammed into her back, and Charlotte fell to the ground. She rolled over to see one of the sailors about to seize her. Charlotte grabbed a handful of sand and threw it in the man's eyes. He shouted an oath and stumbled backward.

Charlotte managed to stand up and start running again, but another sailor was already chasing her. He grasped her forearm and pulled hard, swinging Charlotte around. She stayed on her feet, but couldn't free herself. Charlotte looked at her assailant and pretended to quail. The man laughed. With his guard down, Charlotte landed a kick in his groin. The man buckled, falling to his knees.

"Oy! Mermaid!" Charlotte knew the sound of Robbins's voice meant things had gone badly for Jack. She gritted her teeth and bolted to the rise of the dune.

"You'd better stay if you don't want your boy here to end up in our chum!" Robbins shouted after her.

Charlotte halted and whirled around. To her left, two men held a struggling Jack between them. Robbins's face was bloody. He had a knife in his hand, which he pointed at Jack. The man Charlotte had kicked was still on the ground, moaning. But the sailor she'd blinded with sand was stalking toward her, rage on his face.

Chest tight and blood churning, Charlotte stood rigid. She could see no way out that wouldn't endanger Jack.

"Just go, Charlotte!" Jack's shout earned him a punch in the gut.

"Don't!" Charlotte took a step toward Robbins.

"We don't need to hurt him." Robbins spit into the sand again. This time bright crimson was mixed with the tobacco juice. "Not if you'll keep us company for a little while."

Charlotte didn't move again. She glared at Robbins; a hatred like she'd never known burned beneath her ribs. If only she had a gun or a knife, even a solid piece of wood.

"I think you should let him go." Grave stood on the edge of the sand dune, looking down at the scene.

Robbins shifted his gaze from Charlotte, surprise taking over his features, but soon enough a smirk returned to his face. "I think you'd better turn around and go back where you came from. You look ill. Tangling with us will only make you worse."

Grave ignored Robbins. He came down the slope to stand beside Charlotte.

"Are you hurt?" Grave asked her.

"I'll be fine," she said, then lowering her voice. "Jack."

Grave nodded. He looked at Robbins again. "Please let Jack go."

"Manners don't carry weight with our lot, boy." The sailor gave a snorting laugh.

Tilting his head, Grave regarded Robbins with a slight frown. "Why not?"

Bewildered, Robbins snarled, "To Hades with you and your freakish face."

He took the place of the men holding Jack, keeping his knife against Jack's throat, and told them, "Get rid of him."

One man had his knife drawn, the other held a club. They rushed at Grave.

Grave put his hands out in front of him, palms facing out. The men slammed into him as if they'd hit an iron gate, then reeled back. The knife-wielding sailor wheezed and dropped his weapon. He hunched over, arms wrapped around his ribs, desperately trying to draw breath. The man with the club was wincing, but came forward again. This time Grave lifted his arm and made a fist. When the man reached Grave, swinging his club at Grave's head, the boy brought his fist down on the sailor's shoulder. The crunching sound made Charlotte's stomach seize up.

The man screamed and fell to the sand, clutching at his shoulder.

"Bastard!" The man nearest to Charlotte ran toward Grave. He dove low to avoid any punches and instead wrapped his arms around Grave's calves in an attempt to bring him down.

Grave didn't so much as sway. His attacker came to a sudden stop, grunting as his belly met the sand. Grave jerked his leg free and brought his foot down in the middle of the sailor's back. The sound wasn't a crunch but a crack, and the man's scream was more of a screech. He didn't move again.

The two remaining sailors whom Charlotte had tussled with stared at their fallen shipmates, then bolted away.

That left only Robbins standing. He held the knife to Jack's throat and had Jack's arms pinned.

Grave turned toward Robbins.

"Stay there!" Robbins's voice quaked. "Don't come near, or I'll kill him."

"You need to let Jack go," Grave said in a calm voice.

Robbins watched Grave in horror. "What are you?" His hand trembled so strongly he could no longer grip his knife. It fell to the ground, and Robbins staggered backward. "What are you?" he said again.

Then he ran.

9.

HEY DIDN'T LEAVE the tavern for two days. They spoke quietly and kept away from the windows. Jeannette brought meals to their rooms.

Charlotte and Jack discussed leaving. But they had nowhere to go, and in the end they decided that they'd be more likely to be seen on the run than if they stayed quiet and hidden at the Weir. They asked Thomas and Matilde to listen for any news or gossip that would suggest someone had discovered their whereabouts, but the tavern keepers reported no word other than that some visiting sailors had gotten into a brawl on the beach.

The truth of that "brawl" haunted Charlotte. She'd seen plenty of fights, and she'd killed when she'd had to, but the ease with which Grave could devastate his opponents left Charlotte deeply unsettled. She tried to resolve her qualms by reminding herself that the sailors had instigated violence and had threatened her in particular. But Charlotte could still hear bones snapping and shattering. The agony of the men's cries lingered in her memory. So ugly, so jarring. They stole the brief, sweet thoughts that Jack had planted in her heart—thoughts of a new beginning, a life that could be a sanctuary after so much strife.

But Charlotte knew the truth now. There was no paradise. No place apart. Even the beauty and tranquility of this refuge had been marred by cruel and random brutality. Her sleep had become fitful, marked by visions of broken men and bloodied sands. So when she woke that night, she assumed that once again her mind had managed to pull itself free of another nightmare.

Charlotte propped herself on her elbows and waited for her fluttering heartbeat to settle. She looked out the window, hoping the gentle gleam of moonlight or the sight of winking stars might soothe her. But the moon was either new or snuffed out by clouds. Only darkness, cold and empty, floated beyond the pane of glass.

She lay back, resting her head on the pillow, and gazed up at the ceiling.

The floorboards in the middle of her room creaked.

Holding her breath, Charlotte went rigid. She listened, waiting for another sound or for silence to confirm that her ugly dreams were manifesting frightening noises in her waking imagination. All quiet.

Charlotte let go of her breath and closed her eyes.

Scuff. Scuff.

So soft. Almost imperceptible.

Scuff. Scuff.

Charlotte sat up. Her gaze swept the room, but her vision couldn't pierce the unbroken dark. When she drew her next breath, she caught the scent of brine and tannin.

She quickly rolled over, reaching for the dagger she'd stowed beneath her pillow. Her fingers brushed the sheath.

A hand closed around the back of her neck, holding her down. Another pushed her face into the pillow that swallowed her scream.

Someone grabbed her arms. Rope bit into her wrists as they were bound together.

She was jerked up. As Charlotte gulped air, the hand clamped over her mouth before she could shout for help. Another rope circled just below her sternum and pinned her arms to her sides. Charlotte still couldn't make out her assailants' features, even when they pulled her to her feet.

"You sure you tied her up good, Cooper?" A man's hoarse whisper. "'Cause that's what he said, remember. We have to control the girl, or we'll never get the other one."

Charlotte felt the tip of a dagger between her shoulder blades. "She's not going anywhere," Cooper answered. She felt breath against her ear. "One thrust and you're dead, so you'll do as you're told. Understood?"

The blade bit into her skin, and Charlotte gasped. "I understand."

"Gag her," Cooper ordered his partner. "Then put the collar on."

The kerchief he stuffed into Charlotte's mouth tasted of dirt and sweat. Cool metal encircled her throat, close fitting but not tight enough to choke.

"There's a chain attached to this collar." The man's face was right in front of Charlotte's. His breath a mélange of cloying rot and stale tobacco. "If it's pulled hard enough, something very unpleasant will happen to you. So no fighting us."

Charlotte gave a stiff nod. Her eyes were beginning to adjust to the darkness. She made out the tall, broad shape of Cooper's body.

"Good," Cooper whispered. "Let's get the boy. It's the sickly looking one that we want, Wallace. Get the other out of the way as quick as you can."

Charlotte cursed into the gag.

"Hush now, girl." Wallace shook the chain. It made a metallic tinkling noise that belied its sinister purpose. "It'd be a shame if I had to hurt you."

Wallace guided her to the door. When they reached the hall, Cooper lit a gas lantern. Charlotte squinted through the sudden light. At first the lantern confused her, as did her captors' lack of concern about muffling their approach to Jack and Grave's door, unlike the stealthy entrance they'd made before abducting Charlotte.

Then the troubling realization struck her. The knife against her back, the way she was bound and gagged, the collar. Wallace and Cooper wanted Charlotte to be seen. She was on display.

We have to control the girl, or we'll never get the other one.

Grave. They were after Grave, and somehow they knew about his loyalty, his need to protect Charlotte. Who were these men?

Cooper turned the doorknob and pushed, letting the door swing inward. The lantern light spilled into the room, and Jack sat up. His hand swept under his pillow and then he was on his feet, revolver in his hand, aimed at Cooper.

Wallace dragged Charlotte forward, putting her between Cooper and Jack.

"Not a good idea." Wallace pushed the knife into Charlotte's skin until she cried out. Even with the sound muffled by her gag, Jack knew its meaning. The muscles in his neck and jaw were tight, straining with his anger.

"That goes for you too." Wallace's voice was directed at Grave, who was sitting up on his bed. "Stay right there until we tell you otherwise."

Cooper pointed at Charlotte's neck. "A little prick from a knife won't do harm, but this will. Want to know what it does?"

Jack peered at Charlotte; his eyes traced the chain from the collar to Wallace's hand.

"Get that off her." Jack's voice shook.

Wallace laughed. "Ain't going to happen. But you are going to put that gun down and kick it over here."

Jack bent and placed his revolver on the floor, then kicked it toward Cooper.

As Cooper picked up the gun, Grave asked, "What does the collar do?"

The eerie calm of his voice spooked Cooper, who jumped back and aimed the gun at Grave.

"No need for that, Cooper," Wallace said. "He's a strange one, is all."

Cooper lowered the gun. "So you don't know what a Parisian Ribbon is?"

Grave shook his head.

"See that chain my partner has?" Cooper waited for Grave to nod. "One good tug, and the chain will come free, but when it does, a lever inside the collar is flipped. That sets the tiny parts inside in motion, and what they do is open up the inside of the collar so a wire comes out and the little gears spin and tighten that wire. And they won't stop until all the wire is wound up."

Grave frowned at Cooper. "That would cut her head off."

"Well, you see, the French were fond of folk losing their heads for a few years," Cooper replied. "Hence the name."

Like Grave, Charlotte had never heard of a Parisian Ribbon. She desperately wished she hadn't learned what it could do to her.

"I won't let you hurt her." Grave stood up.

"That's why we're having this conversation," Cooper told him. "So we understand each other. There's a lot of money being offered to bring you in. Money we want.

You don't want us to hurt your friend. If you come with us nicely, we both get what we want."

Sick with fear and anger, Charlotte despised being silenced by the gag. She couldn't speak to Grave, whether to offer words of reassurance or to tell him to ignore the threats and attack the men with the hope that Athene would show mercy to her in that fight. But she could say nothing.

"I'll go with you," Grave said.

"Put the shackles on him," Wallace said to Cooper.

Charlotte knew shackles didn't matter. If Grave wanted to, he could break free of the bonds. But he wouldn't because of her. She was a prop, being manipulated and used. And it was working.

Wallace jerked his thumb toward Jack. "What about that one?"

Jack's drawn features told Charlotte that he was feeling as helpless as she and equally outraged.

"Put him in the cellar with the others," Wallace said. "The contract said no killing, or they'll withhold half the bounty."

Jack's mouth twitched, and he took one step forward.

He jingled the chain. "Don't be getting any ideas, boy. Just 'cause I don't want to kill her don't mean I won't. Half a bounty is better than none. You do as we say, she don't get hurt."

Jack froze.

"Now, get on your knees," Wallace said.

He nodded to Cooper, who came up behind Jack as he

knelt. Cooper took Jack's gun by the barrel and struck Jack hard in the back of the head with the butt of the revolver. Jack slumped to the floor. Cooper bound Jack's wrists and ankles, then heaved the limp body over his shoulder.

"Come along now," Wallace said to Grave.

They followed Cooper out of the room. Then Wallace waited with Charlotte and Grave while Cooper proceeded to the cellar. A minute later, Cooper reappeared without Jack. Wallace took them out the back door.

Cooper's lantern offered sparse illumination against the pressing dark. The wind had picked up. Charlotte's nightdress billowed around and slapped against her body. Cooper and Wallace were taking them toward the sea, but away from the docks and fishing shacks. As they walked, Charlotte fought against the frightening questions chasing through her mind.

What if she or Wallace stumbled and the chain released accidentally? Where were they being taken, and did certain death await at that place? That the Empire had set a bounty for Grave wasn't surprising, but the detail they'd provided to hunters was alarming. It confirmed everything Lachance had suggested about a turncoat in the Resistance. Who had given them up?

Charlotte was certain they'd walked a mile or more when a hulking shape loomed ahead. As Cooper's lantern cast light on the object, it looked as if a giant manta ray had been stranded on the beach. But this manta shone in hues of copper and brass, and its back had been hollowed to accommodate a pilot and passengers. Glass enclosed only the front half of the vessel; the rear was exposed to the open air.

Wallace assisted Charlotte up the small set of steps into the craft. He directed her to one of the rear seats and buckled her into a harness. Wallace took the chair beside Charlotte while Cooper ordered Grave into one of the seats opposite them. Cooper made his way to the front of the craft, strapping himself into a taller chair at the helm. He began turning wheels and hauling back levers. The manta rumbled beneath them. Their chairs began to vibrate, and the entire vessel hummed as it slowly lifted off the ground. Cooper flipped more switches, then took hold of the throttle. The manta swept forward, buzzing only a few feet above the surf as they raced along the shore.

10.

HARLOTTE KEPT HERSELF upright, but inside, a part of her quailed at the sight: the Empire had reduced Boston to rubble, yet left skeletal structures so the devastation could never be forgotten. The only colors that remained were those of death—black char, gray ash. Rumors abounded with regard to Boston's barrenness. Some said the Empire had poisoned the land, ensuring that nothing could ever grow again. Others argued the land was cursed, that Athene abhorred the razing of the city, and her grief had kept life from returning.

The manta sped into the harbor toward the lone dock the Empire had constructed to receive and transport prisoners to the Crucible. A pair of gun turrets capped the end of the dock to dissuade trespassers. Cooper eased off the throttle, and the vessel slowed, gliding toward the shore.

No ships were in port, but a cluster of men stood on the dock awaiting the manta's arrival. All were dressed in military garb except two dockhands. Cooper steered the manta alongside the men and cut the engine. The craft settled onto the surface of the water as Wallace threw a line to one of the dockhands.

Once the manta was tied on, Wallace directed Charlotte to the edge of the craft. The size of the squad awaiting them surprised her. She guessed it was twenty or more men. One of the soldiers reached down to lift her from the vessel, while Wallace clambered up onto the dock to keep the chain of the Parisian Ribbon slack. Cooper disembarked with Grave.

A man from the squad stepped forward. His uniform's adornments identified him as an officer. He looked over Charlotte and then took a much longer time assessing Grave.

"These are the two we've been looking for," the officer said. "Lewis. Chapman. See to it that these men receive their reward. The squad will escort the prisoners to their cells."

"Pardon me, sir," Wallace cut in.

The officer pivoted, his expression making it clear he found being addressed by the bounty hunter very distasteful.

Wallace noticed the officer's disposition as well and ducked his head in respect. "You'll see that I have a contraption on the girl's neck. To keep her in line."

"Yes," the officer replied.

"It's just that it's quite an expensive device." Wallace tugged at his shirt collar. "If I could take it off . . . I have the key right here."

He pulled a minuscule silver key from his vest pocket.

"Hand it over." The officer reached for the key. "And give me the chain."

With some reluctance, Wallace relinquished the key and the chain.

"The collar will be returned to you once the prisoner is secure," the officer told Wallace.

"Of course, sir." Wallace cleared his throat. "Might I have your name in case I need to inquire as to your whereabouts?"

The officer's heavy brow creased with irritation. "Bristow. Major Bristow."

"Much obliged, Major." Wallace bowed, making it clear that he rarely had occasion to do so.

Had Charlotte not been gagged, she would have pleaded for the collar to be removed. The squad, numerous and armed as they were with sabers and rifles, posed enough of a threat that any attempt at escape would have been suicidal. The collar's weight on her neck sapped her strength, a constant reminder of what could happen if the device were activated. But for now she was at the mercy of Major Bristow.

"Form up!"

The squad snapped to attention at Bristow's command. The group divided, half of the soldiers forming ranks in front of Charlotte and Grave, and the others behind them. The major stayed at Charlotte's side.

"Forward!"

They began to march. Charlotte had to walk quickly to match the swift, snapping steps of the squad. They'd reached the end of the docks when two sharp rifle reports sounded. Charlotte twisted her neck toward the sound. The soldiers at her back partially blocked her view, but she thought she saw Wallace and Cooper lying on the dock with the soldiers, Lewis and Chapman, standing over them.

"Eyes ahead," Major Bristow said to Charlotte. "With that Ribbon around your neck, the last thing you want to do is stumble."

Charlotte complied. It seemed incongruous to pity her one-time captors, but Charlotte couldn't rejoice in Wallace and Cooper's fate. Promised fortune, they'd unwittingly brought on their own demise. The Empire's swift, cruel execution of the two bounty hunters wasn't all that troubled Charlotte. Their deaths meant that capturing Charlotte and Grave hadn't been enough. They also wanted to keep the whereabouts of their prisoners a secret, so much so that assurances Wallace and Cooper might have offered to keep silent wouldn't have been enough. All of these things offered clues as to the fate that awaited Charlotte and Grave, but Charlotte couldn't yet discern what that might be.

She *did* know where they were going. She'd known from the moment she'd spied the burned coast. As special punishment for Boston's role in fomenting the War for

Independence, after the entire city had been razed, the Empire had erected the primary internment structure in the colonies: the Crucible. Of all the horrors evoked by the Empire, the Crucible was counted among the worst. Charlotte had never heard it spoken of except in fear. The Crucible was a place that devoured hope. And now she would be locked away inside it. The prison occupied the one-time site of Faneuil Hall, where a skirmish the Revolutionaries had named the Boston Massacre took place. Rallying cries about the unjust deaths of the five men who'd fallen there helped to create a surge of colonial unrest, and eventually the outbreak of war. The placement of the Crucible served as a cruel joke, the fate of Boston demonstrating what a true massacre looked like.

The march from the harbor to the Crucible was brief. Charlotte could hear the place before she laid eyes on it. From the shoreline, she caught the sounds of a steady thrumming, deep groans, and the anguished grind of metal on metal. Then the prison itself was rising before her. A feat of engineering on which the Empire prided itself, the Crucible was constructed of individual iron cubes, each just large enough to accommodate a man. The cubes were grouped in clusters of four with each one fixed onto a joint with a swivel hinge. The joint connected via a long steel arm to a central axis around which the clusters orbited. As the inner axis turned, the swivel hinges of each cluster turned. In addition to turning, the Crucible's arms also rose and descended from the central axis. The Crucible was in near-constant motion, slow but inexorable, controlled from one of the guard towers that ringed the structure. Its movement was halted only to accommodate the entrances and exits of guards and officers.

But before the Crucible stopped for their party, they would witness another mockery of the Resistance. Once she had realized where they were being taken, Charlotte had expected her captors would parade them past the Hanging Tree, but she still wasn't prepared for the stark horror of it. The Hanging Tree wasn't a living thing—after Boston had been burned over, the earth was salted, barren. Instead, the British had erected a tree of their own, a blasphemous replica of the stately elm that patriots had dubbed the Liberty Tree. While the Empire's tree had been forged from metal like the trees of New York's Iron Forest, the similarities between the two sculptures ended there. The Hanging Tree had a hulking trunk of black iron and thick, twisting branches that gave the appearance of forced contortion in their spread rather than nimble grace. The matte black of cold iron made it seem as if the tree still bore scars of the fires that consumed Boston, the trunk and limbs forever charred.

As much as the iron body of the Hanging Tree evoked dread, the sight of strange, gilded fruit hanging from its branches proved far worse, burrowing into Charlotte's mind to leave an indelible, sickening image. If the razing of Boston had served to demonstrate the breadth of the Empire's vengeance, the Hanging Tree bespoke its cruel precision.

The severed heads of America's Revolutionary heroes,

encased in gold, dangled from the black limbs. These eternal death masks glittered in a mockery of the patriots' sacrifice. Charlotte recognized a few of the visages, those features familiar from portraits she'd studied alongside the lessons in Revolutionary history that all children of the Resistance memorized. The noble George Washington and his celebrated officer, Nathanael Green. Charlotte could identify Christopher Gadsden only because whoever had cast his head in gold had, in a cruel twist of humor, added a brass and iron rattlesnake that curled around what was left of Gadsden's neck.

As their line trudged past the tree, Charlotte saw that a ribbon had been tied around the forehead of Patrick Henry, with the words DEATH IT IS crudely scrawled on the silk. She turned her gaze away from the awful monument and snuck a glance at Grave. His eyes were fixed upon the tree. He frowned as they passed by, but his expression was more puzzled than troubled.

Charlotte felt an unexpected pang of disappointment, but quickly chided herself. After all, what meaning could the Hanging Tree have for Grave? He hadn't been raised in the Resistance. No stories had been repeated to him that would have instilled a reverence for the men whose dignity the iron tree so blatantly violated.

The squad came to a halt at a gatehouse that stood in front of the Crucible. The guard inside exited the small structure and saluted Major Bristow, then returned to his station and picked up a speaking tube. Moments later, a bellow like the sound of a giant's hunting horn rattled Charlotte to her bones. The Crucible slowed to a stop.

The gatehouse guard reappeared. He had bundles of black cloth in his hands.

"The hoods," the guard said to Major Bristow.

Bristow nodded, and before Charlotte realized what was happening, the guard was in front of her and her world was enveloped in darkness. An arm hooked under each of her shoulders, and she was dragged forward. Because the threat of her escape was nil, Charlotte decided that temporarily blinding captives must be a measure taken to keep secret the means of entering and exiting the Crucible's cells. The thud of boots on packed ash transformed to a dull ring as she was pulled upward. Her toes bumped against metal stairs. As she was carried, it occurred to Charlotte that the hood prevented her from knowing where Grave was, whether he'd be placed in a cell near hers or somewhere far away. There would be no companionship in the Crucible. No commiserating or plotting.

The whine of metal hinges in need of oiling came from somewhere in front of Charlotte. Her feet no longer knocked against steps, instead sliding on a flat surface. The guards holding Charlotte halted, and she returned to bearing her own weight. Someone pulled the hood from her head, but her surroundings became only slightly brighter. She'd been taken to one of the cells. It was a small, square space. Big enough for a tall man to lie down in, but not much more.

One of the guards cut the ropes binding her, and Major Bristow stepped forward to insert the tiny key into the collar. Charlotte heard a soft click, and the collar loosened. Bristow took the collar and wound up the chain. He didn't say anything before he left the cell. The guards followed. She turned to watch them leave. One of the guards tossed a skin of water toward Charlotte. It hit the floor close to where she stood.

An order, or an act of mercy?

Charlotte thought it more likely the former, given the strictures of this place.

The door closed, and she was alone. Charlotte sat down, staring at the locked door. The skin of water lay untouched beside her feet. She heard a rumbling and then a grinding. The Crucible began to move.

11.

THE METALLIC PUNGENCY of Charlotte's surroundings spilled into all of her senses, as though she had bits of copper and brass resting on her tongue. Worse than the taste of metal was the ceaseless vibration of her cell. As the Crucible turned on its axis and her cell swung on its hinge, Charlotte's body could never rest. Though the movement was slow, it couldn't be ignored and crept inside her so that her entire being felt as though it was being shaken, gently, but without pause. Thus far sleep had been impossible. The only comfort Charlotte found was in laying her fingers against her neck and remembering she was free of the Parisian Ribbon. Its absence still brought her small relief.

Watery daylight filtered into the space through slits on the wall, slim gashes in the steel just below the ceiling. Charlotte wondered if total darkness would have caused greater torment. More fear, certainly. But she suspected that these bare openings, allowing only a trickle of fresh air and shreds of sunlight into the cramped space, induced more agony by reminding the imprisoned of an outside world from which they'd been torn and to which they'd likely never return.

Will I ever return?

Never having had so much time to ponder her own demise, Charlotte now considered her possible fates in the starkest of terms. Death? Likely. Torture? Very likely. She might even count herself lucky if the former happened without any of the latter.

Charlotte shunted aside the notion of escape, at least for the time being. The Crucible's fearsome reputation derived in no small part from the fact that not a soul had ever escaped its mechanized cubes. Those who entered the Crucible were not seen again, except for the occasional gilded head added to the macabre ornaments of the Hanging Tree. Even if others had found ways out of these cells, Charlotte didn't have any of the tools needed to effect an escape. She still wore her nightdress, its hem black with grime after the journey. The soles of her feet were the same shade, and dirt had caked beneath her fingernails. Unpleasant as it was, Charlotte wouldn't waste precious water for washing.

A night and a day had passed, but no one had brought food. The Crucible had not once stopped moving. Though it was hard to judge by what little light entered her cell, Charlotte surmised that it was late afternoon. Soon enough she would be engulfed in darkness and pass another night bereft of sleep while hunger pangs stabbed her.

Better to have no food than no water.

A bellow from outside the Crucible echoed within Charlotte's cell. She clapped her hands over her ears to block the pain of the blast. Only when the sound had faded did Charlotte take her hands away. Her body was still humming from the vibrations of the cell, but she knew the Crucible had stopped moving. Though it felt pitiful, she couldn't suppress the desperate hope that a guard would bring her something to eat. Anything.

The sounds of boots on metal came to her softly at first and then grew louder. She heard men's voices, though she couldn't make out their words. A slot opened on her cell door.

"Stay against the wall, prisoner."

Very little of Charlotte's cramped cell was not against a wall, but she shrank into a corner as best she could.

The door opened, and a man entered her cell. In the dim light, Charlotte couldn't make out his features.

"This won't do," he said. "Bring a lantern."

"Yes, sir."

Charlotte's pulse skipped. There was something about the man who was in her cell. His voice.

He spoke again. "Give her the bread."

Another man came into the cell and set a bundle in front of Charlotte. She snatched it up, unfolding the cloth to reveal the loaf inside. She forced herself to tear off only a small chunk and chew it slowly, though she was mad to rip the bread apart and wolf down great hunks. She took a sip of water before tearing off a bit more of the loaf to eat.

The first guard had returned with the lantern. He handed it to the man, who watched Charlotte as she ate. Charlotte's attention was consumed by her appetite, so it wasn't until she swallowed that she looked up.

The bread fell from her hands.

Her mouth opened, but words died in her throat.

Coe set the lantern on the floor. "I'm told the bounty hunters didn't harm you when you were taken. Is that true?"

Charlotte couldn't nod. She couldn't move.

Her mind refused to accept what her eyes saw, nor could she reconcile the contradiction between the real concern she'd heard in his voice with his shocking appearance. Coe wore the uniform of his office: Commodore Winter of the Imperial Air Force. She'd seen him dressed this way before, and yet now it was different. He was different. His bearing. The tension bleeding off him as he glanced toward the cell door.

Charlotte grappled with her thoughts, searching for an explanation other than the one manifesting starkly before her.

Coe was the turncoat.

"I don't want to hurt you, Charlotte. Please believe that."

Coe was speaking, but Charlotte could barely understand him. The bread she'd just eaten rolled around in her stomach.

"There are many things I hope you'll come to understand," Coe said.

Charlotte hadn't planned to attack Coe. She simply did. Her muscles bunched, and she launched herself off the wall with a shriek. She took Coe by surprise, and when her body rammed into his, he stumbled back but he didn't fall. Instantly, three guards were in the room. Two of them grabbed Charlotte and hauled her away from Coe. The third aimed his rifle at her chest.

"No!" Coe started toward them.

"Stand down, all of you." The voice emanated from a silhouette in the doorway. The man was shadowed, his face masked by darkness, but Charlotte saw that he was very tall with broad square shoulders. Despite the noise of the scuffle, he hadn't shouted, yet his words seemed to resonate through the cell.

The guards who'd accosted Charlotte reacted instantly, almost jumping back as they released her. Coe's response was likewise physical and visceral; he stood at attention, chest lifted, one hand raised in a salute as the heels of his boots snapped together.

The man stepped out of the obscuring dimness, revealing dress that bespoke authority. His navy blue coat was embroidered with gold and adorned with an epaulette. Stars had been stitched onto the shoulder piece, denoting the officer's rank.

Admiral.

Any questions Charlotte had as to this man's identity were dispelled by his features. His face was a weathered reflection of characteristics she'd come to know as those of Coe and Jack, though she could see immediately that Coe bore a stronger resemblance to Admiral Winter while Jack favored their mother. Charlotte even caught a ghost of Linnet in the height and sharpness of her father's cheekbones.

Admiral Winter had dark mahogany hair shot through with silver. His bicorne was tucked under his arm.

"At ease." His second order prompted the other soldiers to drop their salutes, but none of them appeared to relax in the least.

The admiral's gaze fell upon Charlotte, lingered there but a moment, then turned into a scowl when he looked at Coe.

"Considering the ruckus I heard from outside, one would think you had a formidable adversary in this cell," Admiral Winter said. "And yet the only prisoner I see is this girl. Tell me, *Commodore*, how is it that you allowed your captive to attack you?"

Coe understood his father didn't want an answer and looked at the floor in shame.

"Perhaps I underestimate your foe." Admiral Winter turned his attention back to Charlotte. "Lady Marshall's reputation does precede her."

Charlotte refused to quail under the officer's scrutiny and answered his hawklike gaze with a steady glare. Something that might have been amusement flickered in Admiral Winter's eyes. He smiled.

"Courage or bravado?"

She didn't answer.

"My own men are wise enough to fear me," he told her. "Considering your current position, it might serve you better to do likewise."

His condescension disgusted Charlotte. "If I tremble and weep, will you set me free? I think not."

"Freedom is not within your reach, Lady Marshall," Winter said. "But a conciliatory attitude could improve your circumstances considerably."

Having expended what little energy she'd had, yet wanting to show strength, Charlotte leaned against the wall for support. The world had shifted beneath her, toppling all she believed to be real, making her dizzy, weakening her knees.

"Perhaps you need further motivation to develop the proper rapport with me." Admiral Winter turned to the guards.

"Blackwell will stay," he continued. "Commodore, see to your orders."

Coe and two guards saluted Admiral Winter and exited the cell.

"I regret that we're meeting under these circumstances," the admiral said to Charlotte. "Though I am pleased you've had the chance to experience the Crucible—it offers an appropriate lesson."

"I'm not a schoolgirl," Charlotte said. "Stop speaking to me as though you're some kind of teacher."

"But you do have so much to learn," he replied with a chilly smile. "For instance, we needn't be adversaries. It's true that you have much to lose here, but you also could make surprising gains."

His smugness filled Charlotte with disgust.

"Youth is like being carried through life by a strong current," Admiral Winter said. "All you feel is the speed of the river, the thrill of rapids, never comprehending your utter lack of control, your constant peril."

"You talk too much," Charlotte muttered.

His veneer of unshakeable certitude wavered, slipping to reveal a flash of outrage in his eyes, and Charlotte thought he would strike her. Instead, Admiral Winter calmed himself by uttering a disdainful laugh.

"If you prefer a demonstration to words, so be it."

The silence that followed left Charlotte more unnerved than anything he'd said thus far, and she regretted provoking him. The admiral remained mute, stretching the strained quiet that enhanced the threat of his words until Charlotte wanted to twitch with discomfort.

Admiral Winter's smile provoked an instinctive shiver in Charlotte's limbs. He looked over his shoulder at the figures who hovered outside the door.

"Bring him in," Admiral Winter said.

The guards had returned, this time supporting a man between them. The man's head was slumped, his hair shaggy. His legs moved in a semblance of walking, but his body was as limp as a rag doll's, his limbs skeletal. Charlotte's mouth went dry. Was this the fate of the Crucible's imprisoned?

"Good afternoon," Admiral Winter walked up to the prisoner. "I have someone here I'm sure you'll be pleased to see."

The prisoner's head was still bent. A sound like a rasp came from his throat.

"Get him some water," Coe quietly told one of the guards.

When the guard released the man, he teetered on his feet but didn't fall.

Horror and pity choked Charlotte as she watched the poor man. The guard returned with a cup of water. He held it up to the man's lips. The prisoner didn't drink so much as slurp and cough in a way that made Charlotte wonder how rarely he was provided water to drink.

"Now, then," the admiral said. "Say hello to our guest."

The man slowly lifted his face. A matted beard hid many of his features, but not enough to stop Charlotte from gasping and then giving a broken cry.

"Father?"

Charles Marshall had aged like Charlotte's mother, but also differently, not just in the passing of years. Whatever time he'd spent within the cells of the Crucible had drained his life away. He looked more like the husk of a person than a man. He stared at Charlotte, his eyes haunted.

"No," he whispered. "No. Please no."

He began to weep. A coughing fit overtook him.

Tears dampened Charlotte's cheeks as well, her emotions a maddening contrast of sorrow and joy. When Caroline Marshall had told Charlotte her father was gone,

Charlotte had assumed that meant dead. But he was alive! Only the life he'd been sentenced to might have been worse than death.

How long had he been here? When was he captured? Why hadn't her mother told Charlotte and Ashley the truth? She wanted answers, but had no one to offer them.

Maybe their mother didn't know. Perhaps she thought Charles had been killed in battle when in fact he'd been captured.

Her thoughts were dizzying, but Charlotte still walked toward her father, wanting to hold his hands. To offer some comfort.

Coe stepped into her path and grabbed her arm. "No."

"Let go of me," Charlotte snapped, trying to free herself.

"He's ill," Coe told her. "You shouldn't touch him."

Charlotte stopped trying to free her arm. "How ill?"

It was Admiral Winter who answered. "Consumption."

A sickness that was almost always a death sentence, especially without treatment.

Still weeping and coughing, Charlotte's father no longer had the strength to stay on his feet. His legs buckled, and he fell to the floor.

"Take the prisoner back to his cell." Admiral Winter watched Charles with open revulsion.

Charlotte didn't bother to argue. Begging for her father to stay in the room would have been selfish. The exertion of movement paired with the emotional trauma of seeing his daughter in the Crucible would already be taking a horrible toll on his health. Charlotte didn't know if her father would even believe he'd truly seen her, or if he'd come to believe she had been a fevered hallucination. Or a cruel trick concocted by his captors.

The door clanged shut, leaving her alone with Admiral Winter and Coe once again.

Tears still came from Charlotte's eyes, but she kept her voice from shaking. "Are you happy? Did it bring you joy to watch both of us suffer?"

"I'm not a sadist, Lady Marshall," Winter said. "I merely wanted you to be aware of the reality of your situation. And of the choices that lie before you."

"What choices?"

Admiral Winter smiled at her. "There are always choices, but given how you were raised, it makes perfect sense that you wouldn't accurately perceive your options. Allow me to draw back the veil."

He placed his hand on Coe's shoulder. "My elder son offers a fine example of what I want to convey to you. You believe in the Resistance. Why wouldn't you? It's all you've known. You were raised in seclusion, shut away from the world and taught only the lessons that would benefit the Resistance."

Charlotte listened, reviling him but keeping silent.

"The allure of the Resistance reaches beyond its own children. The youth of the Empire, seeking their fortunes, testing the bounds of authority, can become entranced by the myths of liberty and defiance."

Looking at Coe, the admiral sighed. "Neither of my

sons could resist that siren song. I blame myself for being absent through their childhood. My duties required that it be so, but I should have been more vigilant. Instead I presumed loyalty."

Coe flinched slightly. He glanced at Charlotte, and she saw dread in his eyes. Whatever his father was about to say, Coe didn't want Charlotte to hear it. But Admiral Winter didn't continue his story, instead shifting his gaze to Coe.

"Commodore, why don't you tell our guest why you ultimately returned your allegiance to the Empire."

Coe's Adam's apple shifted as he swallowed.

Observing his son's hesitation, the admiral said, "No need to wallow in shame. Those mistakes are in the past. You've been redeemed."

After clearing his throat, Coe looked at Charlotte. "I'd been supporting the Resistance for a little over a year when my involvement with the rebels was discovered."

"By whom?" Charlotte asked, caught off guard by this revelation. Coe hadn't joined the Resistance as a mole. He'd been compromised.

Coe didn't answer, but turned his gaze toward his father.

"One can never be too careful with secret correspondence," Admiral Winter said, favoring Coe with a pitying smile. "Rather than making my son's unsavory alliance with the enemy public, I found more efficacy in turning his errors to the benefit of the Empire."

He gestured for Coe to continue.

"My father offered me a choice. Die for the Resistance or become a hero of the Empire."

You should have died. Charlotte didn't voice her thought, but Coe read it on her face.

"Of course you condemn me, think me a coward, but I didn't return my fealty to my father and Britannia to save my life," he said.

Watching Charlotte's expression fill with contempt, Coe went on. "When I first joined the Resistance, I believed in it. I was happy to call the Empire tyrannical and was ready to struggle to overthrow coloznial oppressors. But once I was inside the Resistance and assessed its capabilities—militarily and politically—I knew the entire movement was doomed. This was no true movement. It was desperation. I knew the strength of Britannia—I'd inhabited its upper echelons my whole life. The leaders of the Resistance are deluded to think they could ever triumph against the Empire's might. All they do is beg crumbs from the French and offer one another platitudes about their righteous cause."

Charlotte couldn't react. Her emotions were too volatile. Rage churned in her blood; she was sickened by Coe's tale. But worst of all, a small part of her was fearful. What if his description of the Resistance was the truth?

"I believe the only hope for a strong, thriving society depends on the survival of the Empire and its unimpeded expansion. My father could have executed me or sent me here to wither away, forgotten. But he chose another option:

he raised me up and gave me new life, new hope, new purpose. He created a way by which I could be absolved of my sins, to be redeemed in the eyes of the Empire. To become its champion and destroy its enemy by devouring it from within."

Charlotte shuddered at the words *new life.* "Athene help us . . . Lazarus. You're Lazarus."

She didn't want to believe, but the moment she'd spoken, she knew it was true. A high-ranking officer of the Empire sympathetic to the Resistance. Part of the story was true, but it didn't end where the Resistance believed it did. Admiral Winter had created Lazarus by leveraging Coe's guilt and fear. If Lazarus was working for the Empire, then everything the Resistance had built its strategies upon—counterintelligence, the secrecy of its own plans, the strength of its ranks—could not be trusted. It was all a lie.

"Coe speaks of your cleverness and strength," Admiral Winter said. "Those are qualities I value. That's why I want to offer you a second chance, as I did my son."

Charlotte opened her mouth to spit a rejection at him, but he held up a warning hand.

"You want to hear what I have to say."

She waited, though her limbs were still trembling with outrage.

"Your father is not beyond hope," Admiral Winter told her. "The Empire has exceptional practitioners of physic as well as the skill of healers from the Temple of Athene. Nothing would be held back in our attempt to restore your father's health . . . if you accept my offer."

Charlotte could hardly breathe. Her body quaked with indecision.

Her father might die from his illness no matter what she did. But could she take that chance, knowing that there was a possibility his life could be saved?

And what to do with the terrible knowledge she'd gained? Impossible as it seemed, she had to get word to the Resistance about Coe's treachery. If she failed to do so, it was only a matter of time before the Empire played a winning hand from its stacked deck and annihilated the Resistance. There was nothing she could do from the Crucible. No escape. She had to find a way out of this place and to get somewhere that she could be found or that offered even the slimmest chance to slip away.

Charlotte had no doubt that Jack would eventually free himself, but would he try to track Charlotte and Grave or would he seek help? He wouldn't go back to New Orleans to contend with Caroline Marshall, even if Ash was there. If Jack contacted Coe, then Jack would only be misled. But if he went to Linnet and Meg for help, they would surely take action. Still, coming to the Crucible would be suicide. There had to be something Charlotte could do to help her friends even in her current predicament. She didn't know how much time she had.

"I do want to save my father," Charlotte said.

"I would have been disappointed if you didn't," Admiral Winter replied.

"What do you want from me?" Charlotte asked.

"In order to proceed with Grave, we need him

pacified." The admiral folded his arms behind him and paced in front of her like an officer inspecting a regiment. "He hasn't tried to escape because we hold the threat of harming you over him."

"And that's not enough?" Charlotte snapped. She hated being the key to Grave's manipulation, but so far she couldn't think of any way to counter Admiral Winter's maneuver.

"In the Crucible it is," he answered. "But we'll soon be leaving for the Floating City, where our work with Grave will truly begin. The Crucible is a place for destruction, not discovery. The experts and facilities we need to fully understand him are in New York. Moreover, I'm hopeful that Grave—and you—will take the change of location as a show of our aims. You will continue to be his traveling companion, and you must ensure that Grave cooperates fully with us."

"No." Charlotte cringed inwardly, not wanting to envision what assignments Admiral Winter had planned for Grave. "Not even for my father."

She closed her eyes, silently begging his forgiveness and Athene's mercy for having to choose.

"Since you are willing to sacrifice your father for Grave"—the heels of the admiral's boots snapped together when he turned to look directly at her—"I'm certain you'd also be willing to sacrifice yourself."

Charlotte didn't respond.

"However," Admiral Winter went on, "you would be foolish to think holding Grave indefinitely is worthwhile to our purpose. His utility extends so far as he can serve us. If he isn't actively supporting the Empire, then our only recourse is to prevent his ever returning to the hands of the Resistance."

"You can't kill him." Charlotte sniffed in disdain.

"I know there are ways he cannot be killed," he replied, his eyes cold. "But by no means have we exhausted the ways that could be attempted. Do you think Grave would survive the heat of the Great Forge? Or bombardment by our air fleet?"

Charlotte had to pull her gaze off him. She didn't know the answer to those questions.

The assured quality of Admiral Winter's tone made her hate him all the more, because he could see he had Charlotte cornered. "You've already shown your willingness to defy the Resistance by spiriting Grave away from New Orleans. What more harm can be done by simply ensuring his survival in New York?"

There was only a hint of truth in what the admiral said. Knowing that Grave wasn't resisting imprisonment was far from telling him to aid the Empire. Some other course had to exist, but for now Charlotte couldn't find it. What she needed was time.

"Very well."

Admiral Winter's smile could have belonged to Hades himself.

"Excellent," he said. "I'll arrange for transport. You'll be provided with clean clothing and food. It's important that Grave knows you're not being mistreated."

Charlotte chose not to respond. She could barely keep her feelings in check as it was.

"You'll speak with him before we leave." Admiral Winter walked toward the door. "Be certain he understands both his and your situation."

She nodded.

"Till tomorrow, then." He stepped out of the cell and was gone.

Coe looked at her, his face pained. "Charlotte—"

"Don't speak to me," she said. "What you've done is unforgivable."

"If you'd let me explain." Coe took a step toward her.

"No." Charlotte raised her fists, making it clear she'd attack if he came any closer. "No more lies."

He gazed at her a moment, then breathed a long sigh before he went to the cell door. Looking over his shoulder at her, Coe said, "I'm sorry it had to be this way."

Then he was gone, too.

12.

GRAVE STARED AT her with his unusual rust-colored irises. Silent.

Guards had arrived at Charlotte's cell as daylight began to seep in through the slit in the wall. They'd taken her, hooded, to a barracks. The hood was removed, and Charlotte was left in a room with a tub of cold water to wash, clean underclothes, and a simple dress. A plate of bread, cheese, and fruit served as Charlotte's breakfast.

Coe brought Grave to the room, ushering him to a chair opposite Charlotte. She was glad to see that, like her, Grave was no longer bound. He appeared calm, and he smiled at Charlotte when he sat. Coe then walked a short distance away, giving a semblance of privacy without moving out of earshot. His presence limited what Charlotte could say, but she hadn't expected she'd be allowed to see Grave without supervision.

Doing her best to convey the duress she was under, Charlotte kept her message plain. They would accompany Coe and his father, Admiral Winter, to the Floating City. While they were in Admiral Winter's care, they were to do all he asked without question.

While she spoke, Charlotte was horribly aware of all the things she wanted to say. She couldn't warn Grave that his life was in peril. She wanted to tell him to run. To forget about protecting her, to discard his unflagging loyalty. She wondered if he'd even listen, were she free to speak her mind. All Charlotte could hope for was that Grave took her simple commands and understood the greater meaning of the silence, of all that was left unsaid. Grave had always been strange, but his mind wasn't feeble. He had to know that her choices were limited. Grave trusted her. But did he trust her enough to know that if she was putting him in harm's way now, she did so only because it offered the means to save them both later?

Grave had been watching her for several minutes when he finally said, "They took the Parisian Ribbon off your neck."

At the mention of the device, Charlotte's hand went to her throat. "Yes."

"I'm glad," Grave said.

He looked at Coe. "When are we leaving?"

Coe regarded Grave, a pleased expression taking over his features. "Within the hour."

When Coe shifted his gaze to Charlotte, his smile was

pained, but also resolved. Her fingernails dug into her palms.

What could she do? She had to find a way out of this.

She drew a surprised breath when Grave reached under the table to take her hand. He grasped her fingers for barely a moment and then let go.

"I'm ready."

Charlotte had no idea what he meant.

13.

O F ALL THE places in the Empire Charlotte didn't want to be, the Military Platform of the Floating City ranked near the top. But she readily admitted the accommodations Admiral Winter had provided were far preferable to a cell in the Crucible. Charlotte didn't know the precise function of the building to which she'd been taken, but from what little she'd glimpsed, it seemed to provide temporary quarters for visiting military officials.

Guards had been posted outside her door, but Charlotte was otherwise left to her own devices. As soon as she'd been left alone, she'd gone to the window, but had immediately ruled it out as a way to escape. The smooth marble walls of the building offered no grips for a climb, and the drop was too far to be sure she wouldn't break a bone.

That afternoon, Charlotte received tea and visitors.

Coe directed his companions to gather around a table as cadets set out trays of sandwiches and cakes.

"Charlotte." Coe gestured to a woman and man, both severe-faced and garbed in military uniforms. "Lieutenants Redding and Thatcher."

"Will the admiral be joining us?" Charlotte asked.

"My father has other commitments," he replied. "He has tasked me with the oversight of Grave."

She nodded, wondering when or if she'd see Admiral Winter again. If Coe had been given full responsibility over Charlotte and Grave's captivity, perhaps she could find a way to leverage her familiarity with him to her advantage.

Indicating the third guest, a man wearing the drab clothing of the Hive and a tinker's apron, Coe added, "And Summing Miller."

Summing Miller twitched in his seat, sneaking anxious glances at his military counterparts.

"Miller here is one of the most skilled tinkers of the Hive," Coe told Charlotte. "He's made great strides in weapons innovation."

"Thank you, sir," Miller said.

"We've recruited him to assist us in the continuation of Hackett Bromley's work." Coe waited for a cadet to fill his teacup, then added sugar and cream.

Charlotte sat up straighter. She hadn't heard anything of Hackett Bromley—Grave's father, or as Grave would say, the Maker—other than that the Empire had taken him into custody.

"Unfortunately, the information Bromley provided hasn't been fruitful," Coe said.

Charlotte glanced at the lieutenants, wondering what their role in this was.

Catching Charlotte's eyes, Lieutenant Redding said, "We hope that you'll be able to provide Miller with valuable insights, given the time you've spent in close proximity to the asset."

Charlotte's eyebrows lifted. "The asset?"

"Grave," Coe said. "Keep in mind, most of us aren't on familiar terms with him the way you are."

"You'll have to pardon me," Lieutenant Redding said quickly. She had a pinched face, made more so by the tight braid ringing her head. "We don't often deal with civilians . . . in this capacity."

Lieutenant Thatcher chuckled, making his heavy jowls shake beneath a thicket of dark sideburns.

A cup clattered. Tinker Miller had knocked over his tea and was mopping up the hot liquid with a linen napkin.

"I'm so very sorry." Miller had begun to sweat.

"No worries, chap." Thatcher reached for a sandwich. "They'll pour you another cup."

He waved at the cadet hovering nearby. While the cadet poured Miller's tea, the tinker watched the cup and saucer like they might come alive and bite him.

Charlotte picked up her cup. "Will you tell me what you learned from Bromley?"

Thatcher and Redding exchanged a glance, then looked at Coe, who nodded.

"Bromley engaged in unique experiments with alchemy," Redding told Charlotte. "Specifically transmutation of organic matter to inorganic."

Charlotte had taken a bite of a cucumber sandwich, but now found it hard to swallow.

Meg stood up. "What is he?" She pointed at Grave.

"Flesh and blood," Bromley answered. "But blood is iron, and bone can become steel. The heart and lungs are but machines. If built with skill, they will run perpetually and perfectly."

"We have his formulas," Redding continued. "And Miller has been able to successfully replicate several of his transmutations."

Thatcher clapped the tinker on the shoulder. Miller looked ill.

Redding hesitated, looking to Coe again.

Taking a sandwich from the tray, Coe didn't meet Charlotte's eyes and kept his tone overly casual. "Where we've run into trouble regards animation."

Charlotte tried not to imagine the specifics of Miller's experiments.

"Do you understand what I've said?" Coe asked.

"Animation." Charlotte stared into her cup of tea. "Life."

"Precisely."

She sipped her tea, biding time until she could form the right question. "Bromley couldn't tell you how he accomplished that?"

"Bromley proved intractable on the subject." Redding's

lips pursed, as if she'd bitten into something very sour.

"Perhaps if I spoke with him?" Charlotte didn't know what state she'd find Bromley in, or if he'd be able to assist her in freeing herself, but she thought it worthwhile to find out. "A friendly visitor?"

Thatcher cleared his throat. "That won't be possible."

Miller covered his mouth with a napkin, as if to cover a cough, but Charlotte thought she heard a quiet sob.

"Why not?" Charlotte asked.

"He's no longer with us," Thatcher said.

She looked at Coe. "You killed Bromley."

"He did not survive questioning." It was Redding who answered.

Coe spoke up. "And that leaves us with inquiries that must be resolved by Grave and you."

Sitting back in his chair, Coe regarded Charlotte with a searching gaze. "Tell me, Charlotte. Do you know how Bromley brought Grave to life?"

Charlotte sipped breath from the air the way she'd been sipping her tea. She had to stay calm.

"I don't know if I understand it," Charlotte said quietly. "But yes. I have some idea."

She carefully set her cup in its saucer. She couldn't risk unsteady hands giving her away when she sensed her only opportunity to escape the confines of the Military Platform was about to present itself.

"And what are those ideas?" Thatcher asked. He rapped the table, making the tinker jump. "Pay attention, Miller."

With her eyes on Miller, Charlotte shook her head. "He can't help you."

Thatcher's furry brows came together. "What do you mean?"

"It isn't the work of a tinker that can animate someone like Grave." Charlotte had to dismiss the impossibility of what she'd just said. There wasn't someone like Grave. There was no one like Grave.

She turned to Coe. "You already know this. Or have you forgotten?"

"Beg your pardon?" Coe straightened, startled by her accusatory tone.

"You were there," Charlotte said. "When we found Bromley in the Hive. You heard his story."

"And?"

"You saw the book he had." Charlotte rested her hands in her lap. She wanted to twist her fingers together, wring them to relieve tension, but she didn't.

"The man was a lunatic." Coe waved a dismissive hand. "You can't tell me you actually believe that nonsense."

Charlotte didn't answer. She simply kept a steady gaze on him.

"He made a machine and gave it life," Coe went on. "But that animation was a result of his designs. The rest was superstition."

"How can you be sure?" Charlotte replied. "Especially given the trouble you're having now."

"Ridiculous," Coe snarled at her.

But Redding watched Charlotte with interest. "I want to hear more about this book."

The lieutenant asked Coe, "Do we have it in our possession?"

Coe shook his head. "Bromley claims he destroyed it. But the contents of that book are immaterial."

"I disagree," Redding said, ignoring Coe's scowl. "We can't afford to dismiss any source of enlightenment."

"What do you have to say about this?" Coe asked Thatcher.

Thatcher shrugged, brushing crumbs off his uniform. "I see no harm in looking into it."

"Very well." Coe wore an expression of disgust. "Charlotte, what can you offer with regard to the mystical aspects of Bromley's work?"

"Nothing . . . on my own," Charlotte replied. She stopped, not wanting to appear too eager.

"Go on," Coe said.

"The information you need is in the Temple of Athene," Charlotte said. "In the arcane knowledge held by the Sisters."

Coe folded his arms over his chest, suspicious and rightly so. "You know very well that only women can enter the Temple."

Charlotte nodded.

"And you expect me to let you go there on your own to get information for us?" Coe sounded almost disappointed by her request.

"Send as many guards as you want," Charlotte said. "And have Lieutenant Redding accompany me."

She held his gaze, hoping her face didn't give anything away.

"I don't see what harm she can do if I'm escorting her," Redding said to Coe.

Thatcher leaned forward. "Sending a civilian to speak with the Sisters is likely to get more results than marching a squad into the square. Redding is more than capable of handling the girl."

"You're underestimating her." Coe reached for his teacup.

Under other circumstances, Charlotte would have been flattered by Coe's comment. Right now it only worked against her.

After taking a few sips of tea, Coe said, "But I see no way around it."

Hope bloomed in Charlotte's heart, only slightly tempered when Coe said, "And I trust Charlotte understands it's in her best interest, and Grave's, to make sure this visit to the Temple occurs without incident."

Redding said to Charlotte, "The Sisters receive petitioners in the morning. I'll come to collect you."

"Before I beg secrets from the Sisters, I have a request," Charlotte said.

Coe's teacup clattered in its saucer. "Let's hear it, then."

"I need to know that Grave is alive and safe," she told

him. "You know that I feel responsible for his welfare."

Thatcher laughed quietly, but Redding stopped him with a reproachful glare.

"He's alive," Coe told Charlotte. "But seeing him is—"

"I think it might be very . . . educational for Miss Marshall to have a glimpse of our work," Thatcher said. "Miller could provide some insights that could hone the questions she brings to the Sisters."

Redding and Coe both appeared taken aback by Thatcher's suggestion. Miller's eyes had gone wild, as if he was desperate for escape.

Without waiting for his peers' assent, Thatcher pushed back his chair and stood. "I'll take them myself. Come then, Miller."

Miller stood. He hadn't touched his tea or any of the food.

"Miss Marshall." Thatcher waited for Charlotte to approach, then offered his arm. His affability made Charlotte wary.

"Lead the way, Miller."

The tinker kept his head down, but marched dutifully from the room. Thatcher and Charlotte followed at a leisurely pace.

The day was startlingly bright outside the dormitory. The sun's rays bounced off the gleaming marble pillars and facades of the Military Platform with such intensity that Charlotte found herself squinting. Miller wove between buildings and gave wide berth to squads performing drills. The drone of airships grew louder as they approached the docks. Charlotte surveyed the sky. Dragonflies zipped nimbly between Gryphons, midweight gunships that lacked the versatility of Dragonflies but boasted superior firepower. Despite their considerable size, the Gryphons were dwarfed by the Empire's Titans, even though the larger vessels were docked at a distance. Their mass forced them to anchor at the far edge of the air docks. Charlotte knew she was glimpsing only a fraction of the Imperial Air Force, and that knowledge made her shudder. Here were the gears of war, the machinery of conquest.

"Fearsome, aren't they?" Thatcher beamed at the airships.

Charlotte didn't answer, chiding herself for her unbidden display of emotion.

The buildings that skirted the air docks lacked ornamentation. Where the majority of the Military Platform strove to impress and intimidate, these structures were designed only for service. Miller entered one of the stark gray loading bays. Sparks flew around a Gryphon's frame as mechanics performed repairs.

On the opposite side of the bay, they paused before two guards standing at attention on either side of a door. With a signal from Thatcher, the guards stepped aside to let Miller pass through. Thatcher and Charlotte followed him into the narrow corridor beyond. The passageway opened into a building smaller than the repair bay. Windowless, the room glowed with phosphorescence that emanated from globes strung along the walls. The filmy blue gleam of the light reminded Charlotte of the bioluminescent fungi that lit the caverns of the Catacombs, but in this strange place, the memory chilled her. In the center of the room sat a long steel box that resembled a train car. On closer inspection, Charlotte decided that it *was* a train car.

Thatcher disengaged his arm from hers. "Wait here a moment."

While Miller hovered nearby, Thatcher withdrew a key from his coat. Once he'd unlocked the door, he beckoned to Charlotte. She walked to the door with heavy footsteps, as if she were slogging her way through deep mud. She'd asked to see Grave, but now that she was here, Charlotte was consumed by dread.

It's better than the Crucible. It has to be.

Miller was inside, lighting lamps to enhance the low blue illumination that already filled the space. The interior of the car resembled what Charlotte surmised Scoff's apothecary and Birch's workshop would look like if forced into the same space and jumbled up. Every nook and cranny was filled with something to catch the eyes. Strange baubles competed for shelf space with vials of liquid. A metal cart held what looked like tinker's tools along with medical equipment.

The dominant feature of the space was a long metal table draped with a sheet. Something was beneath the sheet.

Charlotte couldn't breathe.

Miller took the edge of the sheet and, when Thatcher nodded, drew it back.

Charlotte choked on her scream; only a weak strangling sound trickled from her throat.

Steel cuffs bolted to the table restrained Grave at the neck, wrists, and ankles. His torso had been sliced from the base of his throat to his abdomen. Skin and tissue had been peeled back. Hooked wires pierced the flaps of skin on either side of his ribs, holding them aloft and open like a pair of gruesome wings. Grave's collarbones and ribs lay exposed. Under the light of gas lamps, his bones didn't appear white, but had the luster of brushed steel.

Tears burned in Charlotte's eyes. Despite Coe's promises, they'd seen fit to kill Grave. How could she have been so foolish as to cooperate with someone she knew to be a traitor? She should have made Grave run when he'd had the chance. She should have tried to convince him that protecting her didn't matter.

Unable to move, Charlotte watched Thatcher as he casually walked around the table, surveying Grave's body.

"Miller," he said, "will you take Miss Marshall through your work thus far?"

The tinker cleared his throat. "Um. Y-yes, sir."

He pointed to the flaps of skin tented around Grave's chest cavity. "Piercing the skin presented our first dilemma. It was somehow modified to the point that it neither breaks nor tears easily. What finally worked was a mechanized saw that I refitted with a diamond blade. The skin is remarkably resilient. There's been no degradation of the tissue since we opened him up."

Miller leaned over Grave's exposed ribs. "Here is evidence of Bromley's work I was better able to grasp. You'll see that the bones have been altered—"

"Stop!" Charlotte couldn't bear another word. "This is monstrous! What have you done? *What have you done?*"

She wheeled on Thatcher, who'd finished his inspection and come to stand beside her.

"Why such distress, Miss Marshall?" Thatcher's voice was calm, but his hand moved to his gun holster. "Isn't this what you asked to see?"

"He wasn't supposed to die." Charlotte couldn't hold back her sob.

Thatcher smiled. "And he has not. Has he, Miller?"

"No, sir." Miller stood beside Grave's head. "Are you dead, Grave?"

Charlotte staggered back. Grave's eyes were open.

"I am not." Grave turned his head to look at her. "Hello, Charlotte."

14.

THE CITIZENS OF the Floating City knew Linnet by many names, but few were aware of her true identity. Winning the game of espionage relied on the skill of creating a variety of characters and having the ability to fluidly shift from one role to another. Many spies performed these roles adequately and sometimes well, but the best agents not only made others believe in these fictional identities, but came to fully embrace their alternate lives. Linnet was always Linnet, but when she became Gemma the weaver, who sold her crafts in Temple Square, she was a purveyor of sturdy blankets and simple but pleasing tapestries. If a stationary post didn't suit her task, Linnet could go about the city as Beatrice, a courier who could reliably carry packages from any platform of the Floating City to another and even down to the Tinkers' Faire.

Should one of Gemma's customers encounter Beatrice, or vice versa, neither would suspect their exchanges had been with the same woman. New Orleans was the City of Masks, but Linnet didn't need fabric or feathers to disguise her face. Simple tricks of makeup and adjustments in posture could change her age. Wigs transformed her hair. Her voice shifted to reflect the backstory of each character.

There were others, too. As many as Linnet had need of. But Gemma and Beatrice were two of her favorites, and she cloaked herself in their lives most often.

On this particular morning, Gemma had arrived at Temple Square before dawn to set up her stall. The sun spilled light onto the Arts Platform, kissing the feet of Athene's statue, which towered above her temple, as Gemma finished arranging her pyramid of rugs. She set up easels upon which to display her tapestries, all the while taking note of the petitioners who approached the holy site with solemn steps. Gemma's fellow merchants were of less interest, only because they were familiar. At the moment, none of them were engaged in activities that intersected her own aims.

One of Gemma's regular customers waddled up to the stall. Lilian waddled because she was imposingly pregnant. As burdened as she was, her face held the brightness of a sunflower.

"Good morning, Gemma," Lilian said. She braced her lower back with her palms as she looked over Gemma's wares.

"Good morning, Lilian."

"Do you ever take custom orders?" Lilian reached out to trace the edge of a tapestry.

Gemma left her chair and picked up parchment and quill. "For an extra fee."

"I want something for the nursery," Lilian said. "I thought perhaps a pastoral scene. Rabbits and fawns. Maybe a unicorn."

Gemma had a warm smile and tinkling laugh. Both brought her repeat customers. Now she glanced at Lilian's swollen belly.

"I'd be happy to sketch a design and offer a price," Gemma said. "But I don't know if a tapestry would be ready for the room before the child is sleeping in it."

Lilian patted her stomach with a sigh. "That's true. Let me think on it."

"So you didn't come to the square this morning to order a tapestry?" Gemma teased.

"I seek the Lady's blessing," Lilian said, her smile becoming more thoughtful. "My hour of delivery will soon be here. I want her to watch over me."

"Athene watches over all women in childbirth." Gemma placed her hands over her heart in deference to the goddess.

"I know." Lilian became sheepish. "But I thought it wouldn't hurt to come ask in person."

Gemma offered a comforting smile again. "Yes, of course."

The sound of metal striking stone drew Lilian's attention away. Gemma looked toward the noise as well. What she saw made her brow furrow, but she kept her eyes clear of anything but curiosity. A steam-carriage drawn by a mechanical horse had arrived just outside the square. Three soldiers exited the carriage, followed by a fourth person whose identity was hidden by a long hooded cloak.

"A military detachment," Lilian said. "How odd."

The quartet walked swiftly from the carriage across Temple Square. Two of the soldiers stopped and took up sentry posts at the base of the steps. The third soldier, obviously female, accompanied the cloaked figure, who must have been female as well, into the Temple.

"What do you think soldiers petition the goddess for?" Lilian asked.

Gemma shrugged. "She is a goddess of war."

"Mmmmm . . ." Lilian had already begun to move away. "I hope this doesn't mean a longer wait for the rest of us. I'd better go take my place in line."

Gemma waved her good-byes. Her gaze returned to the soldiers outside the Temple. A visit from the military wasn't of great interest to Gemma. But it concerned Linnet very much.

Gemma went to the cart that stored her extra inventory. She drew out a tapestry woven of royal blue and gold, draping it over the floral tapestry that had been facing the square. When one of Ott's agents happened by, they would recognize her signal and the situation at the Temple would be investigated.

While Gemma continued to ply her crafts in the square, Linnet could wait. If a missive with new intelligence was delivered, Gemma could close down her stall, allowing Linnet to act on orders received.

15

ETITIONERS AND SUPPLICANTS stood in an uneven line that climbed the Temple's stairs and extended into the courtyard. Women of all ages sought the goddess's blessing. Many of those waiting were with child, and some were visibly ill, while others bore no outward signs of the reason for their pilgrimage that day.

The Empire showed no regard for the time and troubles of the petitioners, at least not as demonstrated by the actions of Lieutenant Redding, who hustled Charlotte to the front of the line, passing through the courtyard into the vestibule.

The air in the Temple of Athene was redolent with incense; the light, soft pinks and grays. Somewhere in a distant chamber, women lifted their voices in song. Their melodies reached the vestibule like bittersweet lamentations of ghosts. Four priestesses had taken up posts in front of the sanctuary door. They were seated in pairs, two Sisters each at two tables on either side of the entrance. Temple visitors registered their names and the reasons they sought audience with one priestess, then provided an appropriate offering to the second.

Charlotte doubted Lieutenant Redding had an offering for the Sisters. As the officer stepped to the front of the line with Charlotte in tow, disapproving mutters floated behind them, but none dared voice an actual objection to the military exerting its authority.

The priestess before whom Lieutenant Redding stood gave a disapproving frown. "How may we be of service?"

"We seek the wisdom of the Lady of Mysteries." Redding spoke with a solemnity that made the priestess's eyebrows lift.

"Your names?"

Redding stepped closer, leaning over the table. "The Empire would prefer this audience go unrecorded."

The priestess set down her quill, frowning again. She spoke to the other Sister at the table.

"Sister Penelope, would you please ask Sister Leda to come to the vestibule?"

"Yes, Sister Annelle."

Her name struck a note of recognition with Charlotte. Sister Annelle had been present at Charlotte's last visit to the Temple. That realization brought with it both hope and anxiety.

Lieutenant Redding shifted on her feet, restless and irritated by the delay. For Charlotte, however, any extra attention drawn to their visit made the success of this journey more likely.

Causing a scene or attempting escape was out of the question. If Charlotte pleaded for asylum, the Sisters might try to grant her protection, but she had no doubt that Redding would use as much force as required to retrieve her prisoner—even to the point of violating the sanctity of the Temple itself by bringing a detachment of soldiers into the sacred space. Charlotte wasn't willing to put priestesses or petitioners in harm's way. Fortunately, she didn't need to fight or flee to accomplish what she desired. All she needed was to be seen.

Meg had planned to return to the Temple, and Charlotte could only hope that her friend was still among the Sisters. Not only that, but that somehow in the course of this visit Meg would discover Charlotte's presence and convey that information to Linnet and Lachance.

Murmurs of displeasure grew louder at their backs, making Charlotte smile. Rumors would abound after this visit. Even if she wasn't fortunate enough to cross paths with Meg, hopefully word of the military's disruption of Temple business would fly swiftly through the city to reach the ears of Margery Ott. Lady Ott would certainly investigate the matter, and while that route would prove longer than an encounter with Meg, it could produce the same end result.

Whatever rumblings trailed them could not match Lieutenant Redding's growing displeasure. Her expression made it obvious that she was unaccustomed to anyone balking at or delaying her orders. As they waited for Sister Leda to appear, the officer's gaze swept over the pronaos, taking in the statuary, the burning incense, the contemplative Sisters. Her face showed only disdain.

Charlotte noticed Sister Annelle observing Lieutenant Redding's assessment of the Temple. While the priestess's face remained serene, her eyes were hard as steel. Disapproval wasn't the province of the military alone, it seemed.

Sister Penelope emerged from the cella, followed by a priestess whose face bore the lines of many years and whose silver hair still bore a scattering of bronze threads woven into the long braid that hung down her back. Charlotte was surprised when four more priestesses came through the door to flank their leader.

"Sister Leda, I assume." Lieutenant Redding spoke before either Sister Penelope or Sister Annelle could make a formal introduction. "My name is Lieutenant Redding."

"I am Sister Leda." Her voice was quiet but had resonance like distant, rumbling thunder. "I understand you've requested a visitation regarding the deeper mysteries but have made a further request that this audience remain absent from Temple records."

Lieutenant Redding deigned to incline her head. "It is a matter of security. And of grave import to the Empire."

Sister Leda responded with a tight-lipped smile. "Of course the house of the goddess holds the Empire and its imperatives in esteem. But I'm afraid we have a matter of our own that must be addressed before anything else."

Leda gestured to Charlotte without looking at her.

"Are you aware that this woman is wanted for questioning in regard to the deaths of two Sisters?"

Charlotte blanched as fear skittered down her spine. The Order of Arachne. Meg had seemed confident that she'd be able to resolve that incident. Had she misjudged the inhabitants of the Temple? Was Meg a prisoner of the Sisters now?

"I was not aware." Redding glared at Charlotte. "I am sorry for your loss, but how do you know my companion was involved?"

"We are quite adept at gathering information," Leda replied.

The lieutenant lifted an eyebrow. "Given that Athene's priestesses are not usually prone to violence, I must assume that the women involved were part of the Order of Arachne."

Leda frowned, but nodded.

"I must then also remind you that the Empire does not officially recognize the legitimacy of this group," Redding said. "Its activities have been suspect in the past, and interfering with my business here today will most definitely invite closer scrutiny by the colonial government. It could be decided that the Order should be disbanded. Its rites forbidden."

Several of the priestesses drew sharp breaths.

Sister Leda's eyes flashed, but she spoke calmly. "Athene is a warrior goddess. Would the Empire deny this aspect of her divinity? Are your superior officers so bold?"

"All soldiers pray to Athene before going to battle

and beg her mercy when death draws near," Redding answered. "But the Order of Arachne has been deemed a cult within the greater faith. Extreme iterations of religion are frowned upon by the Empire as they threaten the stability of society."

"It is clear we will not resolve this impasse." Sister Leda lifted her hand.

Wordlessly, the accompaniment of priestesses returned to the cella.

"I will send a formal inquiry to your superiors," Leda told Redding. "But I must insist that your petition be recorded."

"Surely you can make an exception." Redding's smile was more a baring of her teeth than anything else.

"Consider this." The serenity of Sister Leda's voice didn't alter. "All of history is a single tapestry. Our stories, our lives, our deaths form a pattern on the great loom of our lady, Athene. To omit any part of this record will mar the pattern."

Lieutenant Redding looked as if she was considering putting the priestess under arrest.

Sister Leda continued, "You have all our assurances that this record is one of the most guarded secrets of the Temple. The loom of history is woven to honor the goddess. Its vast knowledge is not retained for the purposes of men."

Redding gazed at the priestess for another minute, then she relaxed slightly. "Very well. I put my trust in your discretion."

"Of course, Lieutenant." Sister Leda turned a benevolent smile on her fellow priestesses. "Sisters Annelle and Penelope, I will accommodate the military's special request. Please continue to receive regular petitioners in the cella."

"Yes, Sister Leda." Penelope and Annelle spoke in unison.

Lieutenant Redding barely concealed her disgust at what she viewed as obsequious behavior.

"If you'd follow me, Lieutenant." Sister Leda began to walk away.

Lieutenant Redding and Charlotte followed Sister Leda from the pronaos around the perimeter of the cella. They had almost reached the far end of the Temple when Sister Leda took an abrupt turn to the right. They passed through an alcove and into a narrow, arched corridor. Charlotte gasped in wonder. In what appeared an impossibility, water streamed from the peak of the corridor and followed the curves of the walls. Yet somehow nary a drop spilled onto the ground. The rivulets clung to the marble surface, filling the air with the sound of a river rushing past.

Charlotte heard a sniff of disdain from Lieutenant Redding, as though the officer had decided Sister Leda's choice of location for their meeting had been made with chicanery in mind. That the corridor was intended to impart a message Charlotte didn't doubt, but in her mind this was no mummery, rather a demonstration of true power.

The corridor ended at a door, which had been carved of ebony. It depicted the story of Arachne: a young woman before a loom, her tears and despair, her lifeless body hanging from a tree, her transformation into a spider, and finally, the exquisite beauty of that spider's web.

Charlotte balked at the sight. She hadn't been surprised that the Temple priestesses had resisted Lieutenant Redding's assertion of military authority, but if they were being taken to the Order of Arachne, could anything other than death await? Would the Sisters of the Temple have the gall to murder an officer of the Empire?

Suddenly, Charlotte froze.

What if Sister Leda's route had nothing to do with the Empire or Lieutenant Redding's demand of a solitary audience? Charlotte had killed one of the Order of Arachne, and the Sisters wanted to detain her. Perhaps Sister Leda hadn't given in to Redding at all, instead creating an opportunity to isolate Charlotte.

She stared at the door, more frightened than she'd been even in her cell at the Crucible. She had no weapons. No means for defense. And she didn't believe for an instant that Lieutenant Redding had the savvy or skill to defeat one of the Temple's assassins.

Then Sister Leda's hand was clasping Charlotte's.

"Be not afraid, my daughter." Sister Leda smiled. "The wisdom of the goddess guides you."

Charlotte's fear melted as she looked into the priestess's gray eyes. It was one of the strangest sensations Charlotte had ever experienced. All at once, she knew without a doubt that the blood of the assassin stained her hands and clothes as if she'd struck the killing blow right there in front of Sister Leda and Lieutenant Redding. Yet in the same instant, Charlotte knew that she hadn't been condemned. Somehow, a deep understanding of all that had taken place had suffused not only Sister Leda's mind, but the very walls of the Temple.

"Thank you," Charlotte murmured.

Lieutenant Redding's glance at this exchange was irritated and dismissive.

She's blind to everything that's real in this place, Charlotte thought. *Her mind is forever closed.*

To her surprise, Charlotte was filled with pity for Lieutenant Redding. Even more startling was the unwavering certainty that, no matter what transpired behind this door, Lieutenants Redding and Thatcher, along with Tinker Miller, would never re-create what Hackett Bromley had accomplished. Even if Bromley's actions had been misguided, they had been grounded in belief, love, and profound grief. In desperation. The authenticity, the power of his intent, lay at the center of everything he'd done to transform Timothy into Grave. And that intent could not be replicated.

This knowledge came to Charlotte as both relief and fear. Relief because it meant there would never be an army of indestructible replicas of Grave. Fear because without the possibility of that manufactured power, what reason did the Empire have to preserve Grave or Charlotte? If it was discovered that they served no purpose, how much longer would they be allowed to live?

Fear took Charlotte hostage once more. She believed

that she wouldn't be held accountable for the death of one of the Order of Arachne, but would the Sisters' wisdom extend so far as to protect Charlotte and Grave by keeping the impossibility of repeating Hackett Bromley's experiment a secret?

Sister Leda offered no balm for Charlotte's fresh anxiety. The priestess was occupied with unlocking the ebony door. The sound of the bolt being turned made Charlotte's throat dry. Lieutenant Redding huffed out the breath of one who'd been unnecessarily delayed. Charlotte couldn't see what lay beyond the doorway, but she had little choice other than to follow Redding.

Unlike the straight, smooth walls of the corridor they'd just left, their new path was more like the entrance to a cave: a misshapen circle carved from rock.

They were descending. Other than that, Charlotte could discern little.

It made sense, and yet it didn't. The layout of the Temple of Athene was quite straightforward: the porch at the top of the steps, beyond that the cella where petitioners were received, past the cella was the opisthodomos—a chamber rarely seen by any but denizens of the Temple. If rumors were to be believed, an even more restricted place, the adyton, was set behind the opisthodomos. Only speculative whispers conveyed what transpired in the adyton, if it did indeed exist.

The Temple was made up of rooms within rooms laid out along a straight line. But this new path Sister Leda had taken reflected none of the intention or formality of the

Temple's design. The spiral upon which they trod was built from rough-hewn stone. Charlotte's senses were suffused with the richness of ancient bedrock and the pungency of subterranean streams.

I must be deceived, Charlotte thought. *This is some magic. Illusion or glamour.*

Because the notion of depth was an impossibility. The Temple of Athene hadn't been built upon soil. It was erected on the Arts Platform of the Floating City. There were no depths to be plumbed here. Any tunnels spiraling down would pass through a labyrinth of metal and churning gears, their courses punctuated by blasts of searing steam and boiling water. She should have been seeing markers of industry, not the earth's organic foundations of rock and root.

The question *Is this real?* danced on the tip of Charlotte's tongue, but she dared not speak. She stole a glance at Lieutenant Redding, hoping to glimpse marvel or disbelief, but Redding's face was an unreadable mask.

As they drew farther down the spiral, darkness threatened to engulf them. Charlotte found herself wanting to reach out and follow the path of the walls with her hands, and to stop herself from falling should she stumble. Strange that Sister Leda had brought no source of light to guide their steps. But just as Charlotte believed they were about to pass from shadow into pitch, the path leveled. As they continued forward, impending night retreated into twilight. The corridor widened, and Charlotte could see light just ahead of Sister Leda. The walls continued to curve away from each other, and soon they were no longer passing through a tunnel but standing in a cavern.

A dome-shaped ceiling arched above them, and for some reason gave Charlotte the sense of being shielded from the outside world. Apart.

The center of the cavern featured a round pool, elevated by three steps that ringed its circumference. Pleasant light filled the space, as though a full moon shone on them. But Charlotte could find no source of the light; it seemed to come from the pool itself. A woman sat on the edge of the pool. She was robed in a color that could have been black, midnight blue, or deep purple—the fabric wasn't illuminated enough for a clear distinction. Her hair hung in a long, thick braid that touched the floor. Its radiant white hue rivaled that of fresh snow.

"Come forward." The woman spoke without turning to look at them.

Sister Leda didn't move, but the look she gave Charlotte indicated that she was meant to.

Cautiously, Charlotte approached the pool steps. She sensed Lieutenant Redding close behind.

Something skittered along the highest step. A spider as large as Charlotte's hand.

With a gasp, Charlotte drew back, bumping into Lieutenant Redding.

"You needn't fear them," the woman at the pool said.

Charlotte paid little attention to the word *fear*, instead hanging on to *them*.

She looked around the room more slowly. In the pale

light, along the walls and up the curving ceiling, was movement. Constant movement. Arachnids scurried hither and thither, tending to their business and showing little interest in the visitors. Despite their passivity, Charlotte's mouth had gone dry. There were so many. And of a distressing range in size. Charlotte thought it likely she couldn't see the smallest of them, given the low light in the chamber, but the largest were the size of cats. She also noted dark pockets in the walls, some of which were large enough for her to crawl through. Surely there weren't spiders large enough to fill such holes.

Charlotte looked at Lieutenant Redding. The officer's face was pinched, but she showed no other signs of distress.

The woman beside the pool stood, descending the three steps to stand beside Charlotte and Redding. She stretched her arm out, her long, spindly fingers gesturing to the walls.

"They weave stories for us," she said. "Some true. Some false. All have something to teach."

She looked directly at Charlotte. Her gray eyes were like roiling thunder clouds. "You have a story to tell me today. I wonder if this story will be true."

Lieutenant Redding spoke. "The Empire has no interest in deceiving you, Sister . . ."

"Penthesilea," the priestess answered.

"Thank you for seeing us, Sister Penthesilea. I'm Lieutenant Redding, and this is Charlotte Marshall." Lieutenant Redding's tone was polite, but the set of her mouth indicated her disapproval of the meeting's location.

Charlotte couldn't find fault in that assessment. Though she couldn't tear her gaze from Sister Penthesilea's stormy irises, part of her mind was still panicking about the excess of spiders all around them. Her skin was prickling with the knowledge that the eight-legged beasts were everywhere, quite possibly about to drop from the ceiling onto her head. She barely repressed a convulsion of instinctive disgust.

Sister Penthesilea made a quiet sound that might have been a chuckle, giving Charlotte the distinct impression that the priestess had plucked the fearful thoughts right out of her mind.

"There is a troubling matter that we believe can be assuaged by the wisdom of the goddess and your guidance," Redding said.

"As I said," the Sister replied. "You have a story."

"Charlotte." Lieutenant Redding nodded at her.

Charlotte glanced at the officer in alarm. She'd expected at least some introductory remarks from Redding. Now Charlotte was tongue-tied because the lieutenant wanted her to lie, at least in part, and surely Sister Penthesilea would know any untruth that passed Charlotte's lips. What was she to do? Tell the truth, but not the whole truth? Should she sidle around the parts of the story that would reveal the fact that she was here as a prisoner, not a collaborator?

"You look distressed, my child," Penthesilea said to Charlotte. "Perhaps I can be of help." The priestess folded her hands and rested them on her abdomen. "There was a boy named Timothy. A boy whose life was painful and brief. Then there was a father, an inventor, who used his skills in the hopes of regaining what he had lost."

Lieutenant Redding drew a sharp breath.

Penthesilea smiled at her. "Surely you know the boy's mother now serves the goddess." Her gaze turned to Charlotte. "And this is not the first time you've visited Athene's Temple."

"No." Charlotte's voice was little more than a whisper. "The boy is my friend. I was trying to help him."

Penthesilea nodded, and Charlotte was again filled with the sense that the priestess understood far more than the words Charlotte spoke aloud.

"Are you trying to help him now?" the Sister asked Charlotte.

Charlotte was suddenly aware of a great stillness in the room. The spiders had stopped moving, as if waiting for her answer.

"Yes."

It was true enough. Charlotte was trying to help Grave, just not in the way that Lieutenant Redding believed.

Sister Penthesilea regarded Charlotte for a moment, then reached out and touched the girl's cheek. "You've made sacrifices for this friend. They have not gone unnoticed."

By whom? Charlotte dared not voice the troubling question.

She was surprised that the priestess's touch was cool and soothing. Her long fingers seemed to draw out some of the anguish Charlotte had carried since leaving New Orleans.

"More suffering will come before the end," Sister Penthesilea murmured. "But not without reprieve."

"Please explain the particulars of our problem, Charlotte." Lieutenant Redding's voice was like the crack of a whip.

Charlotte shook her head, feeling as if she were being drawn out of a deep, restoring slumber. "I . . . uh . . . Grave." She paused, clearing her throat. "Grave lives, even though the boy Timothy died from illness."

Penthesilea nodded.

"How could his father, the inventor, accomplish such a feat?" Charlotte glanced at Redding, hoping the question met the officer's expectations. Redding's expression was neither approving nor disapproving.

Something flickered in Penthesilea's irises. Anger?

Charlotte dreaded the priestess's next question. What could it be other than why she wanted to know?

Instead, Sister Penthesilea looked at Lieutenant Redding. "The inventor could not provide you these answers himself?"

Her query startled Redding. The officer blanched, but quickly recovered. "No. He could not."

Penthesilea watched Redding for another moment. "The inventor wielded a weapon as if using a tool. He did not comprehend the gravity of his actions because he was driven by grief and desperation."

"What do you mean he wielded a weapon?" Redding's eyes narrowed.

"Forbidden words. Words of power." Penthesilea shook her head, her face filling with genuine sorrow.

"The Book of the Dead," Charlotte murmured. Then her eyes went wide. She hadn't intended to voice her thought.

But Penthesilea turned a benevolent smile on Charlotte. "You've seen it."

"Yes." Now Charlotte's heart began to race, fearing not Penthesilea's wrath, but Redding's.

"What is this book?" Redding's attention was on the priestess, not Charlotte.

"It was very old," Sister Penthesilea said, though she seemed to be speaking to the room, to the spiders on the walls, rather than to the officer. "And the words it contained were older still. Older than time, perhaps."

Lieutenant Redding could barely contain her contempt. "We found no such book among Bromley's possessions."

Penthesilea's smile held a spark of mischief. "No. You wouldn't have."

"Do you know where the book is?" Redding asked.

"It is no more," the priestess replied. "Or rather, it is transformed. To ashes and dust."

Redding clenched her fists, her knuckles bone white. "You burned it?"

"The Book of the Dead has no place in this world." Sister Penthesilea's face was serene. "To serve the goddess is to rid the world of evils that threaten her people."

Charlotte's stomach tightened. That was why they'd sent the Order of Arachne after Grave. They believed that, like the book that brought life into a boy's dead body, the resurrected life itself was also evil. Did they believe that still?

"And this book was the only thing that enabled Bromley to bring his boy back to life?" Lieutenant Redding asked.

That's not what he did, Charlotte thought, and Penthesilea smiled at her.

Then the priestess answered Redding. "Yes. It was."

Sister Penthesilea turned away, climbing the stair and resuming her poolside repose. "Lieutenant Redding," she said, trailing her fingers through the water, "some mysteries are best left in shadow."

Charlotte followed Penthesilea's gaze to one of the largest crevices in the wall and saw movement, the hint of an appendage black and bristling with spikes of hair, an appendage that rivaled Charlotte's arm in size. The blood drained from Charlotte's face, and she looked at Lieutenant Redding, hoping the officer had taken Penthesilea's admonition to heart. But Redding hadn't bothered to follow the priestess's line of sight; she simply glared at Penthesilea.

Without prompting, Sister Leda stepped out of the shadows where she'd been waiting in silence.

"This audience has concluded," Sister Leda said. "Please follow me."

16.

LIEUTENANT REDDING SEETHED from the moment they left Sister Penthesilea and her spiders. She didn't speak as Sister Leda retraced their path from the depths of the Temple to the perimeter of the cella, but the fury radiating from her body was palpable. For her own part, Charlotte felt as though she was caught in a state between dreaming and waking. She still couldn't grasp the possibility of the place they'd just visited. There were no caves in the Floating City's platforms. Charlotte wondered if they'd actually been in a cavern at all, or if the Sisters had somehow willed that place into existence, ensnaring Charlotte's and Lieutenant Redding's senses for the duration of their visit.

They weave stories for us. Some true. Some false. All have something to teach.

Charlotte was so transfixed by their strange encounter

that only the light of day spilling through the columns of the Temple startled her back into full awareness.

Sister Leda had begun to make an attempt at a gracious farewell, but Lieutenant Redding was having none of it. She grabbed Charlotte's arm so tightly that Charlotte winced. Redding marched out of the Temple, practically dragging Charlotte along.

"Burned it!" Lieutenant Redding was muttering. Charlotte had no idea if she was intended to hear or respond. "Hephaestus's forge, they burned it. No one relinquishes that kind of power. No one."

Charlotte disagreed. Not everyone clamored for power above everything else, shoving all contenders aside in a race to claim whatever prize was sought. She didn't think Sister Penthesilea had lied. A certainty resonated in Charlotte's bones, telling her that the Book of the Dead had been destroyed. And that its destruction was for the best.

But that belief wasn't something she wanted to share with Lieutenant Redding. If Charlotte's captors decided that the process by which Hackett Bromley had brought life into a corpse could not be replicated, then she and Grave were not long for this world. For the time being, she had to offer some succor to Lieutenant Redding's frustration. She just had to figure out how.

They were already at the steps, descending so swiftly that Charlotte almost had to run to match Redding's pace. In the square below, the military escort that had accompanied them to the Temple stood at attention, ready to receive them. Without slowing, Lieutenant Redding transferred Charlotte to a waiting soldier, who ushered her into the enclosed carriage.

Charlotte was shut off from the world once more, and the reality of her circumstance set in. The experience in the Temple had been so consuming that Charlotte's foremost hope had been utterly forgotten. When the idea of visiting the Temple struck her, Charlotte presumed that they would be taken into the cella, as were most petitioners. She couldn't have anticipated the strange journey into a spider-filled underworld. But the difference between the visit she'd experienced versus the one she'd anticipated could mean the failure of her plan. In the cella, priestesses came and went regularly; thus, if Meg had been in the Temple, the cella or the pronaos would have afforded the best opportunities for their crossing paths. Since Lieutenant Redding's request had been treated so uniquely, their exposure to the rest of the Temple had been terribly limited.

An uncomfortable weight settled on Charlotte's chest. The likelihood that Meg had seen her was slim to none. Charlotte leaned her head against the carriage interior, suddenly overcome with exhaustion. She was alone. Charlotte closed her eyes, trying to quiet her mind.

From that stillness came an unexpected voice.

This is not the first time you've visited Athene's Temple.

Sister Penthesilea had known who Charlotte was.

You've made sacrifices for this friend. They have not gone unnoticed.

Charlotte sat up; her heart thrummed not with fear, but possibility.

Even if Meg hadn't seen her. Even if Meg hadn't been present at the Temple today, the Sisters knew who Charlotte was. Within Sister Penthesilea's strange proclamations lay a revelation—that Charlotte mattered. Her life and her choices mattered, for whatever reason, in the divine tapestry that the Sisters wove. They wanted to help her. Whether by conveying intelligence to Meg or some other means, the Sisters not only wanted to help her, they would help her. Charlotte was sure of this.

The desolation that had crept into Charlotte's heart was pushed aside by a new awareness. She had allies of whom she hadn't been aware. These strangers had thrown in their lot with Charlotte and Grave. Though she didn't doubt that the reasons behind their choice differed greatly from her own motivations, Charlotte felt she'd been granted an incredible reprieve. She was not abandoned.

All she had to do now was wait. And survive.

17.

GEMMA USUALLY MEANDERED her way back from the market, but today she'd hurried from the square to return her cart to its storage site. Gemma's work for the day was done, but Linnet's was just beginning. She was eager to reach Lady Ott and learn what intelligence she had gathered regarding the strange military visitation at the Temple.

Her preoccupation with these thoughts made Linnet carelessly less alert to her surroundings than she should have been. As she passed an alley, someone's hands darted out, grabbed Linnet, and pulled her into the shadows. Rather than struggle, she used the momentum of her body against her assailant, letting velocity spin her farther into the alley, dragging her attacker along. Linnet already had her fingers around the hilt of her stiletto when he stumbled and fell against her. She caught his elbow and slammed him into the wall, then pinned him with her left arm, ready to strike with her right.

"Linnet," he croaked. "Wait."

"Jack?"

Linnet backed off and returned her stiletto to its sheath in her bodice, all the while watching Jack with concern. His skin carried a gray pallor, indicative of pain and exhaustion. The sour odor emanating from his body suggested it had been many days since he'd bathed.

"What happened to you?" Linnet asked. "Where are Charlotte and Grave?"

"They were taken." Jack slumped against the wall. He had one arm wrapped around his waist.

"You're hurt." Linnet moved to pull Jack's arm away so she could assess his injury, but Jack grunted and jerked out of her reach.

Her lips flattened in frustration. "Let me take a look. I need to know how bad it is."

"I'm fine," Jack said. "It wasn't bad enough to stop me from getting here, was it?"

Linnet sensed that pushing against Jack's stubbornness would prove fruitless for the time being. "You said Charlotte and Grave were taken—how?"

"Bounty hunters found us," Jack's full weight was against the wall, as though standing on his strength alone would be too difficult. "They bound me and the innkeeper and his family and threw us in the cellar."

Though her heart shuddered, Linnet forced herself to

keep a sensible head. "Do you know to whom the bounty hunters were taking them?"

"They went to the Crucible." Jack closed his eyes, grimacing.

"How can you be sure?" Linnet wished with all her being that what Jack claimed would prove to be untrue.

Jack looked up at her, his gaze sharp. "I went after them."

Linnet drew a hissing breath. "You went to Boston?"

"Thomas overheard the bounty hunters talking about the Crucible when they were tying up his family," Jack said. "I was out for a couple of hours, but when I regained consciousness, he and I were able to work together to free ourselves. When he told me where they were going, I set out to find them."

"How did you manage?" Linnet asked.

"I had to trade my gun, watch, jacket, and all the coin I had for passage to Boston and then to the City," Jack told her.

Her eyes flicked to the protective arm Jack still had wrapped around his midsection. "When did that happen?"

"I'd been keeping an eye on the prison from the cover of some ruins," Jack said. "A lone patrolman came upon me when I decided to leave. I was able to take his gun, but I didn't expect the dagger he'd hidden in his boot."

"Oh, Jack." Linnet shook her head. "It could have been so much worse."

"I know." Jack briefly pulled his hand away from his

wound. Fresh blood had painted his palm scarlet. "But I had to know if Charlotte was there."

"And?"

Jack nodded.

"The Crucible." Linnet briefly closed her eyes, locking the pain away until a time came when she could face it. She didn't let her emotions show, but inside a knife was twisting and tearing through her gut. If Charlotte had been sent to the Crucible, there was no saving her. She was as good as dead.

"She's not there anymore," Jack said, reading the hopelessness on Linnet's face.

Linnet's eyelids snapped up. "What?"

"I saw them leave," he continued. "Charlotte and Grave and some other prisoner on a litter. They boarded a Gryphon with two Dragonflies as escort."

"Do you have any idea where they were being taken?"

"No." Jack sat down, beating his thigh with his fist. "But that's not the worst of it." Suddenly, his voice cracked. "C-Coe was with them."

"What?" Linnet gaped at Jack. "When was he taken? How did the Empire discover he's been working with the Resistance?"

"Linnet." She could hear tears behind Jack's words. "He wasn't a prisoner."

For a long moment, Linnet simply stared at Jack, unable to accept what he'd said.

"You have to be mistaken," Linnet said. "Coe is your brother. He *brought* you to the Resistance."

"It was him." Jack's tears were gone, but his voice was hollow. "My father—our father—was there, too."

"How far away were you?" Linnet pressed. She crouched in front of him. "Are you sure it was Coe?"

"He's my brother." Jack looked at her through red-rimmed eyes. "It was no mistake."

Linnet stood up. "We have to get word to Ott."

"I know."

Linnet's hands were trembling. She didn't want to believe it. She wanted to grab Jack's shirt and scream at him for being a liar.

Coe. How could you?

Of the two Winter boys, Coe had always treated her kindly. He hadn't shied away from acknowledging the blood they shared.

Why, Coe? Why?

And how could she have missed it all these years? Linnet had come to believe, in honesty and without arrogance, that she was the best operative on the continent. But it turned out there was someone better.

"I'm going to see Margery," Linnet said. "Come on."

She pulled his free arm around her shoulder so she could support him as they walked.

"Jack." Linnet hesitated, but then said, "I'm so sorry."

He stiffened, but to her surprise, he suddenly turned and made a sound that was a sigh, then a sob. Jack collapsed against her. She held him while he cried for the brother who'd betrayed them all, and Linnet shed tears of her own. She had lost one brother, but as Jack cried against her shoulder, she knew she'd gained the other.

They entered Lady Ott's home through the servants' door in the alley. The guard posted there, dressed to look like a steward, knew Linnet well and informed them that Margery was in the drawing room. He took in Jack's present state and added that he'd send for the surgeon. Linnet thanked him before helping Jack up the stairs.

"At last." Margery snapped her fan shut as they entered the room. "You won't believe—" Her eyes fell on Jack. "Spear of Athene, what happened?"

"A lot," Jack said.

Linnet was glad to hear wry humor in his voice again.

"So it seems," Margery said. She shooed them back in the direction they came. "We can't stay here—you'll bleed all over the furniture. Down the hall, the door on the left."

The room she directed them to was small, perhaps intended as a nursery, but now furnished with a simple bed, desk, and chair.

"Lie down, Jack," Margery said. She looked at Linnet. "Has Gordon sent for the surgeon?"

Linnet nodded.

Jack groaned as Linnet eased him onto the bed.

"I'm the one who should be complaining," Linnet said, wanting to distract him from the pain. "You smell horrible."

Jack laughed, but his face creased and he pressed his hand tighter to his side.

"Getting you out of those filthy clothes should help with that . . . odor." Lady Ott left the room.

A few minutes later, she returned followed by two maids, one who carried a pitcher and basin, the other bearing a stack of clean linens. They set their burdens on the bedside table and curtsied when Lady Ott dismissed them.

While Linnet poured water from the pitcher into the basin, Margery unbuttoned Jack's shirt. "I don't know if I could tell you what color this shirt will be when it's clean," she teased.

"Blue," Jack said as she helped him out of one sleeve.

"That was the easy one," Lady Ott said. "Now the other."

Jack gritted his teeth while she drew the fabric of his shirt back. Dried blood had secured some of the shirt to Jack's wound. He swore when the blood-crusted shirt pulled at his flesh.

"Linnet."

Margery moved out of the way so Linnet could soak Jack's shirt and skin with water using sodden linens. Bit by bit, she was able to separate the fabric from the wound until it finally came free. Fresh blood flowed from the deep puncture in Jack's flesh, but to her relief, Linnet didn't smell gangrene. Instinctively, he moved to press his hand against the wound again, but she caught his wrist.

"We need to clean this and dress it," she told him. "That will suffice until the surgeon arrives."

"While Linnet tends to that," Margery said, "you can tell me how you came to be in such a sorry state."

Linnet set about flushing Jack's wound with water, and Jack focused on recounting the events of the past days to

Lady Ott. When he reached the point of revealing Coe's deceit, Linnet paused in her work and took his hand. As soon as he completed his tale, Margery began pacing the room.

"This is unfortunate," she muttered, worrying at the pearls around her neck. "Very unfortunate."

Under normal circumstances, Linnet would have anticipated a sarcastic remark from Jack, but he simply closed his eyes and let out a long sigh.

Unfortunate indeed, Linnet thought. She laid the back of her hand against Jack's forehead. *No sign of fever. Small mercies.*

She startled when Margery suddenly clapped her hands.

"Ah well," Lady Ott said, returning to Jack's bedside. "We know the truth of it now and can put this information to use."

Jack didn't open his eyes, but said, "Would you care to elaborate?"

"No." Lady Ott's smile was warm, but her gaze steely. "I'll send word to Roger, but for the moment, that's all."

"Do you think Lord Ott is the best person to tell the Resistance about Coe?" Linnet asked. "He's not officially part of the movement, and he could be cast under suspicion."

"You needn't worry about Roger, my dear," Lady Ott replied. "At this time I wouldn't advise him to share this new knowledge with anyone."

Jack tried to prop himself up on his elbows, but flinched from the pain and lay back down. "Why?"

"If Coe somehow learns that we've discovered his

treachery, Charlotte will be in far greater danger than she's facing now."

"But what if we need help from the Resistance?" Jack argued. "We can't just abandon her."

Lady Ott clucked her tongue. "Of course we can't, and we won't."

"But how—" Jack frowned at her.

"Leave it to me."

18

CHARLOTTE STOOD QUIETLY to the side while Lieutenant Redding relayed the details of their visit to the Temple to Coe and Thatcher. Redding barely managed to keep her temper in check as she spoke, and as the story unfolded, Thatcher's face grew increasingly blotchy. Only Coe maintained a calm demeanor.

"Unacceptable," Thatcher blurted out when Redding had finished her report. "Utterly intolerable."

"Agreed," Redding said. "The situation must be ameliorated."

"Ameliorated?" Thatcher scoffed. "I'll blast that Temple apart and dig through the ruins until we find that book. May I receive the swiftest blow from Hephaestus's hammer if I fail."

Charlotte smiled to herself, enjoying the image of the

god's hammer knocking Thatcher's head right off his shoulders.

Coe, who'd been relaxed in a chair, stood up. "I understand your frustration. Impertinence should never be suffered, and I've long believed the Empire should disband the Order of Arachne."

Redding and Thatcher both nodded vigorously.

"However, do you think it wise to publicly assail the Temple of Athene?" Coe asked. "She is a goddess of the people. The citizens of New York would not be pleased by the desecration of a holy site."

Redding looked at him with indignation. "Would you have us ignore the slight?"

"No," Coe said. "But there are other ways. More subtle approaches."

"That will take time." The red splotches on Thatcher's jowls hadn't faded.

"We have time," Coe replied. "We have Grave, and for the time being, that is the most important fact. We can't risk creating a discontented populace with such a major engagement at hand."

Redding and Thatcher both shot alarmed looks toward Charlotte.

She'd stiffened at Coe's words. Engagement?

Coe waved a dismissive hand at them, though neither looked pacified by his vague assurance.

As shaken as she was by Coe's offhand comment, Charlotte forced herself to focus on the more pressing issue. Believing as she did that the Sisters of Athene intended to help her, Charlotte needed to help them in turn—if she could.

"There's an easier way." Her voice came out rather hoarse, but not tremulous.

With a glance of surprise, Coe asked. "You have something to offer, Charlotte?"

"Yes," Charlotte said, her tone more confident. "You need the Book of the Dead."

Lieutenant Redding glared at her for making such an obvious statement.

Undeterred, Charlotte continued. "The priestesses say they've burned it. And I think they did."

"You're naïve and witless," Redding snapped. "And you have no business—"

Coe cut her off. "Let Charlotte finish."

"What I'm trying to tell you is that even if the book was destroyed, it shouldn't matter," Charlotte said.

"How could it not matter?" Lieutenant Thatcher growled.

"Sister Penthesilea said the book was old, but that the words it contained were even older," Charlotte answered. "Older than time."

"Nonsense religious talk," Redding said. "It means nothing."

"No," Charlotte replied. "It means that there are other books."

. . .

By the time Lieutenants Redding and Thatcher departed, their derisive comments about Charlotte had given way to praise of her keen observation. Thatcher went so far as to clap Coe on the shoulder in approval before exiting the room.

A new plan was in motion. And while it might mean Imperial raids on archives and libraries across the globe, at least it lessened the chance that any of the Sisters would be abducted and tortured while Redding attempted to prove her belief that the Book of the Dead was still hidden in the Temple.

With the other officers gone, Charlotte expected Coe to take his leave as well. Then Charlotte would be alone again.

Wait and survive. Wait and survive.

To her surprise, Coe drew a flask from inside his jacket. Unscrewing the cap, he offered Charlotte a drink.

"It was you." As Charlotte had been reconciling the truth she'd believed in with what had actually transpired over the past month, holes in her knowledge had filled with unpleasant facts. "You poisoned me on the *Calypso*. You think I'd accept a drink from you now?"

"I didn't intend to poison you." Coe shook his head. "But I didn't have enough expertise with the dosage and gave you too much. I sincerely apologize for that. I was very concerned when you became so ill. I felt very close to you that night."

He sounded aggrieved, and she noticed how haggard his face had become.

That wasn't enough to keep Charlotte from snapping, "You almost killed me!"

"I made a mistake," Coe said. "I know you don't believe it, Charlotte, but I do not want any harm to come to you."

While she was tempted to lash out at him again, Charlotte forced herself to pause and take stock. Coe was troubled. He genuinely wanted Charlotte's forgiveness and her good opinion. He needed her to believe he was neither a coward nor a villain.

"Tell me why, Coe," Charlotte said in a quiet voice. "Not what you knew your father wanted to hear, but why you really turned against the Resistance."

He stared at her, disbelieving what she'd said.

"I want to hear it from you," Charlotte pressed.

Coe took another swig from his flask. "Sometimes I don't know if I even remember the truth."

He was gazing ahead, looking through Charlotte rather than at her. "When my father confronted me with the letters I'd received from the Resistance, I knew I was a dead man. I never thought he'd offer a reprieve."

"So you did do it to save yourself," Charlotte murmured.

"No!" Coe stood up and paced a few feet away. "That's not what I did."

Turning back to Charlotte, his eyes begged for her belief. "Yes, I wanted to live. But I didn't make the choice for myself alone. I made it for everyone I care about."

Now Charlotte was on her feet. "Everyone you care about! You betrayed all of them!"

"You don't understand," he said. "I meant what I said about the Resistance. Charlotte, it's hopeless. Truly, brutally hopeless. If the Resistance meets the Empire in an all-out war, the Resistance will be annihilated. They have neither the guns nor the soldiers to defeat Britannia."

"But the French—" Charlotte protested.

"The French." Coe scoffed at her. "You sound like all the rest of them. The French have been perched in New Orleans for four decades. They make beautiful pledges and lofty promises, but they will never abandon their neutral position. They're too afraid to lose the colonies they possess. The British trounced them once on this continent, and they won't risk that happening again."

Charlotte clenched her teeth. She felt like she was losing control of the conversation. She wanted Coe's sympathy, but he was provoking her fears.

"Listen to me, Charlotte," Coe pleaded, a wild hope in his voice. "My father is the only one who can save them."

"What?" It occurred to Charlotte that Coe might be going mad, unable to deal with the guilt and ramifications of his decisions.

"He has power," Coe rushed on. "And he listens to me. If I ask him to give amnesty to members of the Resistance, he will."

"You can't know that." Charlotte frowned. She could tell Coe believed what he was saying, but she was just as certain that he was deceiving himself.

"Do you really think he wants Jack or Linnet dead?" Coe asked. "All my father wants is for the Resistance to fade so the greatness of Britannia can be truly realized. The Resistance is the thorn festering in the lion's paw. It must be pulled out."

"Coe." Charlotte tried to keep her tone kind, despite her frustration. "Even if Admiral Winter was willing to spare the lives of your friends, a handful of the Resistance, what about all the others who will die?"

Coe shook his head, but Charlotte pressed. "And I don't agree with you. The Resistance is not hopeless. I can't speak to France's commitment, but I don't believe that all the men and women who have dedicated their lives to this cause are so misguided that they'd throw their lives away."

"You don't know what I know," Coe said.

"I don't have to," Charlotte countered. "If the Resistance is such a lost cause, why is the Empire so frightened by it? Why do they focus the energies of their military leaders on its destruction? The Empire wants to be rid of the Resistance not because it's a pest, but because it is a true threat. Because it *will* succeed."

Coe stared at her. He was pale, but Charlotte couldn't discern whether anger or fear had robbed his cheeks of color.

He whispered, "It can't be true."

Seizing on his uncertainty, Charlotte said, "Coe, I believe that you don't want to hurt me. I believe that you care about me."

Coe didn't respond.

"You can help me," Charlotte told him.

He walked to the window and rested one arm against the frame. "How?"

Charlotte's heart thudded. "I can't stay here. I need to

get Grave out of that monstrosity of a laboratory and find somewhere safe for us."

"There is nowhere safe," Coe said in a flat voice. He turned toward her, frowning. "Why do you care about him? You keep trying to protect him, despite the danger. He could be an incredible help to the Resistance, but you won't give him to either side."

"He isn't something to be given or taken," Charlotte said.

"You know what he is?" Coe asked.

Charlotte wrapped her arms around herself, feeling a sudden chill. "He's an impossibility. A miracle created because love didn't die when Hackett Bromley's son did. Somehow Grave manifested from that pain and devotion. I may not know what he is, but I know he's innocent." She drew a shivering breath. "I protect him because he shouldn't be treated like a machine or a weapon or a tool. He deserves to simply be."

"To simply be," Coe echoed, then uttered a joyless laugh. "He deserves that? Do any of us get to live that way? From the day we are born, we are thrown into the forge of life; we are hammered and shaped as the world wills. Why shouldn't the same be true for Grave?"

"Because he isn't the same," Charlotte said.

"From all this talk, I'd say you belong with the Sisters," Coe told her. "Go spend your time reading stars and prophesying while the rest of us toil."

His jibe riled Charlotte, but she didn't let it provoke her.

"Will you help me?" she asked.

"If I let you go, my father will execute me," Coe said, returning his gaze to the window.

"You can come with me," Charlotte said.

"If I go with you, the Resistance will execute me." Coe smiled to himself.

"I'll protect you," Charlotte said quickly. "You think you can save our friends by influencing your father. I can do that for you. I won't let them execute you."

Coe pushed himself off the window frame. "I am grateful for your sentiment, Charlotte. It's touching that you would be willing to speak on my behalf. You have more confidence than I that anyone would listen."

"Coe—" She didn't know what else to say, what words would sway him.

"I don't know what to believe," Coe said, speaking more to himself than to her. He started toward the door.

"Coe, wait!" Charlotte went after him.

He was already exiting the room. The door closed behind him.

"Coe!"

The only answer Charlotte received was the sound of a key turning in a lock and a bolt sliding into place.

19.

MARGERY OTT HAD hosted any number of unorthodox gatherings in her lifetime, but this would be the first time she'd staged a kidnapping in her parlor. Quite the adventure. The only troubling part of this endeavor rested in Lady Ott's lack of familiarity with her co-conspirators. Linnet and Jack were close associates, of course, but she knew this Meg only by snippets of intelligence that had been passed on to her. Having always been suspicious of religion, she was predisposed to doubt Meg's reliability in deed and veracity in word. After all, the woman forsook her friends for the Sisters so she might dabble in the arcane. What rubbish!

Then there was the matter of this pirate. Margery had more knowledge of the legend called *Sang d'Acier* than she did of the man she'd been introduced to. Jean-Baptiste Lachance lounged in his chair as if he were in his own house rather than a guest. He was extraordinarily handsome, but too enamored with himself for her taste. Though she knew the pirate's boasts were for show and not a true reflection of his character, Margery still found it irksome.

What was it that had been said of the French champion of America's Revolution, the Marquis de Lafayette? That he was a monument in need of a pedestal. Yes, that was the sort of man Lachance appeared to be.

Sang d'Acier had brought along a rowdy troupe of associates. Meg had asserted that these ruffians could be brought into line at a single word from Lachance. Margery rather wished the pirate captain would get around to saying that word. She had many friends she'd have described as roustabouts, but in her line of work, it was imperative to adjust one's role to whatever setting one found oneself in. Intelligence-gathering proved nearly impossible when an agent was a peacock strutting amid a gaggle of geese. While she'd happily have downed grog in the Quay with these fellows, she would have preferred that they observe appropriate decorum while visiting her home in the Floating City.

Ah well. The hulking men's muscles would certainly be welcome when the time came.

Lady Ott smoothed the front of her plum satin dress and walked to the center of the room.

The company fell quiet, and she allowed herself a small smile of triumph. Through years of partnership, conniving, and love, Lady and Lord Ott had built what was nigh unto an Empire of their own. Theirs was an Empire of secrets, backdoor deals, assassinations, and conspiracy. When the couple were but young things, newly married and madly smitten with each other, their chosen profession had been much more dangerous to their persons. Those were the years when they did the spying and smuggling and, when necessary, killing with their own hands. As their experience grew, their fortunes increased, and their reputations flourished, the Otts were bit by bit able to extricate themselves from the gritty day-to-day tasks of their business and delegate them to their hirelings. Now the couple enjoyed the view from aloft in their expansive domain. The network of loyal associates they claimed hailed from Britain, France, Spain, the freetowns, and the Caribbean, and included Iroquois, Mohawk, Cherokee, Chickasaw, Creek, Seminole . . . the list went on and on. They were aristocrats, bureaucrats, bankers, spies, thieves, mesmers, and mummers.

Hers was an extraordinary life, from which she gleaned great satisfaction.

Thus, news of Coe Winter's treachery caused a painful sting and the sullen bruise of injured pride.

Of course there had been bad apples among the their employees through the years, but Roger and Margery Ott had always been several steps ahead of those who sought their ruin. Coe was the first to fully dupe the reigning monarchs of espionage, and she was eager to repay that favor in kind . . . with interest.

Lady Ott spread her hands in welcome as she addressed the group. "Thank you for gathering here today. You all know why you've been summoned, but let me quickly review the planned operation. Commodore Winter will arrive within the hour. He expects a meeting with me alone. Once he's inside, all of the doors must be secured."

She gestured to Lachance's men, who voiced their "ayes" in acknowledgment.

"You'll keep your posts at the doors," Margery continued, "while Commodore Winter enjoys his tea. Once he's been sufficiently restrained, our real work begins."

"Are you certain he won't be suspicious?" Jack asked. "He didn't make his arrival in the city public."

"I'm sure he has a sound cover story to pacify me," she said. "And Coe shouldn't be surprised that I'd receive word of his presence. He knows we keep close watch on the Military Platform."

"What about the tea?" Jack's anxiety was understandable. The fact of his brother's treachery must have been all the more painful for the younger Winter.

Margery offered him a sympathetic smile. "You needn't worry about the tea, Jack. Coe is aware that I don't take sugar in my tea, while your brother takes three sugars."

Jack nodded, but his jaw remained clenched. Linnet put her hand on his shoulder.

"It will be over soon," she told her half brother.

"Very well," Lady Ott said, shooing them away. "Time to make yourselves invisible."

The group split apart, each person moving to his or her assigned position. Only Meg lingered in the parlor.

"Are you certain you're comfortable facing him alone?" Meg asked.

Margery puffed up in indignation, a retort ready on her lips. But as she looked into Meg's eyes, she saw an old wisdom, and steel.

Perhaps I've underestimated her, just as she's underestimating me now.

Rather than chide Meg, Margery patted her on the cheek and smiled. "My dear, I appreciate your concern. But if you knew me, you'd be aware that's a completely unnecessary question."

Meg was taken aback by Lady Ott's reply. The younger woman considered the elder's face for a moment, then said, "I meant no insult, Lady Ott. Your reputation attests to your expertise in these matters—"

"There's something else, then?" Margery's brow crinkled. "Something that troubles you?"

Meg looked over her shoulder in the direction that Linnet and Jack had exited the parlor. "There's a darkness in this betrayal. Born of jealousy and fear that goes far beyond the politics of war. Coe has been bowed by his father's tyranny. I believe there is no boundary to what Admiral Winter will do to maintain control of the situation. Be wary."

The solemnity of Meg's words chilled Margery to the core. She knew many people sought out Madam Jedda for her gifts of intuition and foresight. It appeared her daughter had inherited the same spiritual abilities.

"I'll keep that in mind," Margery said.

When Meg had gone, Lady Ott returned to her chair. She waited calmly, her mind clear and serene. Though anticipation provoked anxiety in many people, patience had never posed a problem for her. Waiting was an essential part of the intelligence game, and her skill in this arena was finely honed.

A quarter of an hour later, one of the staff announced Commodore Coe Winter's arrival. Another servant showed him into the parlor. Lady Ott stood when the young officer arrived. He was in full military dress. With a broad smile, Coe doffed his hat and bowed. Despite his amiable expression, she noted the dark circles beneath his eyes.

"What a pleasure to receive your invitation," Coe said. "And a surprise."

Margery returned Coe's smile and let her gaze fill with mirth and mischief. "Was it truly a surprise, Commodore? Surely you don't think your arrival would escape my observation."

Coe laughed, shaking his head. "Of course, Lady Ott. You and your husband are farseeing beyond the power of any telescope and more discerning than any magnifying glass or microscope."

"Now you're full of flattery." She laid her hand atop his. "Won't you please have a seat?" She turned to her servant. "Tea, Mr. Bell."

"Of course, my lady."

Coe and Margery settled into their chairs.

"You must tell me what's brought you to the Floating City," she said. "I expected you'd remain in New Orleans to assist Commander Marshall with locating Charlotte. Poor girl, I can't imagine what's gotten into her head."

Coe grimaced. "I wish I knew. I'm fearful for her, and I would have stayed at the Daedalus Tower had I not received a summons from my father. The admiral's will is not wisely ignored."

Margery nodded.

"And I thought I might learn something of Charlotte's whereabouts here," Coe continued. "The Empire is still hunting Grave. If they'd been found, there would be word of it among the officers."

Bell returned bearing a silver tea service. He poured Lady Ott's tea with cream. Then turned to Coe.

"Three sugars, no cream."

"Very good, sir."

Bell poured the steaming liquid into Coe's cup, then added three lumps of sugar. With a curt bow, Bell left them to their conversation.

While Coe stirred the sugar into his tea, Lady Ott asked, "Have you heard anything of Charlotte and Grave since you arrived?"

Coe shook his head. "It's a frustrating situation. I don't think Charlotte realized how much danger she's put herself and the Resistance in."

"She's still young," Lady Ott replied. "And prone to act on impulse."

She watched Coe sip his tea.

"Do you have anything to report on other matters?" she asked, lifting her own cup.

"There's an ongoing debate about redistributing the air fleet." Coe paused and took another drink. "Some of the high-ranking officers believe too much credence has been given to rumors of an overt alliance between the French and the Resistance. They would prefer to have some of our strength in America transferred to the colonies in the East."

"Such reassignments could prove beneficial to the Resistance," Margery said.

Coe began to blink rapidly. "I . . . yes . . . they could."

She sipped more of her tea.

Coe frowned, passing a hand over his eyes. A sheen of sweat covered his forehead. "My apologies, Lady Ott. I fear I may be unwell."

"Have you eaten anything today?" Lady Ott asked. "I know you industrious fellows. All work, never remembering that you need sustenance. Here, I'll have Mr. Bell bring sandwiches."

"Yes." He had another swallow of tea. "That might help."

As Lady Ott reached for the velvet pull to summon Mr. Bell, Coe's teacup slipped from his hand. Tea spilled over the tray while he gazed at Margery in confusion. She continued to smile as Coe slumped in his chair, his head lolling back as unconsciousness swallowed him.

She did pull the velvet rope then, and Mr. Bell appeared

in the next moment. She pointed to the tray. "Would you please take care of this, Mr. Bell?"

"Of course, my lady." Bell moved to collect the tray.

"And let our guests know that we can proceed."

"Right away, Lady Ott."

20.

OE'S SKULL ACHED as though it had just been released from a vise. His first instinct was to rub his temples, but when he attempted to raise his hands, he discovered he couldn't. He lifted his head, blinking in an attempt to clear his blurred vision.

Lady Ott's parlor came into view. Coe was in the same chair he'd occupied when taking tea, but his arms were bound to the arms of the chair, his legs to its legs. He remembered feeling slightly feverish, then dizzy. After that, nothing until a moment ago when he'd woken.

What happened?

Coe had considered declining Lady Ott's invitation. Since Charlotte's abduction, his one-time rigid convictions had become unsettled. For the past two years, he'd adhered to his father's words, to the admiral's assessment of military issues. Under Admiral Winter's tutelage, Coe had found it easier and easier to dismiss contradictory information offered by the Resistance.

But Charlotte was different. Despite being a child of the Resistance, reared to despise the Empire, Charlotte was no sheep blindly following a herd. When her values had been compromised, she had challenged her mother and fled the Daedalus Tower. Charlotte's fealty was to that which she believed true and just. When she fought, it was on her terms. She had courage of a sort Coe had never encountered.

And that was why, despite his doubts and fears, he'd decided to help her.

Leaving the key was the compromise that Coe's mind had finally settled on. He'd offered Charlotte the means to escape her room, but getting out of the building, evading guards—all of that she would have to accomplish on her own.

Most importantly, the Empire still had Grave. Coe doubted Charlotte would attempt to rescue him on her own. By the time she could rally her friends, it would be too late. Events had already been set in motion that couldn't be stopped. The Resistance's fate was sealed.

But Coe still fostered hope that when it was over, Charlotte, if she survived, would understand what he'd done and why. He needed someone to understand.

Ignoring the dull pain in his head, Coe cast his gaze about the room. A rough-looking fellow was across the room stuffing cake into his face while he leaned against the door frame. The man noticed Coe watching him.

"Oy!" the man called, spewing bits of cake from his mouth. "Your man's awake!"

He stepped aside, and Lady Ott came into the room, her skirts swishing over the floor. Walking beside her was a tall golden-haired man who seemed familiar to Coe, but not enough to name.

Coe scrambled to grasp his situation. Obviously, events had turned against him, but to what extent he didn't know. That warranted caution.

With a pained smile, Coe spoke to Lady Ott. "I seem to be in something of a predicament. Is this a prank? Or do I owe Lord Ott more money than I think?"

Lady Ott's returning smile was not friendly. She didn't reply, but waited until Linnet, Meg, and Jack entered the parlor.

The sight of those three sent a fist into Coe's gut.

He tried to keep up the ruse. "Ah, with this troupe involved, I know it must be a prank."

Linnet simply glared at Coe, while Meg eyed him warily.

Jack crossed the room and grabbed Coe by the shirt. "Where are Charlotte and Grave?"

Two answers bloomed in Coe's mind. Two loyalties. Two lives. Who was he—Coe Winter of the Resistance? Or Lazarus, double agent of the Empire?

When he didn't speak, Jack snarled through clenched teeth. "I saw you."

Coe didn't abandon his innocent facade. "Saw me where?"

"The Crucible."

The fist of fear jammed in Coe's stomach now splintered into a thousand cutting pieces.

The game is up.

"So you know." Coe abandoned his amiable expression. Exhaustion overwhelmed him. He didn't remember the last time he'd slept soundly. "You may believe that by putting me in this position you've won a grand prize. But you haven't."

"Capturing you may not be a prize," Linnet said. "But I believe extracting the information you no doubt have will be of great value."

Coe looked at Linnet with distaste. Yes, he'd helped Charlotte, but shaken as he might be, he wasn't ready to abandon his father and the Empire. He'd given too much of himself to the wrong cause. If the ship was burning, he'd go down with it. "What information? Do you really think the Empire would let me serve in any other capacity than gathering intelligence after it was plain I'd once been fool enough to be a rebel? You already know everything I could tell you, because my assignment is simply to relay information about the Resistance."

Hope kindled in Coe's chest. If he could convince them that his role in serving the Empire was only as a mole, it could limit any damage to the Empire's plans.

The man who'd been standing with Lady Ott strolled forward. "I might believe that if you were a low-ranking officer, but a commodore? The son of Admiral Winter?

Such a man is not a pawn in the Empire's game. That man is a bishop, or perhaps even the queen."

Coe tried not to reveal anything through his expression. He knew who the man was now. His French accent combined with Linnet's presence made it clear.

The pirate bent closer. "Ah, but you recognize me? I can see it in your eyes. You should know that I have no love for a man who sets the Imperial navy on my ship like dogs after a hare."

"Yes, I know who you are, *Sang d'Acier*," Coe said, determined to keep as much hidden as he could. "But pirates bring the wrath of authorities on themselves. A hazard of your occupation. Any ships chasing yours have nothing to do with me."

"We're here to identify the turncoat in our ranks," Linnet said, her gaze cool. "Behold our success."

Coe shrugged. "A turncoat? I prefer to think of myself as enlightened. I've reaffirmed my loyalty to the Empire. If you value your lives, you'll do likewise."

"And you take pride in this 'noble' deed?" Lady Ott spoke for the first time. "Perhaps from your perspective you've done something incredibly brave. But had the American Revolution succeeded, Benedict Arnold would be known forever as a traitor and coward."

The laugh that bubbled from Coe's throat was genuine. "If my deeds result in a province being named in my honor, I will hardly complain."

"They won't." Lady Ott's words were spoken with such malice, Coe couldn't stop himself from shrinking back in his chair. He regretted the reflex when he saw her smile of satisfaction.

"It's time you answered your brother's question," she continued. "Where are Charlotte and Grave?"

"Safe." Coe knew making it appear as though he held a gun to Charlotte's head, even in absentia, it would only make things worse for him.

Meg stepped closer. There was a depth in her eyes that made him want to shiver.

"Charlotte is in the city," she murmured. "I've seen her."

"Listen to me. Charlotte is safe," Coe said. "I told her what I'm telling you now. The Empire will grant pardons to any who denounce the Resistance and swear allegiance to Britannia. It's not too late for you."

"Enough of this." The stiletto flashed in Linnet's hand. "The only person running out of time here is you."

She pulled a chair alongside his and sat. "You know where Charlotte is. You're going to tell us how to find her."

"Why would I do that?" Coe was beginning to think that the time for putting up a confident front was gone. He now needed to think about self-preservation.

"I've found that interrogations often drag out unnecessarily," Linnet said. "Out of a sense of propriety or maybe even mercy, no one jumps right to the heart of it."

A cold sweat beaded under Coe's shirt collar.

"We could bruise you or break your fingers." Her voice was chillingly casual. "But will we gain anything from it? I don't think so."

Linnet held her stiletto in front of Coe's face. Then she turned the blade so its point hovered before his right eye.

"Here is my offer, and it comes only once," she said. "Tell us where to find Charlotte, or you lose an eye, brother."

She abruptly stood. "You have one minute to decide."

Linnet left the room, and Captain Lachance trailed after her.

Meg's and Jack's expressions revealed their shock at Linnet's ultimatum.

Coe had to admit that he was stunned as well. Linnet had been right. He'd expected to endure pain and questions and more pain, but only up to a point—the point of saving face while not sustaining injuries that would have lasting effects.

But to lose an eye.

Even putting aside the torment of such a thing, an eye couldn't be replaced. The Empire's tinkers had made great strides in developing mechanical limbs for amputees. But they had yet to create anything of the sort when it came to restoring vision.

Coe appealed to the mercy of his other captors. "Linnet's temper has gotten the better of her," he said to Jack and Meg. "Surely this situation calls for reason over passion."

Jack stared at his brother for several breaths. Then Jack's face twisted and broke; he doubled over laughing.

Coe didn't know what to make of this reaction.

"Reason?" Jack choked out the word. "Reason!"

When Jack straightened, his face was red. He wiped tears from his cheeks; Coe wasn't certain whether they were a sign of mirth or grief.

"You sent Charlotte to the Crucible," Jack said in a low voice. "There is nothing of reason in that place. Only madness."

Coe shook his head. "Charlotte spent little time there and only due to necessity. You know she's no longer there. I assure you she's been provided the utmost comfort since her arrival at the Floating City."

Jack began to laugh again. Coe was frightened by the wildness he saw in his brother's eyes.

"Meg." Coe turned his attention to her. "Tell me you won't abide this reckless behavior. Jack and Linnet are motivated by vengeance, nothing more."

The corners of Meg's mouth tilted up. "You're wrong, Commodore Winter."

Her use of formal address made him shiver.

"They're motivated by love," she continued. "Something I wonder if you've ever known."

Coe's fear gave way to rage. How dare she speak such insults to him? How did any of them risk provoking his wrath? He was the son of Admiral Winter. And while fear of his father had shaped him, love had as well. Hadn't it?

"Do you have an answer for me?" Linnet swept back into the room.

The pirate sauntered in after her, but hung back, letting Meg, Jack, and Linnet close in on Coe.

Linnet stepped ahead of the other two, her stiletto in hand. "Well?"

Coe met her gaze with a flat stare.

"I thought as much." Linnet crouched in front of Coe and lifted her blade. Its point floated a few inches from his eye.

She turned the stiletto slightly so light bounced off the steel of its length. "Tell us where Charlotte is."

Coe spat in Linnet's face. She wiped his saliva away. The stiletto moved closer to his eye.

"Jack!" Coe couldn't take his gaze from the point of the blade. "This is barbarism."

"You and I both know the Empire has done the same," Jack said. "And worse."

When Coe blinked, his eyelashes brushed over steel. He wasn't going to be able to stop himself from screaming if the blade came any nearer.

"I'll tell you!" Coe shouted.

Linnet drew her stiletto back, but only a little. "I'm listening."

Coe was trembling all over. "You'll find Charlotte in Zeus."

When Linnet shot a look at Jack, he said, "That's the visitors' quarters, near the center of the platform."

Linnet nodded. She stood up and returned her blade to its sheath.

Coe wanted to sag in relief, but he forced himself to sit straight and tall. "Savages," he hissed at them.

Jack's eyes were nothing less than hateful when he looked at Coe. "If she's been hurt in any way, you'll lose a lot more than an eye."

Coe's mouth twisted in fury as he stared up at his brother. "I could have had you killed. My orders alone compelled those bounty hunters to spare your life."

"Do you think that changes anything?" Jack said. "Am I meant to be swayed by your grand expression of brotherly affection?"

"Brotherly?" Coe shot back. "You would do well to remember our family. You always whined about Mother, but did you ever think she is simply too weak to be a true helpmeet for our father? Do you understand at all the legacy he wants to create for us? The House of Winter will be the greatest house of the Empire. Yet you treat your inheritance like a burden. Some of the fault is mine. My folly with the Resistance became yours. But I still had hope that when the time was right I would bring you back into the fold."

"I think you'll find you're quite mistaken about who's been deluded." Jack let go of Coe's shirt and turned away in disgust.

"I disagree."

"And Grave?" Meg asked.

Coe knew his smile was cruel, but he couldn't forget the threats they'd made. He wanted them to suffer as he had. "You won't be able to rescue Grave."

"Why?"

"Ask Charlotte when you retrieve her," Coe replied.

"She'll explain. If your little infiltration of the Military Platform is successful, that is."

"Do you want me to get the blade out again?" Linnet asked.

Coe blanched, but Meg waved a dismissive hand. "Better to turn our minds toward Charlotte than waste more time on this wretch."

Linnet turned to the back of the room, where Lady Ott waited. "Where would you like him stowed?"

"The larder, I think," Lady Ott replied. "The cellar would suffice, but Roger has collected quite a number of fine vintages. It would be tragic if this fellow should knock any of them over in a misguided attempt to escape."

"The larder it is." Linnet gestured to *Sang d'Acier*. The pirate whistled, and two burly men entered the room. Lachance's minions lifted Coe up, chair and all.

The men reeked of stale sweat and worse. Coe felt like retching. The room tilted sideways and began to spin. Memories chased each other around his mind, impossible to follow.

No one spoke to him as he was carried from the parlor into the kitchen. The men deposited him in a corner of the larder. Then he was alone.

Throughout his interrogation, Coe had clung to the last threads of his faith in the Empire and his loyalty to his father. The father who saved him. Who had promised redemption.

But that was over. Whether a fleeting dream or a true possibility, the life Coe had imagined as the honored son of the House of Winter—admired by friends whose hearts he'd turned to favor the Empire once more—had passed into shadow. In the hands of the enemy, he was worthless to his father. As much as he wanted to believe otherwise, Coe knew the admiral would prefer him dead over captured.

There was no one to save him now.

21

CHARLOTTE HAD BEEN sleeping when the envelope was slipped under her door. She hadn't intended to nap, but soon after curling up on the velvet sofa, weariness had overtaken her.

The envelope held a key and a note.

I had a choice. So do you.

Coe's words caused a pang in Charlotte's chest. He wouldn't forsake the Empire, but somehow he still felt compelled to help her. She wondered if Coe hoped she would choose to heed his words and stay. Could he really believe that she would choose the Empire over the Resistance?

The Resistance might be flawed, but it existed because of the corruption and abuses of the Empire. Charlotte knew where she belonged and whom she would fight for.

Attempting an escape before the deep of night would have been foolish, so Charlotte was forced to wait for agonizing hours to pass before she slipped the key into the lock and turned it.

No guards were posted outside her room. Had Coe dismissed them, improving her chance of escape?

She closed the door behind her and walked quickly down the hall. While it was hardly ideal, Charlotte could think of no means to leave the building other than the stairs she'd used while being escorted in and out. Too much time would be wasted trying to find alternate exits.

Charlotte hadn't yet reached the stairwell when footsteps in the corridor locked her in place. She could make a run for the stairs, but the sound of her footfalls might prove her undoing. Casting her gaze up and down the hall, Charlotte searched for an alcove or cranny where she could duck out of sight until danger had passed. She found none.

Hiding wasn't an option. That left fighting.

Whoever approached would have to turn a corner before they could see her. That meant a brief window existed where Charlotte had the element of surprise. She might be able to subdue her opponent and then continue to the stairs.

Charlotte crept forward, pressing her body against the wall. The footsteps were closer. Closer. She balled her fists, wishing she had a weapon.

In the dim hall, the figure that rounded the corner was little more than a silhouette. Charlotte lunged. Her body plowed into the stranger's. She'd succeeded in catching him off guard.

"Unh!" His cry of surprise became a whoosh of air flee-ing his lungs. Charlotte drove him hard to the floor.

Charlotte kept her knee planted on his sternum, then raised her fist, aiming to land a blow with force sufficient to knock him unconscious.

Someone grabbed her arm from behind.

"You don't want to do that," a familiar voice said. "Though for a minute I considered letting it happen. Would have been fun to watch."

"Linnet?" Charlotte could barely make out her friend's features.

"I expected to find you locked up," Linnet said. "How is that you're roaming the halls?"

"But . . ." Charlotte turned back to the man she'd at-tacked. "Then who?"

"Not how I imagined the rescue," Jack said, rubbing his chest. "Not at all."

"Spear of Athene," Charlotte muttered. She offered Jack a hand and helped him up. "I didn't know it was you."

"I hope not," Jack said. "Otherwise we need to talk about why you want to kill me."

"How did you find me?" Charlotte asked.

"A fine question," Linnet whispered. "But one that should be answered after we finish rescuing you . . . or rather, come along as you continue rescuing yourself." Linnet's smile flashed in the dim hall. "Unless you think we'll be an encumbrance. You were obviously faring quite well before we arrived."

"Oh, hush," Charlotte said, stifling a laugh. "Just get us out of here."

"My pleasure."

Linnet took point, letting Jack fall in step beside Charlotte. He clasped her hand, squeezing it hard.

Lachance was waiting for them near the door. Given his perpetual air of confidence, Charlotte was surprised to see the pirate looking distinctly uncomfortable. Catching her eye, Lachance plucked at the sleeves of his military costume.

"I can barely tolerate these clothes," he sniffed. "They're so . . . legitimate."

Charlotte covered her mouth to muffle a giggle. Jack laughed as well, but the sound soon became a grunt of pain.

"I told you." Linnet wagged a finger at him. "You shouldn't have come. You'll be lucky if you get through the night without having to be sewn up again."

"You're hurt?" Charlotte ran her eyes up and down Jack, seeking the source of his pain, but not finding it. She felt even worse about ambushing him.

Jack put a smile on. "I'm fine. Nothing to worry about."

Linnet muttered something unintelligible.

"You can scold me as much as you want once we're out of here," Jack said to her.

Ignoring him, Linnet said to Charlotte, "Do you know where Grave is?"

The sight of Grave cut open, unmade, jumped into

Charlotte's mind and caused her blood to curdle with revulsion.

Something in her expression compelled Linnet to ask, "Truthfully, Charlotte, can we help him tonight? Is he somewhere we can access?"

"He . . ." Charlotte didn't want to speak the truth; the truth filled her with guilt and shame.

"Charlotte," Linnet pressed, "we have very little time."

With a reluctant shake of her head, Charlotte said softly, "We won't be able to . . . He's . . . I need more time."

"That's all we need to know right now," Linnet said, comprehending the strain behind Charlotte's answer. "Don't let it gnaw at you. When the time is right, we'll find him. I promise you that."

Linnet took her hand, turning Charlotte's palm over to place a small metal object in it.

"Here," Linnet said. "Put this in your nose."

Still mired in the idea that she was abandoning Grave, Charlotte accepted to the curved bit of copper with a frown.

"Like this." Linnet affixed a similar device to her own nose so the two ends of the open ring pinched the cartilage between her nostrils. "Not exactly comfortable, but you'll be glad for it where we're going."

Charlotte mimicked Linnet's action. The ring did pinch, but Charlotte's nasal passages were suffused with the scent of lavender. Lachance and Jack affixed rings of their own before Linnet led them down the hall. The dormitory was quiet. Charlotte didn't know if that was because her rescuers had silenced everyone who might have raised an alarm, or because the building had been minimally occupied, so there were few souls who might discover her flight.

Linnet paused halfway along the corridor to unlock a door. At first Charlotte thought the door opened to a closet, but Linnet beckoned her forward so Charlotte could see that beyond the doorway was a trapdoor set into the floor. Linnet opened the trapdoor to reveal a chute that plunged into darkness. Even through the potent lavender oils on her nose ring, Charlotte could detect the cloying and sour odors of rot.

"Rubbish?"

Linnet smiled sweetly. "After you, kitten."

Pinching her nose to ensure the ring wasn't jarred free whenever and wherever she landed, Charlotte climbed into the chute. She pushed off the edge, then she was flying, flying, flying. The pitch wasn't steep enough to be frightening, but it did send her whooshing down the slick metal tube. Then for a moment she was hanging in the air until she landed with a soft *whumph* atop a lumpy pile of detritus.

Charlotte tried not to look at what she'd landed upon. She clambered over the uneven surface until she found her way off the trash heap and onto solid ground. She heard another body land in the rubbish, and soon Linnet was scrambling toward her.

"Not too bad," Linnet commented to herself. She reached out to pluck something from Charlotte's hair. "You've got—"

"Thank you." Charlotte cut her off, not wanting to know what from the mass of garbage had affixed itself to her head. She hoped whatever it was wouldn't leave behind the stench of this place, which was doing all it could to fight past the filtering perfume of her nose ring.

A subsequent thump and thump announced the arrival of Jack and Lachance. When the two men had climbed down from the heap, Linnet gestured that all of them should follow her. She led them to the perimeter of the room, which appeared to be the receiving point for a number of garbage chutes. Their progress was accompanied by the occasional sound of discarded items adding themselves to the rubbish piles.

Linnet suddenly crouched down, then disappeared. Charlotte bent to see how her friend had vanished and discovered an air shaft. She crawled forward, guided by the sound of Linnet ahead, as almost no light penetrated the shaft. Swallowed by that dimness, their small party moved slowly, making it nearly impossible for Charlotte to determine the distance they traveled.

Without warning, the sound of Linnet's clothing scraping along the walls stopped. Charlotte froze, holding her breath and releasing it only when Linnet's quiet words traveled back to her.

"There's a ladder here. You'll have to feel your way up the rungs."

"Okay," Charlotte answered.

She heard Linnet's boots clang against the ladder rungs, keeping still until the sound came from above. Charlotte inched forward, one hand out, until her fingers brushed against metal. She moved her hands along the chute wall and found the protruding ladder. Staying crouched on the balls of her feet, Charlotte let her hands lead the way up the rungs, pulling herself to standing when she couldn't reach any higher. Then her feet followed and she began to climb. From somewhere above came a steady, loud humming sound, and rushes of air pushed at Charlotte, growing stronger as she made her way up the ladder. She heard the whine of hinges, and muddled light from the city drifted into the shaft. The light winked in and out as it was obscured by Linnet scrambling from the hatch.

Charlotte kept climbing, and the light increased, though it never became bright. When she reached the open hatch, Linnet offered Charlotte a hand.

"Careful, now," Linnet said. "There isn't a lot of room up here."

Charlotte frowned, unable to comprehend the reason for Linnet's caution. Once she was out of the hatch, Charlotte understood the warning perfectly, and she didn't like it at all.

"I'll admit it gets a bit tricky now." Linnet moved her grip from Charlotte's hand to her elbow, steadying her as her mind accepted her body's location.

The air shaft terminated at a fair distance from the garbage repository . . . under the platform. The loud hum had transformed into a chorus of roars generated by the trio of massive propellers that held the platform aloft, each of which covered nearly a third of the platform's belly. Wind from the great turbines buffeted Charlotte and Linnet.

Where they'd exited the hatch was a small landing with a protective fencing around its edge. Its design suggested it should accommodate only one person at a time, likely for maintenance purposes alone.

Jack's head emerged from the hatch.

"You'll have to wait until one of us is off," Linnet told him.

Off? Charlotte made a full turn, examining the landscape—or rather, airscape—off each side of the landing. She didn't see anywhere they could go. The only object she spied was a thick cable of tightly wound metal that swooped down and disappeared into a low-hanging cloud bank beneath them. Charlotte started to look away, but her gaze was drawn back to the cable. Dread began to coil beneath her ribs.

That icy anticipation grew when Linnet said to Jack, "Ask Lachance to hand up two of the riders."

Jack's head ducked beneath the opening. When he reappeared, he threw something that looked like a tangle of metal and leather onto the landing. He offered a second jumble of materials and parts to Linnet.

Linnet shook out the object in her hands until leather straps dangled. Charlotte caught sight of buckles, and her heart lurched with apprehension.

"This is a rider." Linnet held the thing out for Charlotte to examine. Each of Linnet's hands held the edge of a thick metal cylinder that was open at the bottom. She turned the opening to show Charlotte what was inside. "The wheels ride the cable like trains would a track. You'll loop the straps around your shoulders, and a third strap buckles around your chest. It's not comfortable, but it will do the job."

Charlotte glanced at the cable once more. The line was obviously intended to moor small craft belonging to maintenance workers while they serviced the platforms. Linnet grabbed one of Charlotte's arms and threaded it through one of the loops. Charlotte abandoned the hope of trying to ease her anxiety about the imminent descent and waited for Linnet to finish buckling the harness.

"Reach your arms over your head," Linnet said.

When Charlotte did so, Linnet made adjustments to the lengths of straps that connected the back of the harness to the wheeled mechanism. Linnet brought Charlotte's fingers to clutch the wooden handle on a slender chain that dangled from the cylinder.

"This is the brake," Linnet told Charlotte. "When you're closing in on the landing below, be sure to slow down. You probably wouldn't knock yourself out if you hit it at full speed, but you could break some ribs."

Charlotte nodded.

"I'm going to head down first, so I'll signal when you should reduce your speed." Linnet gazed over the edge of the landing. "If I can. That cloud bank looks pretty dense."

"Great," Charlotte muttered.

Linnet patted her on the shoulder. "You'll be fine, kitten. If things do clear up below, try not to look down."

Charlotte offered a thin smile as Linnet donned her own harness.

"When I'm away, let Jack know he can come up." Linnet clamped the rider onto the cable. "He'll help you attach the rider to the line."

She eased herself over the railing. With one hand she clung to the landing while she clasped the brake handle with the other. She let go of the railing.

The cable buzzed as Linnet sailed away, faster and faster, until she disappeared into the clouds.

Charlotte swallowed several times in an attempt to soothe her dry throat. Her voice still cracked when she called, "Jack. Linnet's gone."

Jack pushed himself out of the hatch and onto the landing. He stood and leaned over the railing, following the path of the cable.

With a low whistle, he said, "That's going to be quite a ride."

"Have you done this before?" Charlotte asked.

"Only once," Jack said. "It's not as bad as it looks."

He didn't sound convincing.

"Well, then." Charlotte squared her shoulders. "Linnet said you'd show me how to connect the rider to the cable."

"Happy to," Jack said with a teasing smile.

Charlotte moved closer to the point on the rail where the cable attached to the landing. Jack secured the cylinder to the thick metal cord.

"You know to brake before you reach the other side?" Jack asked.

"Yes."

As much as her heart was flinging itself about her chest, like a wild bird trying to escape a cage, Charlotte didn't think she was about to plunge to her death. She truly didn't.

But just in case.

Charlotte turned to Jack. She hooked one of her arms around his neck and buried her hand in his hair before she pulled his head down and pressed her parted lips against his. Both of Jack's arms went around her. He drew her against him as the heat of the kiss flooded her body.

"I am the last person to stand in the way of love." Lachance's voice came from the hatch. "But perhaps this is not the best time for such things?"

Charlotte drew back. She met the pirate's mischievous gaze with a resentful glare. He only laughed and pushed himself up to sit on the edge of the hatch opening.

"See you on the other side," Jack said quietly. Charlotte smiled at him.

Emboldened by the kiss, Charlotte climbed over the rail. She mimicked Linnet's movements so that she had one hand on the brake handle while the other held the railing, keeping her aloft.

Her heart made its protest again, hammering her ribs. Charlotte knew that this would be the most difficult part: letting go. Her mind could fix on the facts of the harness and the rider and Linnet waiting on the other side. But her body only screamed its awareness of the long, long fall to the earth. Hanging suspended between terror and release could easily send one into madness.

But that was where Charlotte seemed to be trapped.

"I'm not going to have to pry your fingers off, am I?" Jack said. "Because I'd feel awfully bad about it."

His words made her laugh, and her laughter broke her paralysis.

Charlotte released the rail. And she was soaring, down, down, down. The cloud bank rushed up to meet her. Thick, silver mist left kisses like dewdrops all over her face. Then she was free of the clouds and though she knew she shouldn't, Charlotte looked down. Fear and amazement twinned in her blood. Far below she could see the Iron Forest, its metal branches dull in the absence of sunlight. She pulled her eyes away from the ground directly underneath and gazed into the distance. Beyond the island of Manhattan, the sea was a patchwork of grays and blues, restless and sullen under the overcast sky but brilliant in those places where shafts of sunlight pierced the clouds.

A sharp whistle caught Charlotte's attention. Looking ahead, she saw that she had passed beneath one of the lower platforms and was swiftly coming upon a landing at which Linnet waved emphatically.

Charlotte pulled on the brake. The rider screeched in protest as metal clamped against the cable. She was still moving quickly, but under control. She pulled the brake again, slowing even more as the cable began to rise to meet the landing. Linnet leaned over the railing, extending a hand to Charlotte. Releasing the brake for fear that she'd slow too much on this brief upward slant and come up short of the landing, only to dangle helplessly, Charlotte didn't use the brake again until she could almost reach Linnet's hand. Then she pulled the brake as hard as she could. The rider shrieked, and Charlotte jerked to a stop as her fingers closed on Linnet's.

"Pretty good for the first time." Linnet grinned at her.

Charlotte could only smile back. She was breathing hard, not from fear, but exhilaration.

When Linnet had finished helping her over the railing and they'd released the rider from the cable, they both turned to wait for Jack's approach.

Tracing the route she'd just followed, Charlotte asked, "Has anyone ever gotten stuck?"

Linnet laughed, nodding. "More than once."

"What happens then?" Charlotte shivered at the idea of being suspended, motionless between the landings.

"You have to pull yourself the rest of the way."

22.

THE REMAINDER OF the escape route proved far less harrowing. Rather than being forced to squirm through another series of ventilation shafts, they had alighted upon a landing fitted with permanent ladders connecting the upper surface of the platforms with the machine works that kept the structure aloft.

By the time they reached the Market Platform, it had begun to rain in earnest. Swollen drops crashed onto Charlotte's head, face, and shoulders. In less than a minute, her clothes were sodden and she shivered from the cold. Linnet led their beleaguered party through the deluge, her head down, trudging ever forward. Despite the unpleasant weather, Charlotte felt wave after wave of relief at being free of the Military Platform and once again in the company of her friends. Jack walked beside her, his fingers twined with hers from the moment he'd climbed over the railing of the second landing. She grasped his hand fiercely, needing the connection—she'd been far too close to never seeing him again.

Lady Ott's apartments offered a much welcome refuge from the cold. When she ushered them in, Charlotte rushed forward to embrace the woman.

"Oh, no, no, no." Lady Ott nimbly avoided Charlotte's outstretched arms. "As delighted as I am to see you well and here, my dearest, you reek like Hades. I'll have my maid prepare you a bath."

She sniffed the air, casting a glance at each of the others with consternation until she finally pinched her nose. "Baths all around, I'd say."

Though Charlotte had considered Lady Ott's insistence that they all thoroughly bathe before attending to other business quite irksome, she was now grateful for their host's obstinacy. The hot water and steam soothed aches from her muscles and the lingering tension from her ordeal. And once she'd removed her nose ring and become fully aware of the powerful stench that hung around her like a pestilence, she knew Lady Ott had the better sense of things. Charlotte was happily rid of the clothes Coe had provided during her captivity and hoped Lady Ott would choose to burn them.

Clean and freshly dressed, Charlotte went to join Lady Ott in the parlor. When Charlotte entered, Lady Ott set aside her glass of sherry and came to embrace her.

"Now I can welcome you properly." She folded Charlotte into a fierce hug. "I can't begin to tell you how relieved I am that you are with us again and that you appear well."

"I'm quite well," Charlotte replied.

"I'm also relieved to hear that." The speaker had been partially hidden by Lady Ott, but now came forward.

"Meg!" Charlotte rushed into her friend's arms. When they drew apart, Charlotte said, "I trust it was you who set my rescue in motion."

"In part," Meg said. "I learned from the Sisters that you had visited the Temple under watch of a military escort. But it was Jack who told Linnet of your initial capture."

Charlotte nodded, not wanting the memories of bounty hunters and the Crucible to seep into her mind and strip away the contentment she could bask in for the moment.

"But it wasn't until we had Coe that we were able to determine where you were being held in the city."

The room became airless as Charlotte took in Meg's words. She stared at her friend.

"Charlotte?" Lady Ott's voice seemed to come from very far away. "May I offer you something to steady your nerves? Sherry? Or a brandy, perhaps?"

"No." Charlotte fought back the sense of unreality. "I'm fine."

She turned her eyes on Meg, wanting to be sure of what she'd heard. "You have Coe? Here?"

"Yes." Meg's brow had furrowed with concern. "Lady Ott was able to lure him here, and we were able to take him captive without difficulty."

The barrage of emotions assailing Charlotte had caught her unawares. Now that she understood their provenance, she was able to hold them in check.

"Where is he?" Charlotte asked. *He left a key.*

At the moment, she didn't know if she was ready to face Coe. But she would be. By Athene, she would be. Coe could be fundamental to Grave's safe return. Charlotte didn't want to leave her friend in the Empire's hands a moment longer than necessary.

Lady Ott made an exasperated sound. "Where hasn't he been? I kept him in the larder for a time, but that proved untenable. He gave the kitchen staff too much of a fright, no matter how often I assured them he was tightly bound. Then I shut him into one of the guest rooms, but I couldn't bear the thought that he'd enjoy all the lovely natural light that room afforded him. In the end I put him in the cellar . . . though only after I'd had all the wine removed."

"We have yet to thoroughly interrogate Coe," Meg said. "We wanted to ensure you were safe before anything else."

"I understand," Charlotte said. "And I'm incredibly grateful, but I'm ashamed to have left Grave behind."

Meg and Margery exchanged a glance.

"We were told an attempt to rescue Grave would be futile," Meg said.

That's why Linnet questioned me in the way she did.

"By Coe?" Charlotte asked. *Who else?*

Meg nodded.

Charlotte's grief over Grave's absence smoldered,

becoming rage at Coe—the instigator of these sorrows. Then she remembered the key. The note.

I had a choice. So do you.

It didn't seem like the Coe who had betrayed them could be the same person who'd helped her escape. And who would he be now that he'd been taken prisoner? When he hadn't been exchanging insults with Jack, Coe had struck Charlotte as steadfast, skillful, and intelligent. She didn't think those qualities could be fabricated. Was that the true Coe, the man who remained when the Empire, the Resistance, his father had all been stripped away? If it was, Charlotte held on to hope that her friend-turned-adversary might somehow be redeemed. Only time and trial would reveal his true nature. She had to reach the Coe she believed existed beneath the treachery, beyond the fear and shame that bound him to his father.

"Coe can get Grave back for us," Charlotte said. "He has to."

"There are many things Commodore Winter should be made to do for us," Lady Ott spoke in a gentling tone. "He has much to answer for."

A familiar, uneasy chill settled over Charlotte. Once again she found herself at a crossroads, where it was likely her priorities differed from those of her companions. Of course Coe's crimes against the Resistance would be considered of greater import than retrieving Grave. Charlotte's hands balled at her sides as she grappled with her emotions.

The last time she'd been put into this position, she'd run. She didn't have anywhere to run this time. More than that, when Charlotte had fled New Orleans, it had been to escape her mother's and Coe's machinations regarding Grave. Circumstances had drastically shifted since then. Coe was a prisoner. And Charlotte couldn't know how her mother would react upon learning that her co-conspirator was in fact an agent of the Empire.

The people surrounding Charlotte now were her friends. She trusted them. Despite the strength of her fears, she wouldn't let her feelings overcome her belief that together they would find a way to help Grave while still serving the goals of the Resistance.

The Resistance . . .

Alarm charged through Charlotte's limbs. "We need to talk to Coe now."

"What is it, Charlotte?" Meg asked.

Charlotte waved the question off. "Gather the others. Have Coe brought here—"

Pausing, Charlotte looked at Lady Ott. "Unless you'd like to have us question him in the cellar?"

"No, no." Lady Ott smiled at Charlotte, though her gaze was full of puzzlement. "It would be far too cramped."

"I'll get Linnet, Jack, and Lachance. We'll retrieve Coe," Meg said, her expression as bemused as Margery's.

When Meg had gone, Lady Ott said, "Something put spurs to you, my dear. I must confess I'm quite desperate to hear what it is."

Charlotte's smile was stiff, but determined. "It's something everyone needs to hear."

"Very well." Margery gestured to the silver service with its sparkling crystal glasses. "Are you certain you won't have something to drink?"

"No, thank you." For what was about to happen, she needed to be sharp. She didn't want to be softened in any way, only relentless.

Standing straight, Charlotte stared at the door where Coe would enter, while Lady Ott chattered about quotidian things to which Charlotte paid no mind. She wasn't worried that her host would think her rude or take offense. She knew the older woman's running chatter was more to ease her own nerves than to engage in real conversation.

Charlotte heard their footsteps before Linnet and Meg came into the room. Lachance and Jack followed, Coe held between them. His wrists were bound. The scowl on his face faded when he saw Charlotte.

"I could say I'm surprised, but I'm not." Coe smiled at her. "You made your choice."

"Yes," Charlotte answered, ignoring the puzzled, inquiring glances of her friends.

Rather than address Coe again, she turned to her companions. "What was the last communication the Resistance received from Lazarus?"

At first no one replied; the already tense room simmered with unease.

"Charlotte, I say this without wanting to give offense," Jack said at last. "You're not at the rank required to be involved with intelligence coming from Lazarus. Only a small circle within the Resistance has access to him."

"Just tell me."

Charlotte's cutting tone made Jack glance at Lady Ott. When the older woman nodded, Jack said, "Nothing of great interest, and the information has been confirmed by other sources—"

"Go on," Charlotte said.

"Lazarus encouraged us to seek better terms with the French before moving forward with any offensive measure," Jack told her. "He said the Empire is in the process of refitting and redistributing its air and naval craft. They won't be prepared for major action anytime soon."

"But wouldn't you want to take advantage of their lack of readiness?" Charlotte pressed. "Why wouldn't that be the ideal time for attack?"

"In some ways it would be," Jack replied with hesitation. "But Lazarus relayed the dates of craft dispersal, and in six months, the majority of the naval fleet will be in the Mediterranean and the air fleet distributed evenly between the continents, significantly reducing their capabilities here. That's when we should strike, and it gives us time to negotiate more balanced terms of alliance with the French. At the moment, they're pushing for territorial oversight of any lands we take from the Empire. We'd prefer complete independence."

Charlotte nodded. "I understand the reasoning behind that point of view. But it will lead to the Resistance's downfall."

Jack stared at her in disbelief, but Lady Ott walked straight up to Charlotte, peering at the young woman with hawk-sharp eyes.

"Why do you say that, Charlotte?"

"Because Lazarus has been lying." Very deliberately, Charlotte held her gaze, then slowly moved her focus to Coe, then back to Lady Ott.

Lady Ott's face drew taut with distress. "No. It can't be."

"I'm sorry," Charlotte said. "But it's true."

"What?" Jack glanced between the two women. "What are you talking about?"

Margery turned to face him, her expression grief-stricken. "Your brother is Lazarus."

Jack actually laughed. "That's ridiculous."

"Is it really?" Coe smiled placidly, gazing at his brother. His eyes lit with satisfaction as he watched Jack's incredulity become horror. "You've always underestimated me, Jack, despite my being your elder."

Charlotte watched the brothers' exchange, abhorring the appearance of Coe's prideful, vicious side.

"I didn't think I could loathe you more," Linnet whispered. "I was wrong."

The confidence and satisfaction in Coe's expression didn't flicker. He took time to regard each of their reactions as if he were enjoying the first bites of an exquisite dish.

He is two people, Charlotte thought. Part of him was still the hopeful youth, wanting to change the world, but his other self had been created when Coe surrendered his fate to his father. The latter Coe was her enemy, and Charlotte would do whatever it took to defeat him, while hoping that victory didn't also mean the untainted side of Coe was past saving.

"This goes beyond Coe. Your father conceived the plan," Charlotte said to Jack. "He learned that Coe had joined the Resistance and used Coe's life as the bargaining chip to turn him. Lazarus was what Admiral Winter contrived as the best way to put Coe to use."

"Our father . . ." Jack stared at Coe with a mixture of fury and regret.

Meg was the least troubled by this revelation. "A clever ploy. Admiral Winter's son would be in a unique position to operate as an effective double agent."

"And he has been," Linnet murmured, her expression mirroring Jack's. "Remarkably effective."

"Well, that's at an end," Jack said bitterly. He leaned over Coe, letting his anger drive out whatever sympathy he might have had for his brother. "You may think Winter blood is worth preserving, but I don't share that belief. I'll be happy to see you executed as soon as we turn you over to the Resistance."

"No." Charlotte moved between Jack and Coe. "We won't be handing Commodore Winter over to the Resistance without securing their promise to spare his life."

Linnet and Jack both gaped at Charlotte. Even Coe was taken aback.

Meg kept a reasoned tone. "Why would we do that, Charlotte?"

"Coe has committed grievous crimes," Charlotte answered, her gaze fixed on Coe. "He knows that. But I believe Admiral Winter shares in the blame. If we show mercy, I hope that Coe will give us what aid he can. And there are things we need him to do."

"Such as?" Jack sounded incredulous.

Though Charlotte wanted to say *Grave*, she instead replied, "He can tell us what the Empire's plans are. Something is about to happen. An *engagement* was the word he used, as I remember."

Coe began to shake his head.

Charlotte smiled at him. "Regretting your words, Commodore?"

"Do you think the Empire is about to launch an attack?" Linnet frowned. "Even if Lazarus, or Coe, was feeding us false intelligence, there haven't been any other signs of those kinds of preparations being made. Lazarus isn't our only operative."

"But how many operatives was Coe aware of?" Charlotte countered. "I'm sure it wasn't all of them, but could it have been enough that he would have been able to influence the information they gathered?"

Linnet's frown deepened, and Lady Ott answered for her. "Yes. It is possible."

"Then we have to assume we know nothing," Charlotte said. "And if Coe values his life, he will tell us the truth now. We could use pain to pry information from him, but I want to offer a choice."

Coe glared at her, but the anger in his gaze was matched by sadness.

"Charlotte could be right," Lady Ott said. "I believe that the commodore is most concerned with self-preservation; thus, he knows it's in his best interest to do what we ask."

Coe's eyes remained fixed on Charlotte, but he didn't contest the statement. Lady Ott caught Charlotte's eye, and Charlotte gave a slight, affirming nod.

Lady Ott addressed their captive. "I won't claim I speak for all of us, but I want it to be clear that should you attempt to double-cross us, it won't be a matter of handing you to the Resistance. I'll have no qualms about shooting you on the spot."

Coe didn't speak. His shoulders sagged.

He would help them. Charlotte was certain of it. But she could find no joy in this victory. At some point, Coe had been broken, and she didn't believe it had happened in this room or on this day. But as she watched him crumple inwardly, defeated and resigned, Charlotte felt not only grief, but also fear.

What would happen to a man when he abandoned himself?

23

THE MOOD IN Lady Ott's parlor was grim at best. The fact that Coe had been locked away in the cellar once more provided little satisfaction, given what they'd learned.

"There's no time," Jack muttered. "Even knowing what we do, I doubt we'll withstand the attack."

"You can't assume that," Linnet said. "All we can do is prepare as best we can. But there's no time to waste. We need to get word to the officers so they can begin a counterstrategy. Doubtless, once it's clear that Coe has been taken, the Empire will take action. The attack will occur as soon as they can reasonably manage."

"I'll send word to Roger immediately," Lady Ott said. "He can reach the right people in a timely fashion."

She exited the parlor so swiftly that her skirts left a breeze in their wake.

Meg took a seat in the chair beside Charlotte that minutes ago Coe had occupied.

"You've done a great service, Charlotte," Meg said. "You may have just saved the Resistance. But you have yet to tell us about Grave, and I know you must be concerned for his welfare."

Having held her emotions in check while trying to adhere to the ideal of a greater good, Charlotte felt her eyes well up at the kindness in Meg's voice. She nodded, unable to speak for the moment.

"Where is he?" Meg asked gently. "What's happened to him?"

"He's in a makeshift laboratory near the air docks." Charlotte concentrated on the facts to keep her voice from breaking. "They have a tinker studying him in an attempt to learn how to replicate Hackett Bromley's experiment."

Meg sighed. "The Sisters in Athene's Temple suspected as much. What fools they are to meddle with such power."

"Do you think Bromley was a fool as well?" Jack's question was curious, not hostile.

"In a way," Meg replied. "But his madness was driven by grief. He understood what he was risking and was willing to accept the consequences. The Empire desires only a great weapon. They have little regard for the forces behind the miracle that is Grave."

"They won't be able to make an army in Grave's likeness," Charlotte said with conviction.

Meg nodded. "They don't know how to access the

other realm from which spirits might be drawn into a vacant body. Even if they obtained the rites in the Book of the Dead, they do not have the faith required to manifest the spell."

Although she'd felt certain she was right, Charlotte was relieved to hear Meg's confirmation. "They don't know that. I couldn't afford to let them think their efforts were futile . . ."

"You were right to protect Grave, Charlotte," Meg said. "And we will find a way to rescue him."

Charlotte closed her eyes, her voice quaking. "I don't know how we can . . . What they've done . . ."

"What have they done?" Jack asked. Charlotte was surprised by the fear in his voice.

She looked at him, drawing strength from his concern for Grave.

Charlotte told them what she'd seen. The horror of it. The seeming impossibility of it.

When she'd finished, they were all silent. The visceral depiction of what Grave had endured, was still enduring, suspended their movements. Jack looked as if he were about to be sick, Linnet's expression was one of aghast amazement, while Meg kept her face an unreadable mask.

Several minutes passed before Meg said, "You'll need help if you want to save him."

"But who can help me?" Charlotte asked, frustration making her seethe. "No one understands who or what he is. I know him better than anyone else, and I have no idea what to do."

"Someone *else* might be able to," Meg said. "The right mind. Sufficient belief in the extraordinary."

"Io!" Jack exclaimed. "That's who can help you."

"Aunt Io?" Charlotte asked, startled by Jack's outburst.

Jack's excitement had him practically babbling. "You know her as Birch's aunt, but the rest of the Resistance— by Hephaestus, the rest of New Orleans—know she's the most brilliant tinker of her generation. If anyone can bring Grave safely through this ordeal, it's Io."

"Aunt Io," Charlotte repeated softly. The idea planted itself in her heart and bloomed into hope. It wasn't her reputation for genius that moved Charlotte; it was Birch's admiration.

"Jack is right," Linnet chimed in. "I don't mean this in a cruel way, but Io is . . . crazy enough to think of a way to recover Grave. She could, um, fix him?"

Charlotte nodded, and nodded, and nodded. She couldn't find words. Grave wasn't lost. She wouldn't break her promise. Somehow, she was going to save him.

24.

THE WAITING WAS awful.

They spent a day and a half in Lady Ott's apartment, restless and on edge. Until they received word from New Orleans, they were paralyzed as well as plagued by the fear that somehow—however unlikely—Coe's abduction would be traced to Lady Ott. They watched through windows and spoke in hushed tones. While they took meals together, their conversations were strained and brief.

On the afternoon that news finally arrived, Lady Ott swept into the parlor bursting with enthusiasm.

"Roger has negotiated your return to New Orleans," she said matter-of-factly. "To say he's smoothed things over would be an oversimplification, but enough has changed in the meantime that you won't be condemned for leaving. However, there are conditions attached to this arrangement."

"Do those conditions involve Grave?" Charlotte asked. As much as she wanted to rejoin her friends in New Orleans, she couldn't abide any plans on the part of the Resistance to use Grave just as the Empire hoped to. If they demanded his return as a condition of cooperation, Charlotte didn't see how she could agree. But it wasn't just Grave. Ever since she'd escaped the Military Platform, Charlotte had worried what the consequences for her father might be. It all depended on the chain of command. Had her father already been transferred to a medical ward? How closely was his status being followed? If Admiral Winter still saw Charles Marshall as a bargaining chip, then Charlotte's liberation could put her father in grave danger. By contrast, if Winter had dismissed her father's importance the moment the deal at the Crucible had been made, then Charlotte's choices likely had little to no bearing on her father's fate.

Lady Ott's eyes were sympathetic, but her tone brusque. "In part, my dear. But let me speak to that in a moment, for more immediate issues must command our attention."

Charlotte nodded, ignoring the impatient questions that circled through her thoughts. Her father's face still flashed in her mind. As much as she wanted to, Charlotte knew nothing she could do at this point would guarantee his health or safety. She offered a silent prayer to Athene, asking the goddess to watch over her father. The Resistance needed her now. Grave needed her.

"Unsurprisingly, their foremost concern is gaining custody of Commodore Winter," Lady Ott said.

Jack muttered something unintelligible.

After sliding a chastising glance in his direction, Lady Ott continued. "Coe is a valuable bargaining chip, but even his worth can't fully alleviate the Resistance leaders' concern regarding your return to the Daedalus Tower."

"What would convince them?" Charlotte asked.

"A demonstration of your commitment to the cause," Lady Ott answered.

"Not Grave." Charlotte's hands were on her hips. "They can't have him."

"Let me finish, Lady Marshall."

The sharp reprimand made Charlotte's cheeks warm with embarrassment. "My apologies, Lady Ott."

Margery smiled. "Roger made it clear that you are not the only one who has taken Grave's care as a personal responsibility. We have declared our intent to ensure his welfare. And believe me, the Resistance has a firm grasp of the resources we have at our disposal to enforce our will."

"Thank you," Charlotte whispered. She would never have asked for such a show of support from the Otts; to have it offered voluntarily left her overwhelmed with gratitude.

"If Grave isn't the issue, then what does the Resistance want this show of loyalty to be?" Jack asked.

"In truth, your loyalty isn't at issue to the same degree as Charlotte's," Lady Ott said. "Roger convinced the Resistance officers that you left the city because you were compelled by . . . baser instincts." She coughed politely.

Jack rubbed the back of his neck. "How flattering."

"All in all, their opinion of you is good news. If I were you, that's how I'd take it," she told him. "It's likely they were amenable to my husband's interpretation of your actions because they want your flying skills when the British attack New Orleans."

Jack shrugged.

Lady Ott's expression became grim. She went to a chair and took a seat, folding her hands on her lap. "The Resistance entered the final stages of negotiations with the French regarding an assault on the Floating City," she told them.

Charlotte drew a sharp breath. "When?"

"The information we've gleaned from Coe suggests an imminent attack on New Orleans," Lady Ott said. "Defense of the city is the first priority. However, if the outcome of that battle is in our favor, the French want an immediate strike against the Empire, before they can regroup and mount a proper defense of their own. The target the French have selected is the Floating City."

Jack gave a low whistle.

"What does this plan have to do with the conditions of our return?" Charlotte asked.

"Not only do the French want to muster as much of a surprise attack as possible," Lady Ott said, "but they also want to create alarm that will mislead the forces stationed in New York as to the nature of the attack. This diversion will be executed by a small group of operatives. The mission is high risk, but both the Resistance and the French believe it could significantly benefit them."

"They want us to complete this mission?" Charlotte asked with a frown. "Aren't we having this conversation because they don't trust us?"

Jack barked a cold laugh. "They trust enough to put us in harm's way. Better us than their own."

"It may seem harsh," Lady Ott said. "But Jack's assessment is correct. Taking on this assignment demonstrates your willingness to sacrifice yourselves for the cause. If you succeed, you'll be welcomed as heroes of the Resistance. If you fail . . ."

"If we fail, it won't matter," Charlotte finished.

"Do you have any specifics of this assignment?" Jack asked. "What's the diversion?"

Lady Ott nodded slowly. "You're going to destroy the Great Wheel."

25.

THE FIRST TIME Charlotte had glimpsed New Orleans's massive iron walls, she'd been awash with expectation and hope. At that point, the city had represented the end of a hard journey. A victory.

Now as the walls loomed taller and taller, Charlotte couldn't view her approaching destination with anything but ambivalence. Despite Lady Ott's reassurances that the Resistance would honor their side of the agreement, Charlotte restlessly paced the deck of the nondescript flatboat hurried along by the Mississippi's powerful current. The trip from New York had been quick. Their small party consisted of Lady Ott, Meg, Linnet, Jack, and Charlotte—along with Coe, who was not only in manacles but also under constant guard. They'd taken the Otts' Scarab from the Floating City to the airfield closest to New Orleans without crossing into its restricted airspace. Being forced to shift from the speed of air travel to the much slower pace of the river made the final leg of their journey seem torturously long, even though the flatboat slid through the water much more swiftly than the lumbering steamboats they passed.

Charlotte watched the city draw near and felt the painful thud of her heart against her ribs. It wasn't fear of imprisonment or punishment that made Charlotte eye the high metal walls as if they were a beast rising from the Louisiana bayous. What she dreaded was betrayal. She was afraid of entering the Daedalus Tower and discovering that she was caught up in a war machine over which she could exert no influence. And though she wouldn't be facing the Resistance leadership alone, the number in her party had been reduced. Jean-Baptiste Lachance had returned to the sea, setting sail to rendezvous with his men in Barbados. His departure hadn't surprised Charlotte, but Meg's decision to remain in New York had.

"I want to keep an eye on any unusual activities around the Temple," Meg had told Charlotte. "I doubt the military would be so bold as to raid a holy site, but I can't make any assumptions."

What about Ashley? Charlotte had wanted to ask. When it had been determined that they'd be returning to New Orleans, Charlotte had been hopeful that the pair would be reunited under happier circumstances than their last disastrous encounter. But any such reunion was going to be delayed for the time being.

Linnet joined in Charlotte's restless turns around the deck.

Looping her arm through Charlotte's, Linnet said, "Remember, kitten. You're not facing them alone."

"Is my discomfiture so obvious?" Charlotte asked. When she faced the leaders of the Resistance, especially her mother, Charlotte wanted to present an unwavering front. If Caroline Marshall sensed hesitation or weakness, Charlotte would hold no sway in whatever negotiations took place.

"To me it is," Linnet replied. "But it's my job to look beyond the masks people wear. Don't fret. You can call up courage when you need to. I've seen it."

Charlotte smiled her thanks and was surprised to see an unexpected weariness on her friend's face.

"Are you unwell?" Charlotte asked.

Linnet's answer laugh had a bitter edge. "I suppose I am."

"What's troubling you?" Charlotte took the other girl's hand. "Let me help."

"I fear I am a lost cause, kitten," Linnet sighed, but when she saw how Charlotte's expression became drawn with fear, she laughed again. "Oh, darling, you needn't worry about me. What plagues me isn't fatal. At least I hope not."

Charlotte frowned. "Won't you tell me what's wrong?"

"It's shameful," Linnet said. "You'll think less of me."

"Surely not!" Charlotte said, all the more puzzled.

Linnet's shoulders slumped in defeat. "I miss him."

Charlotte stared at Linnet so long that Linnet growled. "Don't make me say his name."

"You mean Lachance?" Charlotte asked.

Linnet uttered a noise of disgust that Charlotte took as a yes.

Charlotte decided it best not to giggle, though she wanted to. "It's not so bad. Missing someone."

"For me it is."

"But why?" Charlotte asked.

When Linnet didn't answer, Charlotte said, "I know he's a pirate, but I think he's quite nice."

Nice wasn't the best word to capture all that was Jean-Baptiste Lachance, but at the moment it seemed like the most diplomatic choice.

"I don't care about his being a pirate," Linnet said. She withdrew her arm from Charlotte's, placing her hands on her hips and squaring off against the other girl. "I care that I miss *him*."

Charlotte quirked her lips, trying to unravel the mystery that was Linnet's distress.

Reading Charlotte's obvious confusion, Linnet threw up her hands. "I've sworn to myself since I was a girl that I would never lose myself for love of a man. I'd sooner find a tunnel leading to Hades." Shaking her head, Linnet gazed at Charlotte with baleful eyes. "Why do you think I didn't want to kiss him?"

"You already knew how you felt about him," Charlotte said softly. "But you'd been able to lock it away." Her heart cramped in sympathy, knowing full well the futility of burying such powerful emotions.

"And that blackguard had to demand a kiss!" Linnet shook her fist at the sky. "He knew exactly what he was doing."

Charlotte considered Linnet's outburst, then said, "Why does revealing your affection for him mean you have to lose yourself?"

"Because that's how it always happens." Linnet gave Charlotte a withering look. "I've seen it too many times to count. I will not swoon while my brains dribble out of my ears."

With a slight nod, Charlotte continued, "What about Lord and Lady Ott? Do you think either of them are lost?"

Linnet regarded Charlotte warily, as if she were being led into a trap. "They're exceptional."

"Aren't you and Lachance exceptional?" Charlotte countered. "You're a spy. He's a pirate. That's hardly ordinary."

Linnet pursed her lips. "I suppose."

"Couldn't you find a way to be with him and not betray who you are?" Charlotte's voice became sly. "Perhaps you're afraid of a challenge."

After glaring at her for several moments, Linnet whispered, "Wicked girl."

Charlotte laughed, and Linnet took her arm again.

"I'll not admit that you're right," Linnet said. "But I'll take what you've said into consideration."

"If anyone can create a romance that thrives on

independence and adventure, it's you and Lachance," Charlotte told her.

Linnet cast a sidelong glance at Charlotte. "What about you and Jack?"

A smile tickled the corners of Charlotte's mouth. "Ask me after we get through the storm that's about to break."

No sooner had the words passed her lips than the shadow of the Iron Wall spilled onto the deck and covered them, blotting out the sun.

26.

AFTER THE FLATBOAT had passed through the gates of the Iron Wall, the vessel proceeded directly to a dock where Lord Ott awaited their arrival. He immediately came forward to assist Lady Ott as she disembarked, kissing her lightly once she was safely off the boat. He greeted the rest of their party with a broad smile, but the lines at the corners of his eyes seemed deeper. Charlotte saw his age in a way she hadn't before. He kept his arm locked around his wife's waist, as if afraid to be parted from her even for an instant.

"Linnet will take you to the Daedalus Tower," Lord Ott told them. "Once you're assured that your differences of opinion with the Resistance have been reconciled, she'll join us at *La Belle Fleur*."

"You're not coming with us?" Charlotte asked. The idea filled her with startling anxiety.

"We never set foot within the Tower," Lady Ott said.

"While our allegiance is unquestioned by the Resistance, we must maintain the semblance of neutrality in the wider world."

Charlotte nodded, understanding but wishing this news didn't render the ground beneath her feet unsteady.

Lady Ott reached out and touched Charlotte's cheek. "Don't fret, my dear. Believe me, your mother and the other officers know very well what our position in this matter is."

Charlotte nodded again, hesitated, and then asked, "Are you going to stay in the city? The British fleet could arrive at any time."

"We have a vessel waiting in the Quay," Lord Ott said. "When enemy ships are sighted, we will take the necessary precautions."

Lady Ott offered her a compassionate smile. "You're under no obligation to remain in the Tower, Charlotte. If you choose to cut ties to the Resistance, you'll receive no judgment from us. Come to *La Belle Fleur*. Take refuge on our ship. When it's time to leave the city, you'll be safe. That offer extends to any of your friends as well."

The wave of relief and temptation that swept over Charlotte was so strong it almost made her knees buckle. A way out. An escape hatch.

At the same time, she knew that was a path she'd never take.

"Thank you," Charlotte told the Otts. She had no idea what she'd be feeling after her meeting in the Daedalus Tower, where she'd want to be.

"Of course, my dear," Lady Ott said. "Keep in mind that once the Imperial fleet is spotted, you have only one quarter of an hour to reach us before we leave the city."

"Again, I thank you," Charlotte said.

"Be brave, Charlotte," Lord Ott added. "But most of all, stay true to yourself. You've done a marvelous job of that, thus far. As much as it has on occasion infuriated me when those choices have come as a surprise, the truth of your heart is what should always guide your actions."

Linnet clucked her tongue. "Before this gets too sentimental, I think we should go."

"Be well, my dear," Lady Ott said. Her eyes flicked to Linnet. "Of course I'd never presume to tell you what to do, but I trust you'll keep your head amidst the inevitable chaos?"

"Always," Linnet replied. She turned to Charlotte. "Time for your family reunion."

The Daedalus Tower seemed smaller and less imposing than Charlotte remembered. She supposed her memories had been tinged by the awe of first impressions, of being introduced to the hidden operations center of the Resistance. Now she saw its characteristics more clearly: a space utilitarian and spare, functional but cramped due to the need for a secret and secure location.

An attachment of midrank soldiers awaited them at the end of the corridor that ran from the Sintians' Warehouse to the Resistance hideout. The soldiers took possession of Coe, and Charlotte was more than glad to be rid of responsibility for him. When their escort moved toward the heart of the Tower, Linnet hung back.

Charlotte stopped, turning to her friend with a questioning gaze.

"This is where I exit, kitten," Linnet said.

Charlotte's pulse skipped. Being separated from Lord and Lady Ott was one thing, but the idea of Linnet's absence was far more difficult to bear. She frowned. Surely Linnet wasn't afraid.

Reading Charlotte's expression of dismay, Linnet took her hand. "I'll be fighting for you and with you, Charlotte. But this isn't my kind of battle. Don't worry. We'll be together again soon. I promise."

Charlotte gave Linnet's fingers a quick squeeze, not trusting herself to speak. Linnet turned away while Charlotte followed the soldiers.

Jack leaned over. "I'd hold your hand, but this doesn't seem like an appropriate time."

His teasing words brought lightness back to her heart, and Charlotte threw him a quick smile.

They were led to the same room where Charlotte had been taken by her mother the first time she'd visited the Daedalus Tower. Caroline Marshall and a fellow officer were waiting to greet them. Ashley stood slightly to the side. He offered Charlotte a brief smile of welcome, but his icy glare quickly settled on Coe. Coe returned Ash's gaze steadily, but a shadow of regret flickered over his features.

"Welcome back, Charlotte," Caroline said, but her

voice held no warmth. She regarded her daughter with what appeared to be tolerance, but nothing more. "I'm glad to see you safe. You've been through quite the ordeal."

Her eyes shifted to Coe. "And you've brought this turncoat so punishment can be meted out as warranted by his crimes. Do you have anything to say for yourself, Commodore Winter?"

"Hail, Britannia," Coe answered in a flat tone.

Caroline nodded to the soldiers who'd escorted Charlotte and Jack through the Tower. "Take him to the cell that's been prepared."

Coe didn't struggle as he was removed from the room, but he did call out, "Enjoy this petty triumph while you can. It's the only sweetness of victory you'll ever taste."

Charlotte heard the desperation in his shout. *He needs to believe he was right. It's the only thing he has left to hang on to.*

When he was gone, Caroline said to Charlotte, "We're indebted to you. Coe's treachery could have brought about the end of the Resistance."

And that's the reason you're willing to forget about Grave, Charlotte thought.

"Any word on the British fleet?" Jack asked.

"We know they're on the move," Caroline replied. "And we expect their arrival by day's end."

The skin on Charlotte's arms prickled. So soon.

"Are we ready?" Jack's brow crinkled with concern.

Caroline gestured to one of her companions. "Commander Harrington, please bring them up to speed."

A tall, spindly man whose face was dominated by a thick, shaggy mustache of mottled gray and brown stepped forward. "When we first learned of an imminent assault by the full force of the British fleet, we feared we would not be able to withstand the siege. However, new information has come to light that drastically improves our chances."

"What new information?" Charlotte asked.

"It seems our sometime friends, the French, had not been completely forthright about their own military capabilities in the North American colonies," Harrington answered with a slight scowl. "They have a much more substantial arsenal at the ready to defend New Orleans than we knew of. And they have additional forces hidden throughout the Caribbean, waiting to be called upon in the event of an offensive maneuver."

Jack whistled. "That does change things."

"Indeed." Harrington's displeasure had vanished, and his eyes now shone with eagerness. "Should we manage to rout the British here, the French have made it clear they are both prepared and willing to make a counterassault that could break the back of the Empire on this continent."

"A counterassault on the Floating City," Charlotte said, echoing what Lady Ott had already told them.

Harrington nodded.

"You think they can take the city?" Jack sounded incredulous.

"The French don't intend to take the city," Harrington said. "They plan to destroy it."

"But . . ." Charlotte had been bracing herself for an

unpleasant confrontation with her mother. Now her thoughts turned only to Grave. Grave who was in New York and was no longer viewed as of interest to the Resistance. "How soon?"

Jack's face was drawn as well.

His mother.

Charlotte saw her father. His broken body at the Crucible. Admiral Winter had promised Charles Marshall would receive the best medical care the Empire had to offer. Did that mean he'd been moved to New York?

When Harrington hesitated, Caroline spoke instead. "That all depends on what befalls us once the British arrive. Our hope is to significantly reduce the capabilities of their fleet. Our allies are optimistic that the outcome will be in our favor. If that goal is achieved, a surprise attack on New York can commence, and it will be undertaken by the French, staged from the Caribbean."

"Are you sure they plan to destroy the entire city?" Jack spoke carefully, but Charlotte heard the tension in his voice. "Not just the Military Platform?"

"To take down the Floating City is to ruin the crowning achievement of Britannia's colonies," Harrington replied. "The French have been waiting for the opportunity to land a crippling blow on their enemy. This is that opportunity."

Charlotte's pulse crackled in her veins. How much time would she have to get to the city, retrieve Grave, and get out again? And what about Meg? They'd have to find a way to get word to her so she could flee the city with her mother. But would Meg want to evacuate all the Sisters in

Athene's Temple? Such a thing wouldn't go unnoticed, and could ruin the element of surprise the French were counting on. And what about Jack's mother and other civilians? Again, Charlotte saw her father's face. What of him?

"Charlotte." The fears rushing through Charlotte's mind must have been plain in her expression, because Jack spoke her name softly and with concern.

"So much could happen so quickly," Charlotte said, trying to tamp down the true sources of her anxiety. "I'm trying to grasp it all."

"You don't need to concern yourself too much," Harrington said with a patronizing smile. "When it comes to the move against New York, most of us will be bystanders."

Charlotte answered with a wry smile of her own. "But not us."

"We were pleased you were amenable to our proposal," Harrington said.

Charlotte continued to wear her smile, but didn't otherwise respond.

"There's really nothing more to add," Caroline said, shifting her weight in a rare show of discomfort with the turn in conversation. "Quarters have been prepared. You should retire while you still can. When the attack begins, you'll be taken to an interior shelter that will be safe from any bombardment. If we prevail against the British siege, you'll be retrieved and taken to a military vessel that Jack will pilot for your mission."

Ash coughed, and Caroline shot him a sidelong glance.

"Your brother insists on accompanying you," Caroline told Charlotte. "Despite the fact that he has no need to prove his allegiance."

"Good man," Jack murmured, and Ash flashed a smile at him.

"There are others who've volunteered their skills," Ash added. "I'll fill you in."

"You're at liberty to decide whom you deem necessary to complete this mission," Caroline told Charlotte, but the slant of her mouth was disapproving. No doubt her mother had envisioned an infiltration of the Floating City by seasoned Resistance operatives, not a ragtag group of displaced youths. Charlotte met her mother's gaze without flinching. Caroline might doubt the abilities of Charlotte's friends, but Charlotte had no doubts that they would see the mission through to the best of their abilities, or beyond.

Caroline turned her back on Charlotte and Jack to dismiss them.

"Mother, I need to speak with you and Ash," Charlotte said. "Privately."

Caroline stiffened. "Considering the preparations we're in the midst of, I'm certain whatever you have to say can wait."

"No, it can't."

Something in Charlotte's voice stopped her mother from arguing further. Ash stepped closer.

"I'll be in the Command Turret," Harrington told Caroline, then said to Jack, "Flight Lieutenant Winter, we could use your assistance with the air defenses."

"Of course." Jack shot a worried glance at Charlotte, but followed Commander Harrington to the door.

When the room had cleared, Charlotte leveled a stony glare on her mother. "Did you know Father is alive?"

"What?" Ash stared at Charlotte in disbelief.

The color drained from Caroline's face. "That's not possible," she whispered.

"I saw him," Charlotte said.

Ash's hands were trembling. "Where?"

"At the Crucible." Breaking her gaze from Caroline, Charlotte turned to Ashley and took his hand. "He's very sick."

"With what illness?" Ash asked.

"Consumption." Charlotte flinched at the memory of her father's emaciated body. His racking cough.

A choking sound escaped Caroline. She put her hands over her face and began to shake her head.

Charlotte's outrage wavered. Had their mother genuinely believed that her husband and the father of her children was dead?

"Admiral Winter promised that Father would be seen by doctors," Charlotte said weakly. She had little faith in Winter's promises. And even with treatment, Charlotte knew, his prognosis wasn't good. In the time that had passed since the admiral had used Charles Marshall as a bargaining chip, the illness might have killed him.

Caroline lifted her face. "No one comes back from the Crucible. No one."

Charlotte was surprised to see that her mother was dry-eyed, despite her initial show of emotion.

"It would have been folly, suicide even, to treat his absence as anything other than death." Caroline seemed to be reassuring herself, rather than addressing her children.

So she had known. Charlotte couldn't stop herself from asking, "How could you give up on him? Why didn't you try to find him?"

"Charlotte." Ash's reprimand was thick with sorrow. He tried put his arm around their mother's shoulders, but she shrank from his touch.

Charlotte didn't acknowledge her brother's cautioning tone. "What happened?"

"He fell." Caroline stared ahead, as if watching the horrible memory play out before her. "The British soldiers swarmed over him. We couldn't reach him, and we had to retreat."

Forcing her gaze back to Charlotte, Caroline said, "I didn't think he survived. Athene's mercy, I didn't know. But even if I had . . . retrieving prisoners is unheard of. To be taken is to be lost, and we must fight on."

She stared at her hands, twisting her fingers together. "Charles . . . I did . . . I did what I had to do. "

Charlotte gazed at her mother, feeling more and more alienated from the woman. If Charlotte adopted the attitude that Caroline clung to, Grave was already forsaken. How could her mother abandon someone she loved? To have believed Charles dead was one thing, but now that she knew the truth, she refused to do anything but justify her choices.

Caroline Marshall might have decided her commitment to the Resistance took precedence over all, but Charlotte refused to do the same.

"I don't know where he is," Charlotte spoke through clenched teeth. "But if I can find him and bring him back, I will."

Caroline nodded, then walked away.

Ashley watched their mother leave. When he turned to Charlotte, his eyes were bright with grief.

27

HARLOTTE!" PIP WAS a blur of green hair and flapping arms rushing at Charlotte. "You're back!"

Charlotte caught Pip in a tight hug, then shared more dignified embraces with Birch and Scoff.

She'd found her friends in the workshop amid showers of sparks and glowing hot metals. Wary of being scorched due to her lack of protective garb, Charlotte coaxed her friends away from their work station and into the corridor.

"We've been worried," Birch said once they were huddled together just outside the workshop.

Guilt bit into Charlotte. A sudden, secret departure had been needed to protect Grave, but she'd never wanted to abandon her friends. "I'm sorry I left so suddenly. And without saying anything."

"We know you had your reasons," Scoff said, but the

heavy silence that followed made it clear that her friends needed Charlotte to give those reasons.

"I'll tell you everything that's happened," Charlotte said. "But it's urgent that I speak to your aunt, Birch. Do you know where she is?"

Birch frowned. "When she's not in the workshop, she's usually in her quarters. We could look there."

"Please." Charlotte gestured for him to lead the way. "Quickly."

As they hurried through the Tower, Charlotte felt her friends' unanswered questions hovering all around her. Though she was ashamed at having left them without explanation, Charlotte was comforted by their seeming lack of anger or resentment. Their trust in her allayed a good deal of her anxiety.

Aunt Io answered the door after Birch's second round of knocking. Moses was perched atop her head like a strange crown amid her vivid blue hair.

She surveyed the faces watching her in anticipation. "My goodness, look at all of you. Something's afoot, is it? And not just these rumors about an impending attack. No sense worrying about that. If the British are coming, so be it."

Io stepped back from the doorway. "Come in. Come in."

When they were inside, she ushered them into her small sitting room. "Tea?"

Charlotte cleared her throat. "Thank you for offering, and I don't mean to be rude, but I'm afraid I need to speak you immediately."

Io peered at Charlotte. "I haven't seen you for some time, have I? No, I don't think I have."

"I've been away," Charlotte said.

Io continued to look at Charlotte. "Are you the one they've all been fussing about? Did you steal their mechanical boy?"

"I didn't steal anything," Charlotte blurted out. "And Grave is—" She stopped herself. "Please. Let me explain."

"I'm listening, dear girl. I hope you won't bore me. My mind tends to wander when I'm bored, and when that happens, I'm inclined to interrupt and change the direction of conversation. Or to leave the room." Io settled on a velvet pouffe.

Though Charlotte wouldn't have described her experiences over the past weeks as boring, she worried that Io's idea of what was or was not interesting might be very different from that of the ordinary person. However, as Charlotte recounted everything that had transpired from Grave's abduction in New Orleans to the present moment, Io appeared attentive, if not quite riveted.

When Charlotte finished her tale, Pip stared at her with huge eyes. "I can't believe you were in the Crucible. Was it as horrible as they say?"

Horrible wasn't word enough to describe that place, but Charlotte nodded.

"An awful place, yes," Io said. "But a marvel of engineering. Quite ingenious."

"Io." Charlotte folded her hands, almost prayerful, in

her lap. "I need your help. I think you're the only person who could rescue Grave."

"The boy who was captured with you?" Io asked. "You plan to go back for him?"

"I have to," Charlotte said, her eyes downcast. "I can't abandon him."

"Your friends came for you when you were being held in the city," Io said. "But they had no intentions of retrieving your friend?"

"We couldn't." Charlotte wrung her fingers. She could still see Grave laid out on the table. She looked at Io, hoping the woman's face would push that horrible image away. "Because of what they'd done."

Aunt Io's eyebrows went up. "They were experimenting on him?"

Charlotte nodded. "They wanted to find out how he could . . . what he . . . They hoped to replicate the process that allowed Hackett Bromley to bring his child back from the dead."

It wasn't entirely accurate, but it was the best Charlotte could muster.

"What a puzzle!" Io put her hand level with her forehead. Moses scrambled onto her palm. Io cupped the little bat in her hands, gazing at it. "Mechanics allows us to pull off incredible feats. My dear nephew restored the gift of flight to this fellow."

She petted Moses under the chin with her pinky. He chirped with contentment.

prove pivotal should Grave need any sort of rehabilitation after his ordeal. Keep pondering, my dear boy. That's how breakthroughs manifest."

She ruffled Scoff's hair. He beamed and blushed.

Bizarre as it was to approach Grave's condition with any positivity, Charlotte found Io's disposition deeply comforting.

"As long as he hasn't been completely dismembered, it should be a straightforward project," Io added, tapping her forefinger against her cheek absentmindedly.

"Dismembered?" Pip's mouth formed an O of disbelief.

Noting the girl's distress, Aunt Io abandoned her musing and said, "No fear, child. If he's in pieces, we can still put him back together. But we may have to transport the parts back to my workshop in order to do a proper job."

Charlotte was revising her opinion about how much comfort Io could be relied on to provide.

"You really think you can fix Grave, no matter what they've done to him?" Pip asked, clearly still shaken by the idea that her friend might be found in parts rather than whole.

"If my theories about how he operates are sound, then yes," Aunt Io told her. "I will admit, however, that a key component of Grave's existence lies beyond my grasp. Or the grasp of any tinker, I'd wager."

Io clucked her tongue, pensive. "Ingenious mechanics are at work, but that's not all. You'd better ask your friend from the Sisters of Athene about the . . ." Io began to wave her arms and wiggle her fingers while she made bizarre humming sounds. "You know. That sort of thing."

"Magic?" Charlotte asked.

"Whatever you want to call it." Io stopped her mummery. "All I know is that what keeps your friend alive is more than machinery. I can work with the machinery—and the alchemy—that affect him. If there's a problem with the other side of things, I won't be of much use."

"I don't think what they've done has affected that part of Grave," Charlotte said. "Despite being vivisected, he didn't appear to be in any pain. And he spoke to me."

"Yes," Io said. "Highly unusual."

Charlotte thought it very possible that there could be no better description of Grave than "highly unusual."

"But what are we if not ready to meet a challenge?" Io said, smiling at Pip and Scoff. "We'll be an exceptional team."

"Don't you even want to know what the mission is?" Charlotte asked.

"Details always prove frivolous, my dear." Io stood up. "All that matters is the heart of the mission. Of course there are preparations to be made. Gather your things. Don't dally!"

"It's not a matter of details," Charlotte said. "Pip is too young. I won't put her in that kind of danger."

"Charlotte!" Pip objected, quickly blushing as she caught the childish whine in her voice.

"It's not just rescuing Grave," Charlotte told the girl. "The French are about to launch an air siege on the city with the aim of destroying it. I don't know how much time we'll have. We could very well end up in the middle of a bombardment."

"Danger is danger. I need to work as swiftly as possible," Io countered, with a dismissive flap of her hand. "And that means I must have assistants who understand the instructions I give them. You, my dear, are no tinker. But Pip is."

"You don't understand." Charlotte frowned. "I was allowed to return here only after committing to carry out a mission for the Resistance. I have to do that before I can rescue Grave. The risk involved—"

"Risk is risk." Io flung her arms wide. "Without risk, no great deed would ever be done."

"I can help, Charlotte, and I want to," Pip said. "It doesn't matter what the mission is. If you're fighting, I fight with you. That's what we do."

Charlotte saw flint in the girl's eyes and then she saw herself at Pip's age.

It's time. Charlotte felt the pang of the bittersweet realization. I can no longer try to protect her.

She smiled at Pip, knowing what an important moment this would be for the girl.

Pip's eyes widened when Charlotte didn't offer further objections. A grin lit up her face. "Thank you!"

Aunt Io caught Charlotte's eye, giving her a nod of approval. "With a bit of luck, we can be on our way before this dreaded attack everyone has been going on about."

The alarms began to sound.

"Ah well." Io smiled wistfully. "The wheel of fortune is ever turning."

28

OSES HAD LAUNCHED himself out of Birch's pocket at the sudden flood of noise, and now darted around the room, swooping from corner to corner and squeaking along with the blare of the alarms.

"At least we have a pleasant place to wait this out," Io shouted over the din. "A benefit of having quarters on the interior side of the tower. A bit stuffy, but less vulnerable in the event of a siege. Though sieges are quite rare, and breathing stuffy air is something one has to deal with every day."

Aunt Io moved toward her kitchen. "Please make yourselves at home. I'll get that tea ready now."

"Stay with Io," Charlotte told her friends. "And as much as you can, try to prepare for our mission. I have no idea how long this attack will last."

"Where are you going?" Birch asked.

"To find Ash and Jack," Charlotte said.

Outside Io's quarters, the Daedalus Tower was a chaos of sound and movement. Soldiers rushed to their battle stations, while support crews gathered to create supply lines and triage sites. Charlotte ran up a flight of stairs and stopped on the landing. She leaned out over the rail, trying to spot her brother or Jack. But it was Caroline Marshall whom she saw first; Ashley was a few steps behind their mother.

Charlotte hurried back to the main corridor and wove her way through the current of bodies. Ash and Caroline flicked in and out of her vision as Charlotte dodged men and women who were hurtling past, intent on their goals and pausing for no one.

Ash caught sight of her. "Charlotte! Here!"

When she drew close, Ashley grabbed her arm and pulled her alongside him. He kept moving forward, and Charlotte realized that wherever they were going, their mother was leading the way. When Caroline reached a staircase, she began to climb swiftly, to the second story, then the third.

"Mother, wait!" Charlotte called.

Caroline turned, stopping midflight on the staircase.

"Where are we going?" Charlotte asked.

"The Command Turret," her mother answered.

Charlotte began to shake her head.

"What's wrong?"

"I should be in one of the gunwells," Charlotte argued. "So should Ash. We can help with the defense."

"It's been made clear that your status within the Resistance is contingent upon your execution of the mission," her mother said. "I won't discuss the matter any further."

Charlotte fell into a bitter silence.

"As for Ashley," Caroline said, "I've requested that he remain with me. I don't feel the need to explain my reasons to you."

The tightening around her mother's eyes provided a hint as to what those reasons might be. No matter how steely a mask Caroline Marshall tried to wear, Charlotte could see the grief behind it. Caroline wanted Ash with her because he was her son and she couldn't bear the thought of losing him.

Charlotte looked into her mother's eyes and saw something that had been absent when they'd first been reunited, something Charlotte hadn't realized she desperately wanted: fear for her daughter's safety, doubt of her own beliefs, but most of all, love, a mother's love. Charlotte nodded, now understanding that Ash had stayed at their mother's side for this reason.

Caroline gave Charlotte a tight smile and turned her gaze to Ashley.

"The Command Turret it is." Ash tried to keep his tone light. "Lead the way."

• • •

The Command Turret stood at the center of the east wall. Ash, Charlotte, and their mother ascended the spiral staircase inside the tower for what felt like ages. When they emerged from the enclosure of cylindrical iron walls onto the observation deck, where metal had been exchanged for reinforced glass, Charlotte gasped.

Every part of the city seemed to be moving. The air pulsed with vibrations as long-dormant machines came to life, readying themselves to meet the encroaching attackers. Running as she was, Charlotte had no time to observe New Orleans's transformation from city of gaudy delights to war machine. But out of the corners of her eyes, Charlotte caught glimpses of telescoping barrels as they shot out from turrets, rendering once unadorned metal columns spiky enough to rival a porcupine's back.

A cluster of French officers and a few from the Resistance were gathered around a map table. Brass speaking tubes dangled from the ceiling, ready to carry orders from command to other stations in the city.

The British fleet had massed on two fronts, southern and eastern. Imperial warships gathered on those horizons like approaching storm clouds. Charlotte could name the ships by their signifying characteristics: Cyclops, with its massive single cannon; Scylla, whose broad body supported numerous snakelike arms, each of which had a gunner at its tip; Colossus, the spherical vessel from which small fighters like Dragonflies could be deployed. Behind the gunships Charlotte spotted transports, which housed infantry who would parachute to the ground when the order was given. No doubt there were Rotpots aboard the transports as well, ready to snatch fleeing civilians. These were the invading force that would overrun the city when its walls had been breached.

Could the Iron Wall be breached?

Charlotte didn't doubt that the heavy gun of any Cyclops could eventually break down even a wall as stout as that of New Orleans.

But the walls wouldn't matter if any Imperial ships made it past the blockade of antiaircraft fire that would assail the attackers as long as there was ammunition to feed the hungry weapons. Should that line of defense fail, New Orleans could simply be bombarded from above, annihilated with terrible ease.

The panoramic view from the observation deck made Charlotte simultaneously feel omniscient and helpless. She could see everything, but do nothing. Her heart quaked at the great mass of ships drawing ever closer. So many. There were so many ships. Here was the might of Britannia that had quashed Napoleon in Europe and now looked to overrun the world.

Charlotte found it difficult to imagine how this force could be stopped.

She was startled out of her dark thoughts by the eruption of artillery fire, but at a much greater distance than any coming from the turrets that guarded the city walls. She tracked the sound until she saw bursts of light shooting from within the cover of the swamp just past the southern shore of Lake Pontchartrain. Flashes from the ground were soon mirrored by those from the sky as the warships returned fire.

The surface of Lake Pontchartrain began to stir. At first its waters simply shimmered and trembled, but the mild disturbance erupted into violent agitation as the whole of the lake began to bubble and froth. Tall spouts of water leapt high above the lake's surface. From within each spout objects shot into the sky like bullets from a gun barrel. At first the projectiles appeared to be metallic cylinders, but as they hurtled forward, large pieces of metal sloughed off like discarded cocoons. When the outer casings had fallen away, the crafts hidden inside came to life.

"Wasps," Ashley breathed.

Smaller than a Dragonfly, a Wasp was broken into three segments, head, thorax, and abdomen, mimicking its namesake. The pilot guided the ship from a narrow cockpit, while the gunner commanded a 180-degree range at the tail. The two operators were separated by the machinery at the center of the craft. Their engines filled the air with a high-pitched, buzzing whine as they swarmed toward the British ships.

British Dragonflies began to drop from the Colossus ships, moving to engage the rebels' Wasps. Charlotte knew that Dragonflies were valued for their speed and maneuverability, but it quickly became clear that the Wasps were both swifter and more nimble. They darted through the sky, forcing the Dragonflies to give chase and drawing them dangerously close to the larger warships. Some Dragonfly pilots knew better than to play this game, but others tried to mimic the sudden spins and hard banks of the Wasps to disastrous effect, temporarily losing control of their crafts and becoming vulnerable to enemy fire; in the worst cases, they rammed their own warships.

Charlotte sipped the air in small, shallow breaths while she watched the Wasps and Dragonflies battle for dominance of the skies. Her racing pulse and quick breaths came from a certainty that had fixed itself in Charlotte's mind.

Jack was piloting one of those Wasps. She was sure of it.

When the notion first occurred to her, Charlotte tried to dismiss it. After all, hadn't she and Ash been denied an active role in this battle? But that reassurance quickly melted away, because Jack was different. He was a skilled pilot. A former officer in the Imperial Air Force. And the Resistance thought he was misguided, led astray by base passions, but not a traitor like Charlotte. He would be an incredible asset against the British attackers.

He was out there. Flying. Risking his life.

Whenever Charlotte saw a plume of smoke trailing from a Wasp as it fell from the sky, she thought her heart would stop. Her hand was a fist pressed against her breastbone as she whispered a prayer to Athene, goddess of war, to lend her aid to Jack Winter.

Standing beside Charlotte, Ash watched the battle unfold, his face pale and stern.

"He'll be all right," Ash murmured. And Charlotte

realized he was speaking to himself, not to her. She didn't want to lose the man she'd fallen in love with. Her brother didn't want to lose his best friend.

"Eastern front, prepare to engage." The tinny voice echoed through the observation deck.

Charlotte forced herself to turn away from the southern field of action and look east. While she'd been watching the Wasps and Dragonflies, the warships approaching from the east had drawn frighteningly close.

"Take these." Caroline Marshall put two small nubs of wax into Charlotte's hand and gave another pair to Ash. "Put them in your ears, like this."

Caroline fitted the bullet-shaped piece of wax into her ear, blocking the canal. Charlotte did as her mother said, and the world became muted. A moment later, she was incredibly grateful for that.

The turret began to vibrate and hum. She could hear whirs and rumbling.

Artillery fire burst from the turrets along the eastern wall. The blasts seemed deafening even with the protection of the wax plugs. Each shot reverberated through Charlotte's skin, traveling through her flesh until her bones rattled.

Again.

And again.

And again.

Charlotte had to steady herself by gripping a rail.

In the distance, incendiary petals blossomed when the

guns found their targets. Dragonflies exploded in the sky and dropped to the earth. Smoking wounds marred the pristine hulls of Cyclops, Scylla, and Colossus alike.

But the airships encroached farther upon the city.

An enormous crash sent shock waves through the turret. Charlotte was thrown off her feet, as were most of the occupants of the Command Turret. She crawled to one side of the deck and pulled herself up. Where one of the gun turrets on the eastern wall had stood was a cloud of thick, oily smoke.

"The Cyclops is in range," one of the officers said.

"Countermeasures," their commander responded.

A grinding sound rose from beneath the turret. Charlotte pressed her forehead against the glass and looked down.

The base of the eastern wall was suddenly pocked with dark circles from which metal spheres rolled. When the spheres hit the ground, legs sprouted from their round bodies, and like spiders, they skittered forward, stopping only when directly beneath a British warship. Projectiles shot from the top of the spiders' bodies, barbed shafts like harpoons, strong enough to pierce a warship's hull. With the harpoon embedded in the ship, the spider rose swiftly in the air as if on a silk thread, and the bottom of the sphere opened to release a figure, a person, who appeared doomed until a parachute bloomed overhead, slowing their descent. If the former occupant of the spider reached the ground safely, he or she began a desperate retreat toward the wall. The abandoned vehicle continued its ascent until it reached the ship. Its legs dug into the hull, and it clung there. Until—

BOOM.

Where the spider had attached itself to the ship, only a gaping hole remained. Vessels shuddered and twisted in the air. Some began to drift toward the ground, while others barreled to their demise.

A fist tightened around Charlotte's heart as she watched the spider operators fleeing the battlefield. She wondered what type of person could muster the courage to volunteer for this assignment: there was the hope of escape, but though survival aids were in place, the chances of making it back to the wall were terribly slim. Many of the spider pilots were dead before they reached the ground, their parachutes or their bodies riddled with gunfire from Dragonflies. Others were shot down as they fled toward the city.

And yet the spiders continued to emerge from the wall.

"Incredible," Caroline murmured. "I thought the claims they made about these new craft had to be exaggerated. I was wrong."

Charlotte watched as a spider's harpoon pierced the hull of a Scylla and began to follow its thread toward the bottom of the ship. This spider's pilot didn't make it to the ground, but he wasn't shot down. He fell directly into the path of a Dragonfly, his body crashing through the vessel's cockpit, sending the aircraft into a death spiral. Oblivious to its pilot's fate, the spider continued to rise, latching itself onto the ship.

The smaller fighters had caught on to the spider's method of destruction and sought desperately to interrupt the cycle of attachment and eruption. Destroying the spiders without hitting the warships proved almost impossible, however. One Dragonfly hurtled toward a spider that was ascending to a Scylla and managed to shoot it down before it could reach its target. But the gunfire triggered the explosive in the spider. Shrapnel from the blast pierced the Dragonfly, killing its pilot, and the out-of-control aircraft smashed into the side of the Scylla it had been trying to save.

The Scylla lurched sideways, then began an inexorable spiral toward the ground. Not swift enough to maneuver from its path, one of the transport ships became tangled in its limbs and was pulled down with it. The two ships spun, locked in a deadly embrace, until they slammed into the earth. Flames erupted all around the crashed vessels, punctuated by explosions as the ships disintegrated. It was terrible and glorious to watch.

Cheers filled the Command Turret, but the surge of triumph Charlotte felt was accompanied by a sickening wave when she thought of the infantry aboard that transport. Charlotte had never shrunk from blood or cowered in a fight. She faced and killed her enemies. She never hesitated to defend herself or those she loved. But never had she witnessed death on this scale. War that was all-consuming.

The eastern approach to the city was rapidly becoming a graveyard for warships. Heaps of crumpled metal licked by flames dotted the landscape.

Charlotte moved to the southern side of the observation deck. Wasps and Dragonflies still chased each other through the air, but Charlotte noted that the Dragonflies were now significantly outnumbered by the Wasps. As on the eastern front, smoking wreckage littered the shores of Lake Pontchartrain.

Charlotte's gaze was still locked on the darting aircraft in the south when a triumphant roar went up from the officers.

To the east, the handful of warships that had managed to evade the onslaught of spiders were turning away from the city.

The British had begun their retreat.

"It's over," Ash said.

Charlotte didn't reply. Her mind was already on the Floating City and its terrible, imminent fate. The siege of New Orleans may have ended, but Charlotte's battle was about to begin.

29

HARLOTTE AND ASH hurried through the Tower, ignoring the celebration that had overtaken the Resistance hideout. Charlotte needed to gather her friends as soon as possible and to find a way out of the city.

But first she needed to know if Jack was safe.

Their mother had directed them to the entrance by which the Wasp pilots were most likely to return to the tower. By the time Charlotte and Ash arrived, a crowd had already formed at the door. Congratulatory shouts and whoops of victory greeted the airmen as they stepped into the corridor. Charlotte's view of the entrance was mostly blocked by bodies. She shoved her way forward, but the crowd was surging ahead too, surrounding the pilots to clap them on the shoulder or hoist them into the air.

Tangled in the celebrants, Charlotte began to shout

Jack's name. At the same time, she struggled to break free of the throng.

"Charlotte!"

For a moment, Charlotte thought she'd imagined Jack's voice. A manifestation of hope that was only wishful, not real.

But the call came again. "Charlotte!"

"Jack!" Charlotte turned in a circle, seeking Jack while trying to stay in one place despite the bodies knocking against her.

She turned again and there he was, standing in front of her.

Charlotte threw her arms around him. "Thank Athene."

She kissed his neck, his chin, his cheeks, his forehead. The press of her lips against his warm skin confirming that he was here, alive, out of danger.

Jack began to laugh. "Charlotte, please."

"What?" Charlotte drew back to look at him.

"Let me kiss *you*." Then his lips were on hers.

When they parted, Charlotte's skin was tingling from the crown of her head to the tips of her toes.

Ash found them at the edge of the crowd.

"Good to see you, mate." He grinned at Jack.

"It's good to be seen." Jack clapped Ash on the shoulder.

The three of them left the din of victory behind and headed for Aunt Io's quarters.

Birch answered the door. "Is it over?"

"You couldn't hear?" Charlotte asked.

"I thought the gunfire had stopped," Birch answered. "But Aunt Io didn't want us to leave until we had 'official' word that it was safe to do so."

"Consider this your official word," Jack said.

Io appeared behind her nephew. "Oh, good! You're here and not dead. There also don't appear to be gaping holes in the Tower. Does that mean we won?"

"The British retreated," Jack told her.

"Is that not the same as winning?" she asked, but didn't seem to expect an answer because she immediately went on. "We've done as much preparation as we could here. I'll need to go to the workshop, and Scoff needs to collect some things from his apothecary."

"Scoff has his own apothecary?" Charlotte looked to Birch for confirmation.

Birch nodded.

"When we have all we need, where should we gather?" Aunt Io asked Charlotte.

Charlotte balked. She didn't have an answer. They needed a ship, a fast one, but not the one the Resistance wanted to provide. Even a British ship that had been commandeered by the rebels might raise suspicion. What she needed was a well-known ship. One that could approach and dock in New York without drawing attention.

"How soon do you think Lord and Lady Ott will return to the city?" Charlotte asked Jack.

"I'd guess they'll come back whenever they deem it safe," Jack said. "That could be anytime."

Charlotte ground her teeth. Anytime wasn't soon enough. Not only was the timing of the Otts' return unknown, but reaching their Scarab would require a trip up the Mississippi. Still, they didn't seem to have another choice.

"Tell everyone to meet at *La Belle Fleur* when they're ready," Charlotte told Birch and Io. Turning to Jack and Ash, she said, "I hope the Otts decide the city is safe again sooner rather than later. In the meantime, I need you to bring Mother a message, Ash. Tell her the mission will go forward, but there's been a change in plan."

The refined clientele of *La Belle Fleur* cast curious glances at the seven guests who'd seated themselves in the tea room and ordered cake.

Cake had been Aunt Io's suggestion.

"I didn't have any cake to offer you when we had tea earlier," Io said. "And I must confess I am ravenous. Who knew that weathering a siege would work up such an appetite?"

And so Charlotte found herself sitting at a table where a three-tiered silver serving dish had been filled with exquisitely decorated tiny cakes. Unlike Io, Charlotte had not found that the siege encouraged a strong appetite. Cake didn't appeal to her at all. She was rather surprised that the hotel was serving tea and cake, given that no more than an hour ago, the entire city had faced possible destruction. But that was the strange thing about people. Charlotte supposed that there was a strong likelihood tea and cake would be present even if the world was about to end.

Charlotte had positioned herself so she could watch the lobby while her friends ate. Impatience gnawed at her. They had to reach the city before the French fleet arrived, or they'd have no chance of rescuing Grave. Or any of the other retrievals that were about to be attempted. Meg and Madam Jedda. Jack's mother. Charlotte's father.

Charlotte was doing the best she could to keep her father's plight from taking her mind and heart hostage. She knew going on a wild search for him through the city would be futile, not to mention foolish. She understood that leading meant focusing on what could be realistically accomplished, not what one could only wish for.

"If you lot stay here much longer, the reputation of this hotel will be in jeopardy."

Charlotte pivoted to discover Linnet's arm resting on the back of her chair.

"Where did you come from?" Charlotte asked.

"A girl must have some secrets." Linnet smiled. "Come with me. Lord Ott is waiting."

"How did he know we were looking for him?"

Linnet arched an eyebrow. "Do you really need to ask? Why else would you be in the tea room of *La Belle Fleur*?"

Charlotte blushed. It was an obvious explanation.

"Don't worry, kitten. I forgive you."

• • •

Lord Ott hadn't returned to *La Belle Fleur*, but was waiting for them at the docks.

"Margery suspected you'd be looking for a way out of the city," Lord Ott said to Charlotte. "This boat will take you into the Delta. A Scarab will be waiting for you."

"You smuggled an aircraft into the restricted area?" Charlotte asked.

Lord Ott puffed up. "Some things are much easier to accomplish when there's a battle to draw attention."

He looked at Jack. "I assume you can pilot the Scarab."

"You assume correctly."

Returning his attention to Charlotte, Lord Ott said, "You won't have any trouble docking my ship on the Market Platform. But docking will be the least of your worries once the French fleet arrives."

The spectre of French airships bearing down on the city made Charlotte shiver. "So many will die."

"We're doing what we can to mitigate civilian damage," Lord Ott told her. "My people have been quietly moving families to the mainland. Even so, losses will be massive, but it's something."

Charlotte nodded, only slightly consoled by his words.

"Is the fleet already closing in?" Ash asked. "Will they be bombarding the platforms when we arrive?"

"There's been no news," Ott replied. "But the French will want to exploit the advantage of this victory. They'll strike soon."

"Then we have no time to waste," Linnet said, hopping from the dock onto the boat. She laughed at Charlotte's puzzled expression. "You didn't really think I'd let you go without me?"

Aboard the Scarab, Charlotte couldn't sit still. Jack piloted the craft, and the earth rushed by far beneath them. The passenger cabin had been designed for comfort. It featured high-backed chairs and long, satin-upholstered benches accented with silk-covered pillows. Charlotte wished she could sit and calm herself, to carefully resolve her mind to the task at hand, but her limbs were abuzz with anticipation, and her heart beat with the frenzy of a moth trapped in a glass.

"How do you plan to infiltrate the Military Platform?" Ash asked his sister.

Charlotte didn't have an immediate answer. Stealth? Force? Disguise? A combination of all three?

She could see the worry on Ash's face. He wouldn't be with them. Nor would Jack. The two boys had tasks of their own.

While Jack went to collect his mother, Ash would seek out Meg at the Temple and ask the Sisters for any news of their father and his whereabouts. If, by some miracle, Charles had been transferred to the city and hadn't remained at the Crucible's facilities, Ash would try to reach him. Though Jack would return to the Scarab and wait for the others, Ash didn't plan to rendezvous with their group after he'd visited the Temple.

That part of the plan had been at Linnet's prompting.

"If the Sisters don't have their own escape route out of the city, I'll give you my favorite dagger," Linnet said to Ash. "And I *love* that dagger."

That left only one piece of their mission unresolved— getting to Grave and freeing him from military custody.

"We're going to use our mission for our own ends," Charlotte told the group. "Not just because the French asked for a massive diversion."

"Bringing down the Great Wheel will certainly get attention," Linnet said. "And you actually have the means to get it done." She pointed to Birch and Io. "You have two tinkers here."

"And me," Pip interjected. To further her point, she left her seat and burrowed onto the bench between Birch and his aunt. Io put a fond arm around the girl's shoulders, and Birch gave Pip an encouraging nod.

"Three tinkers." Linnet smiled at Pip. "I'm sure they're very good at blowing things up."

"Oh, yes, very, very good." Scoff laughed.

Birch scowled at him.

"Don't be cross," Io said to her nephew. "Blowing things up is a very important step on the path to innovation."

"All right." Birch leaned back in his chair. "We're going to blow up the Great Wheel. That will be . . . invigorating?"

"Better not to guess until we've done it," Io replied firmly.

"Can you do it?" Charlotte looked at the trio of tinkers. All of their eyes had become alarmingly bright with anticipation.

"We'll need to have a look at the supplies Scoff brought," Birch told her. "He might have some components that would amplify a blast."

His expression suddenly darkened. "What about the people in the Wheel's carriages?"

Charlotte's chest was tight. The French had demanded the Wheel be attacked, but there was no denying that it was a civilian target. Given that the ultimate goal of the French fleet was to destroy the entire city, casualties on the Wheel were likely considered insignifcant.

"The Wheel stops taking passengers at midnight," Linnet said. "If we complete the mission before dawn, the carriages should be empty."

"Thank Athene," Charlotte murmured.

"No passengers. Good." Birch started to smile again. "You've given us quite the task. I hope we're up to it."

"I'm not worried about you lot getting the job done." Linnet was frowning. "That's the easy part."

"What's the hard part?" Scoff asked.

"Getting to the Wheel," Linnet answered. "It's always guarded, but the city's bound to be on high alert now. Security will no doubt have increased."

"She's right," Jack said. "And we won't know what we're up against until we get there."

"Then we have no choice but to plan our attack immediately before we execute it." Charlotte's brow furrowed with concern. She didn't like going in blind.

Linnet, on the other hand, was grinning. "Excellent. I'm at my best when improvising."

"For the rest of our sakes, I hope that's true," Jack said glumly, but he was smiling.

"Oh, it's true."

"There's also the question of placement," Io interjected, her mind still grappling with the logistics of an explosion. "The best point to detonate any device would be at the axis. But to get to that height, we'd need an army of squirrels. If we had more time, I might be able to manage that—"

Charlotte was shaking her head, but Pip exclaimed, "You don't need squirrels. You have me! I'm a brilliant climber."

"No, Pip," Charlotte said. "This isn't like any forest or cliff climb. A fall would be fatal. We'll just have to place the explosives somewhere around the base."

"But I have my pinwheel!" Pip stated with a frown.

"Of course!" Aunt Io patted the girl on the head. "That's the perfect solution." Io turned to Charlotte. "We'll be sure to build as light a device as we can manage."

Charlotte's brow furrowed. "What are you talking about? What pinwheel?"

"I know what I'm doing, Charlotte." Pip clasped her hands together in a pleading gesture. "You can trust me."

Drawing a long breath, Charlotte nodded. "Promise me you're not being reckless."

"I promise, I promise." Pip had traded loose pigtails for a single long braid, but it still swung madly when she hopped with joy about the cabin.

30.

THE TREES OF the Iron Forest had never appeared more skeletal than they did that night, clothed in pale fabric of moonlight and steam. The engines that kept the Great Wheel revolving sent clouds of moisture into the air, filling the dark woods with warm fog. Noise from machinery muffled whatever sounds of life teemed on the platforms above.

Their group of eight conspirators had docked at the Market Platform. The mood on the usually buzzing center of the city's commerce was subdued. News of the fleet's demise in New Orleans had suffused the Floating City with an ominous air. The people they passed on the streets hurried by with heads down, avoiding the eyes of their fellows.

Linnet led the way to one of Ott's shops, within which was hidden an elevator to the island of Manhattan. Once they'd been deposited on the ground, they'd taken a route that retraced the path Charlotte had followed with Coe after the Imperial raid on the Tinkers' Faire. The memory triggered a pang in Charlotte's chest. When she'd first met Coe, he'd impressed her with his bravery and confidence. Learning the truth of his character was like biting into a ruby red apple only to discover rot and worms at its core.

Charlotte gazed up at the glittering wheel moving in its languid revolutions, oblivious to the threat lurking at its base. She watched for signs of movement inside the carriages when they passed close to the earth and was relieved when she saw none.

The maintenance grounds for the Great Wheel were surrounded by a tall iron fence and a locked gate, neither of which would have impeded their entry. The guards were another matter.

While the others waited beneath the forest's cloak, Charlotte crept to the edge of the trees to peer from behind a thick iron trunk. From her vantage point, she counted eight men, but the Wheel blocked her line of sight to any guards posted on the opposite side. Best to assume they'd be pitted against double the number she could see, if not more.

On light feet, Charlotte hurried to rejoin her friends. They crouched in a circle.

"Eight on this side," Charlotte told them in a low voice.

"And likely eight on the other," Jack said.

Charlotte nodded.

"I'd wager that there are at least two pairs of roving patrols around the perimeter as well," Linnet added.

Ash shook his head. "That's too many for a direct assault."

"Then we'll draw them out," Charlotte replied. "If we can separate them, we'll have a better chance of taking them down one at a time."

"Or three at a time," Linnet offered. When Jack threw her a withering look, she added, "I'm not saying I want to fight more than one at a time. It's simply prudent to be prepared."

"We can't afford the time it will take to fight them all by playing hide-and-seek in the woods," Ash said. "The French fleet is on its way. The Wheel has to be taken down before they arrive."

"The way the mission was presented, I think we could interpret that bit as optional," Jack offered.

"What are you talking about?" Ash asked.

"Well, they did keep saying *if* you succeed," Jack replied. His tone was teasing, but Charlotte suspected he was at least a little bit serious.

Charlotte waved off the suggestion. "Unpleasant as it may be, you know as well as I that *if* meant 'if you don't die,' not 'if you don't give up.'"

"No one's giving up." Ash's sudden anger caught Charlotte by surprise. "I know we don't all share the same opinion of the Resistance, but I still believe in their cause. I still say the Empire must fall."

Charlotte put her hand on Ash's arm. "We aren't going to abandon the mission, and you're right that time is working against us."

Addressing the group, Charlotte said, "The priority is getting Pip inside the fence and up to the Maintenance Platform. Linnet and Io will go with Pip. Linnet picks the lock. Io can offer any last-minute changes to the device. Both of you, if needed, will defend Pip as she climbs.

"Before you make a run for the gate, the rest of us will draw as many of the guards into the forest as we can. Hopefully we'll eliminate them or hold their attention long enough for Pip to place the device and detonate it. Once that happens, I doubt the guards will care about catching us."

"Probably not," Jack said.

"Pip's group, head to the far eastern edge of the forest and wait until the guards have left," Charlotte said. "If some stay behind, you'll have to take them down."

"We'll manage," Scoff told her.

"It's time," Charlotte told them. "Good luck."

When the infiltrators had gone, Jack began to laugh.

"What?" Charlotte frowned at him.

"It just occurred to me that we're about to create a diversion for our diversion," he said with a grin.

"Ugh." Charlotte rolled her eyes.

"Let's divert, then," Ash said. "I'll take the north side."

"I'll draw them to the west," Scoff said.

"Near east side sounds good to me," Jack added.

Birch looked at Charlotte. "I guess that leaves us the south approach."

"I'll take the south," Charlotte replied. "I need you to climb a tree at the edge of the forest and keep an eye on the situation at the Wheel. You're good with the long rifle. Take out any threats to Pip's squad."

"I can do that." Birch selected the sleek-barreled gun from their array of arms and went to seek a suitable perch.

Charlotte looked to her remaining friends. "Anything else?"

No one spoke.

Charlotte nodded, and the group broke apart.

The southern approach to the Wheel's base was the very point from which she'd first assessed their opponents. The eight guards she'd observed earlier were still there. Charlotte watched them, trying to get a sense of their alertness. They rarely spoke to one another and moved with quick, jerky reflexes. High tension, then. That could work to her advantage. Fear easily gave birth to confusion and chaos, and the Iron Forest was a catalyst for those unstable emotions.

Charlotte fitted the carbine to her shoulder and took aim. Another shot rang out before she pulled the trigger, but the sound didn't startle Charlotte, nor did it mar her aim. She squeezed the trigger, and one of the guards crumpled.

Shouts filled the air, and the remaining seven guards charged toward her position, guns at the ready. Charlotte dashed from the edge of the forest, trying to stay within the cover of its shadows.

More shots rang out.

After a brief sprint, Charlotte ducked behind a tree and raised the carbine again. She could hear the guards crashing through the forest, but she had yet to find a second target.

A flicker of movement caught her attention.

A flicker of movement behind her.

Charlotte threw herself to the ground, and a moment later, metallic rings sounded from the tree trunk as bullets struck the place she'd been standing. She rolled over and scrambled to her feet. Her eyes tracked through the trees, searching for her assailant. The guards from the Wheel hadn't overtaken her, so it had to be one of the patrols.

At her back, the seven guards she'd led into the metal woods drew closer. Charlotte needed to fire at them again, but she couldn't risk turning her back on this new threat.

She continued to track south, moving with stealth rather than speed. The men pursuing her were running. Before long, they would overtake her.

"Halt!"

The shout came from her left. Charlotte froze, turning her head. A guard had his rifle trained on her, but what arrested her attention was the creature held back by its master.

Charlotte couldn't believe what she was seeing. It was an armored rat. The rat clawed at the ground, straining against the chain gripped by its master.

"Drop your gun." The guard shook the rat's chain, and it reared up as though it had been given a promise of imminent release. "You don't want me to set her on you."

Charlotte agreed. The rat's beady eyes were already devouring Charlotte in anticipation of sinking its teeth into her flesh.

She could try to run, and she might be able to evade the rat, but not if the guard shot her legs out from beneath her. Charlotte began to lower the carbine. She didn't know what to watch more carefully, the guard whose gun was trained on her or the rat.

Shots still rang through the air at irregular intervals. Some of the blasts were closer than others.

The drum of footfalls was closer still.

"Identify yourselves!" the rat guard shouted. He kept his gun aimed at Charlotte, but she could tell he was nervous, unsure whether the approaching din signaled the arrival of friends or foes.

The guard's gaze slipped from Charlotte toward the noise coming from the woods.

Knowing this might be her only chance to flee, Charlotte bolted. A rifle report boomed in her ears, but the guard's shot had missed. She ran faster.

Charlotte kept the line of her flight jagged, darting behind trees, changing direction. Angry, confused shouts filled the woods. She turned again and then pivoted around a large tree. She crouched against its trunk.

Running had been a temporary solution, but it wouldn't serve the larger aims of Charlotte's mission. She needed to lessen the threat that followed her. And that meant waiting for the guards to catch up.

And the rat.

I wish I had Pocky.

It was a fleeting desire. Pocky would have served Charlotte well against the rat, but wouldn't have been much use against the guards.

Charlotte could hear their approaching steps now. She raised the carbine. A guard appeared between the trees ahead. Charlotte took aim, waiting for him to come in range. She fired. The bullet's impact knocked him off his feet. He didn't get up again.

Answering shots rang out all around. The guards weren't bothering to aim, but all it would take was one lucky bullet to bring Charlotte's mission to an end.

She stayed low when she moved to the cover of another tree trunk. She changed her position one more time.

Another guard came into her sights. She fired and immediately dropped to the forest floor in anticipation of the volley to come. Shots filled the air once more, but not as many.

Charlotte crawled to the next tree. Another soldier fell prey to her carbine. She dared to maintain her position and was rewarded with another successful shot.

As she scrambled to another site of cover, a searing pain lanced along Charlotte's upper right arm. She heard the gunshot in the next moment. Dropping to the ground, Charlotte rolled several times until she was curled against a tree trunk.

One glance at the wound told Charlotte the shot had only grazed her. She sat up, pressing her back to the tree as she contemplated what her next move should be.

The woods had grown strangely quiet. She no longer heard boots stomping through the trees. Either the soldiers had decided Charlotte was no longer worth pursuing or something else had claimed their attention.

I have to get back to the Wheel.

If somehow the remaining guards had been alerted to the threat posed by Pip's squad, they could be returning to their posts.

Charlotte stood up, but went still when she heard a soft scuffling nearby. She'd only begun to turn in the direction of the sound when the rat's head appeared from around the opposite side of the tree trunk. Its muzzle was crimson with gore, and its nose was lifted, twitching as it scented Charlotte's blood.

There was no time to aim. The rat was too close. Charlotte grabbed the gun's barrel as the rat leapt. She swung the butt of the carbine as hard as she could, and it vibrated in her hands at the impact. The rat squealed in pain and then it was on her.

The creature was weighty on its own, but the armor gave its body a crushing force. Charlotte smashed into the ground. She would have been pinned had her blow to the rat's head not forced it to the side. Charlotte was on her feet while the rat still shook its head, dazed from the blow.

Charlotte raised the gun once more and brought its butt down between the rat's eyes. There was an awful crack before it slumped to the ground. Charlotte's fingers still gripped the barrel tightly. Her heart was pounding as she watched the rat, waiting for any sign of life. It remained still.

By the time Charlotte reached the Wheel, whatever battle had been fought there was over. From what she saw, Charlotte guessed it hadn't been much of a contest. Guards lay at random places in the stretch of ground between the forest and the Wheel's base. Birch had done his job well.

Scoff and Ash had taken up sentinel posts in front of the entrance to the Wheel's mechanical stations. Ash waved as Charlotte approached, but frowned when he saw she was bleeding.

"It's not bad," Charlotte told him before he could ask.

"There's Jack." Scoff nodded toward the eastern edge of the forest.

Jack wasn't so much coming toward them as stomping his way out of the trees.

"Please tell me someone else had to fight a rat." He was scowling.

"A rat?" Scoff asked.

Ashley looked puzzled as well.

"I did," Charlotte said.

"What?" Ash gave Charlotte a curious glance. "Rats?"

"Armored rats," Jack told him. "Just like the good old days."

"Heap rats?" Ash shook his head in disbelief. "The Empire doesn't train Heap rats."

"Apparently they do," Jack said. "Though not very well. The one I faced turned on its master as soon as it smelled blood. Took care of two guards for me."

Charlotte wondered if the guards who'd been behind her hadn't given up the chase after all.

"How's Pip doing?" Jack asked.

"See for yourself," Scoff pointed at the Wheel's axis.

High above them a tiny figure was approaching the heart of the Wheel. The sight stole Charlotte's breath. She rushed through the gate to join Io and Linnet, whose eyes were fixed on Pip.

Charlotte marveled at Pip's speed. The ascent was even longer than Charlotte had imagined, but Pip was practically flying up the ladder. Charlotte wanted to laugh at how much Pip did mirror the nimble motions of a squirrel.

When Pip reached the Maintenance Platform at the wheel's axle, her body was almost too small to see. Charlotte squinted as she tried to follow the girl's progress. At last, Pip's tiny form moved away from the giant axle. But rather than returning to the ladder, Pip walked to the edge of the platform.

Io took Charlotte's arm. "Now you'll want to scream, dear. But please don't."

Pip jumped.

A scream did rise in Charlotte's throat, but sheer disbelief in what she was seeing stopped her cry's escape.

Pip raised one arm, and Charlotte saw that the girl was holding an object that looked somewhat like an umbrella. The top of the umbrella was spinning, and Charlotte realized that Pip wasn't falling. She was floating.

"Hephaestus's hammer," Linnet murmured. "What is that contraption?"

"She invented it." Io clucked like a proud mother hen. "Heaps of potential in that one. So creative."

Pip's feet touched the ground, and she twisted the handle of her device. The whirring of a motor slowed and then stopped, as did the spinning petal-like canopy above her head.

Pip ran up to Charlotte, breathless with excitement.

"That was astonishing," Charlotte said.

"Did you like it?" Pip brandished the device with pride. "I call it a Pinwheel. It's very useful."

"You're quite the clever little thing." Linnet eyed Pip. "You should speak to Lord Ott. I think he'd be eager to employ you."

Pip grinned.

Linnet grabbed Pip's hand. "Yes, yes, huzzah for Pip, but we have to go!"

Charlotte blinked away her amazement as she remembered the ticking clock high above them, counting down to massive destruction.

"Time to run," Birch said.

He took off. Scoff and Birch were at his heels, with Io, Linnet, Pip, and Charlotte close behind.

Birch shouted a warning to Jack, Ash, and Scoff when he passed them, and a second later, they were running too. They didn't stop until they'd reached the wide tree trunk that housed Ott's secret elevator shaft. Linnet moved to pull the branch that would reveal the elevator door, but Birch stopped her.

"We need to wait for the explosion," he said. "We don't want to be stuck in that elevator if the blast radius is great enough to interfere with its machinery."

Linnet's eyes widened slightly, and she nodded.

"Are you sure we're far enough away?" For the first time that night, Pip sounded afraid.

Birch put his arm around her. "It will be loud, and the ground might shake, but we aren't in danger."

They stood, huddled together beneath the metal tree, and waited. A terrible quiet seemed to fill the forest, like the sudden silence of woods when a predator appears.

A bright flash illuminated the wheel before the roar of the explosion reached them. Charlotte covered her ears. All around them, the metal forest vibrated with the power of the blast. The ground shuddered.

Then, again, quiet. For several moments, Charlotte could only hear the rapid strikes of her heartbeat.

Something low began to swell in the air. A long, weary groan followed by a keening that pierced through Charlotte's ears, making her wince.

Pip gasped and clapped her hands over her mouth.

The Great Wheel began to tip away from the Floating City.

What had been a horrendous, shrill noise became a chorus of shrieks as metal screamed and carriages dropped from the outer rim of the wheel, falling like overripe fruit to the earth. Beneath the ceaseless high-pitched cries rose a deep groan. The death bellow of some mythic beast. And the Great Wheel fell.

31.

HE MARKET PLATFORM was in chaos. Fearful cries mingled with blaring alarms as panic seized New York's citizens. Smoke billowed at the edge of the platform where the Great Wheel had once taken on passengers.

Witnessing it all, Charlotte was suddenly filled with grief. She understood what was happening and why, but her mind clung to other memories of the Floating City. And while its platforms suffered the bloat of the Empire's indulgences, the city could also claim true beauty, real innovation. Its inhabitants weren't all blind servants of the Empire, hateful of the Resistance. They lived and worked, surviving and thriving in whatever ways they could. But now all the city's residents would be subject to the same violence, destruction, and suffering. They would bear the responsibility for decisions over which they'd had no control.

How many here would die without purpose?

The buzz of aircraft filled the sky as Dragonflies zoomed toward the wreck of the wheel.

"This is where we part ways," Linnet said.

Charlotte nodded. They had no time for sentiment or fear. Jack met Charlotte's gaze briefly before he went to find his mother. Ash was bound for the Temple.

Though the city had already begun to tilt toward chaos, for the moment its quotidian functions were still in operation. Grave's rescue party boarded the trolley and rode it to the Military Platform. The scene they encountered upon disembarking was one of panic, but the organized sort. Uniformed men and women ran in every direction, responding to whatever orders they received.

"Follow my lead," Linnet told them. "Walk swiftly and keep your head up. Act as if you belong here."

They moved in an orderly fashion, lined up in pairs, and kept a clipped pace as they crossed the platform toward the air dock. Far fewer vessels were stationed at the platform than when Charlotte had last been there. Many were now smoldering ruins outside the walls of New Orleans. Those that remained were rumbling to life, preparing to answer the attack they believed was already under way.

Linnet's assessment of the situation proved accurate. They were largely ignored as they made their way toward the warehouses. It wasn't until they reached the door that gave entry to Grave's prison that they encountered an obstacle. The guards posted outside had not abandoned their posts, despite the alarms sounding beyond the walls of the warehouse.

"Who are you?" One of the guards stepped in front of Linnet. Without hesitation, she dipped her hand into her bodice. Her stiletto flashed, and a crimson line appeared on the guard's throat before he could raise his weapon.

The second guard's eyes bulged as he watched his companion stagger, clutching at his neck while blood spurted through his fingers. When Linnet grabbed the petrified guard's rifle, he barely seemed to notice.

Charlotte drew her pistol, leveling its barrel at his head. "Open the door."

The guard fumbled with the key, but managed to unlock the door. Once they were inside the passageway, Charlotte nodded at Linnet, who slammed the butt of the rifle into the back of the guard's head. He slumped to the floor.

Charlotte ran down the passage, bursting into the laboratory. She found a scene eerily similar to the one she'd witnessed when she'd first been taken to this place.

Grave was still splayed on the table. His body dissected and laid open to the world. Tinker Miller stood beside him. He held a scalpel, but his hand trembled.

"You will stop working only when I tell you to stop working!" The barked command came from Lieutenant Redding, who glared at the quailing man.

Redding whipped around to face Charlotte. "What's the— You!"

"Yes," Charlotte said, smoothly cocking her pistol. "Me."

She shot her in the head.

Lieutenant Redding fell to the ground.

Miller dropped to the floor as well. He wrapped his arms around his knees, rocking back and forth as he wept.

Charlotte's companions rushed into the room.

Linnet drew a hissing breath when she saw Grave. "Athene's mercy."

Io pushed Linnet aside and strode matter-of-factly to the table. She turned to look at the others with a smile. "Not dismembered!"

Ignoring Io for the moment, Charlotte hurried past her and leaned over Grave's face. His eyes were open, but he was staring at the ceiling.

"Grave?" Fear tinged Charlotte's voice.

He blinked, then his distant gaze focused on her. "Charlotte." He smiled.

"Are you . . . all right?" The question seemed ridiculous under the circumstances, but Grave understood Charlotte's concern.

"Yes," he said. "I think my body is sound, but I had discovered that while Tinker Miller was . . . working . . . it was more pleasant for me if I could go away."

"You mean in your mind?" Charlotte asked.

"Yes."

She wanted to ask where his mind could go, but there wasn't time to ponder such mysteries.

Io, Birch, and Pip hovered over Grave's mutilated body. His rib cage had been cracked, and his body cavity further opened. More flaps of skin were stretched out and pinned down like insect specimens. Pip's face had lost some of its color, but she inspected Grave without flinching.

"Fascinating," Io murmured.

"Aunt Io?" Grave turned his gaze toward her. "Why are you here?"

"To put you back together!" Io reached out to touch his cheek in a gesture of warmth that surprised Charlotte. "You're not in pain, are you?"

"No." Grave said. "But I don't like this. I don't like how I feel. I don't like not being able to move."

"Of course you don't," Io replied. "Who would?"

She turned her attention to Birch and Pip. "Now. Hand me the tools that I ask for, and when I need your assistance, do exactly as I say."

Deciding it best that she get out of Io's way, Charlotte said to Grave, "You're in good hands. I'll be right over there."

Grave nodded. It was a strangely normal movement, given that his head was one of the only parts of his body still intact.

She smiled at him and began to turn away.

"I knew you would come, Charlotte."

Her throat closed, and tears gathered in her eyes. He'd been here so long. Alone. She didn't deserve such faith.

"I'm so sorry, Grave," she whispered.

"I'm not," Grave told her. "Don't be sad."

Charlotte nodded, trying to hold back her tears.

"Now, Grave," Io said, "we're going to begin. I want you to tell me if anything feels wrong. It won't do any good for us to put you back together incorrectly."

"I'll tell you," Grave answered.

Charlotte made her way to Linnet, who was standing over Tinker Miller. The man was still shivering and rocking.

"What should we do with him?" Linnet asked.

"Nothing," Charlotte said. When she looked at Miller, all Charlotte felt was pity. "He didn't want to do this."

Linnet shrugged. "If you say so."

The pair watched as Io and her assistants worked painstakingly to restore Grave's body. Most of the procedures Io performed herself, though she occasionally called upon Birch or Pip, or both, to aid her. What Charlotte found the most fascinating were the moments when Io summoned Scoff to her side. At her bidding, Scoff would produce a vial or a flask or a pouch and administer the substances inside as Io directed. Some were thick and viscous; others, shimmering and light as dust motes. Some required precise and minimal application, while others were spread liberally over Grave's torso.

"Alchemy?" Linnet whispered to Charlotte. Her expression was as mesmerized as Charlotte's.

Charlotte could only nod.

An hour passed. Then another.

Io was bent over Grave's chest, stitching his skin back into place with metallic thread, when the building shuddered. In the distance, Charlotte heard a boom. The building shuddered again.

"I'll be right back," Linnet said, and disappeared into the passageway.

Casting a glance at Charlotte, Io said, "Only a bit longer."

Charlotte bit her lip and nodded.

More ominous sounds, closer ones, reached into the laboratory.

Linnet returned. "The French fleet is here. We have to leave."

Her warning was marked by an explosion that made the building not only shudder, but rock. The cart covered with surgical tools tipped over, its contents clattering onto the floor.

"Just a few minutes more." Io gritted her teeth in concentration.

Charlotte's nails dug into her palms. Linnet paced beside the door.

The frequency of blasts increased. Charlotte heard the roar of large engines, signaling the arrival of heavy-gunned warships.

"There!" Io stood up. "Scoff. The ointment."

Scoff dipped his hand into a jar and rubbed shiny, silver paste over the stitches in Grave's chest and abdomen.

"Silly me," Io huffed. "You're still shackled to the table. Linnet?"

Linnet started toward the table, but Grave said, "There's no need."

He sat up. The steel cuffs that had bolted his arms to the table sprung loose as if they were paper, as did the collar at his neck.

Io nodded with pleasure, then beamed at Birch, Pip, and Scoff. "You see? We did an excellent job. Well done!"

Though Io seemed to be taking all of this in stride, the rest of the group were staring at Grave in amazement.

Grave swung his legs over the side of the table and hopped down. He bent his knees and stretched his arms.

"This is much better."

"I'm delighted," Io said. She snapped her fingers at the dumbfounded group. "Get a move on. We don't want to be blown to bits, now, do we?"

32.

WHATEVER ORDER HAD existed when Charlotte and her companions entered the warehouse had vanished with the arrival of the French fleet. The air docks burned, and the platform shook as the bombardment continued.

They ran for the trolley.

"Everyone in the first two cars," Linnet ordered. She pulled Charlotte into the front car with her. "The automated settings will get us killed. We'll never make it off the platform without more speed." Linnet leaned down and pried a compartment open with her stiletto to reveal a control box filled with buttons and levers. She punched three buttons and pulled hard on the largest of the levers.

"Manual controls engaged," the tinny voice of the trolley announced.

Linnet grasped what Charlotte had thought was an emergency brake.

"That's the control?" Charlotte tried to mask the alarm in her voice.

With a grimace, Linnet said, "It's the emergency brake, but when you activate manual control, it also becomes the accelerator. That's all we can do, speed up and slow down."

Linnet shoved the brake forward, and the trolley lurched on the tracks.

"Hang on!" Linnet shouted to the passengers in the second car.

The trolley hurtled forward, screeching along the rails as it was forced from the leisurely pace for which it had been built into breakneck speed.

Charlotte was about to tell Linnet to slow down, but when she turned, she caught sight of what was happening to the platform behind them. The largest of the warships had crossed into firing range of the city. Their fury now rained down on the highest platforms. The Governor's Platform, the pinnacle of New York, was in flames, and its turbines were beginning to fail. Unable to maintain equilibrium, the platform was slowly tilting away from its horizontal plane toward a vertical position. At the same time, it was falling. In minutes it would collide with the Military Platform.

"Go faster, Linnet," Charlotte breathed, though she doubted the other girl could hear her or that the trolley wasn't already being pushed to its limit.

The tracks angled down as they crossed the threshold from the Military Platform and descended onto the Market Platform. The incline gave the trolley more speed. The cars began to quiver.

An explosion rocked the Military Platform, its impact shuddering down the tracks. The cars jolted sideways. Charlotte felt the right side wheels lift off the tracks. Pip screamed. The trolley thudded back onto its rails as the track began to level out and, at the same time, to curve.

Linnet swore. "We're going to hit this turn too fast."

She hauled back on the brake, shouting, "Brace yourselves!"

Sparks flew as the wheels shrieked in protest. The trolley entered the curve. They were slowing. Slowing. But the momentum of their descent pulled the cars too far into the turn. The trolley surged to the left. A horrible jolt threw Charlotte back against her seat and then they were floating as the wheels jumped the tracks. The cars were airborne for only seconds before the platform rushed up to meet them. Charlotte gripped the side of the car as tightly as she could, but the impact of the crash wrenched her from her seat. Her body slammed into Linnet's. The car was falling, and Charlotte's world was spinning. She hit the ground hard. All the air rushed out of her lungs. Her body had stopped moving, but she could still hear people screaming and metal crumpling.

Charlotte sucked in a painful breath, forcing her lungs to work. She wheezed, then took another breath as she pushed herself onto her hands and knees. There was pain, but the bruised sort. She could put weight on her hands and her feet. Her muscles responded when she told them to move. She was dizzy, and she put her hands on her temples, waiting for the wooziness to fade.

When she trusted herself not to fall, Charlotte stumbled forward, moving toward the jumble of smoke and gilded metal that had at last come to a stop in Temple Square. Charlotte couldn't believe how far she'd been thrown from the wreck, but then the cars had probably kept moving after she'd fallen free.

"Charlotte!"

She turned to her right. Linnet was running toward her. A gash ran from her temple to her jaw, but she appeared otherwise unhurt.

"Are you hurt?" Linnet asked, her eyes tracking over Charlotte's form.

Charlotte shook her head. When she spoke, her voice was a croak. "The others?"

"I don't know."

Together they approached the wreckage. The trolley cars lay on their left side.

"Birch!" Linnet called. "Scoff! Pip!"

They had to climb up the roof of the trolley so they could peer inside the second car.

Birch was lying prone toward the rear of the car, while Scoff's body was splayed between the first and second cars. Charlotte couldn't see Grave, Io, or Pip.

"Birch!" Linnet shouted.

Birch groaned.

"Thank Athene." Linnet lowered herself into the car.

Charlotte was about to do the same when a deafening crash wrenched her head around.

Having shaken off the disorientation of the crash, Charlotte could now perceive the Governor's Platform clearly. She watched with horror as structures, vehicles, and the small, forsaken bodies that were people slid from its surface. This chaos of projectiles struck the Military Platform, which in turn began to buckle. Its sides slowly lifted, curving inward as the Governor's Platform crushed its center.

"Linnet!" Charlotte didn't have to explain.

"We have to get them out." Linnet put one of Birch's arms over her shoulder and helped him to his feet.

Charlotte braced her legs over the side of the car and reached down. "Hurry!"

Birch grasped Charlotte's wrists as she gripped his. With all her strength, Charlotte pulled him up, levering the weight of her lower body against the car. When Birch's torso cleared the trolley window, he was able to push himself the rest of the way.

"Can you help?" Charlotte asked.

"I think so," Birch said. He took the same position as Charlotte and leaned over the car.

Linnet had Scoff on his feet. One of Scoff's arms was dangling at an impossible angle.

"I'm going to have him stand on my shoulders, so you can grab his chest," Linnet called to them. "We don't want to damage his arm any further."

Birch nodded. Linnet dropped to one knee and braced her arms against a seat. Scoff climbed onto Linnet's shoulders, using his good arm to steady himself by finding handholds in the interior of the car.

"Okay, Scoff," Linnet said. "I'm going to stand. Steady now. Steady."

"I'm all right," Scoff told her, but his face had gone white with pain.

With a sharp groan, Linnet pushed herself up. Scoff's head rose, then his shoulders cleared the window.

"We've got him," Charlotte called as Birch wrapped his arms about Scoff.

"What about the others?" Charlotte asked Linnet. "Do you see any of them in the front car?"

"They're not here." Linnet frowned. "They must have been thrown from the car like we were."

But they hadn't returned to the wreckage. That meant they weren't conscious, or . . .

"I'm coming out."

Charlotte started to reach for Linnet, but the other girl had crouched low. Her body burst into motion like a spring uncoiling. She grabbed the frame of the window and pulled herself out. Linnet paused to look at the crashing platforms above them.

"Let's find the others."

"Charlotte!" Birch was calling from in front of the first car. "Here!"

They hurried toward the sound of his voice and found

him crouched beside the crumpled car. Pip was sitting there crying. She didn't appear to be hurt, but she couldn't stop weeping.

Charlotte went to her. "Pip, are you wounded? Can you move?"

"He saved me," Pip breathed through her sobs. "He held me till it was over."

Pip had been thrown from the front of the trolley. Charlotte tracked the path from where the girl was sitting farther into the square until she saw Grave. He was standing over a body.

"Oh no." Charlotte ran. She knelt beside Io's unmoving form. The woman's eyes were closed. A trickle of blood seeped from one corner of her mouth.

"I couldn't shield them both," Grave said. "I'm not big enough."

"You protected Pip." Charlotte laid her ear against Io's chest. Hoping for the faintest heartbeat, the shallowest breath. But there was only silence.

A sob welled in Charlotte's throat, but she swallowed it. "You saved Pip," she said to Grave.

Grave stared at Io, his face etched with a sadness Charlotte had never seen in him.

"Aunt Io?" Birch had reached them. "Oh no. Aunt Io! No." Birch dropped to his knees. He grabbed Io's hand and pressed it to his cheek. "No. No. No."

Pip and Scoff hovered nearby.

"I'm so sorry, Birch," Pip cried. "I'm so sorry."

Birch was shaking his head.

"We can't stay here." Linnet spoke quietly. "The city is falling. We don't have much longer."

"I don't want to leave her," Birch said. "She doesn't belong here."

"Grave can carry her." Linnet nodded at Grave. "We'll bring her home."

That seemed to give Birch enough strength to stand up. Grave gathered Io in his arms.

"We should run," Linnet said.

With what little strength they had left, they ran toward the docks of the Market Platform. They could only hope that the docks were still intact and that Jack was waiting for them at the Scarab. Charlotte had to shut out the horror that surrounded them. Everywhere people wailed and screamed. The air had a metallic bite that Charlotte knew was the saturation of panic. But to think about it, to let in the devastation of so many lives, was to give up. She wouldn't get off the platform alive if she stopped for even a moment to consider what was happening to everyone and anyone who lived in New York.

Smoke thickened as they closed in on the docks. Shops serving the trading vessels that frequented the platform were ablaze. The air stabbed at Charlotte's lungs, making her cough, and her eyes watered.

Linnet suddenly stopped. "No!"

The despair in Linnet's cry made Charlotte's skin crawl. A moment later she knew why.

Nothing lay beyond the shops at the edge of the platform. The docks were gone.

They stared into the emptiness. Pip was still crying softly, her head tucked against Birch's shoulder.

"What do we do?" Scoff murmured.

A shape swooped overhead accompanied by the buzz of an engine.

"We need to take cover!" Linnet pivoted, searching for shelter.

"Wait!" Charlotte peered into the smoke. The aircraft was circling, descending. It was moving too slowly to be a fighter.

A bulbous silhouette appeared faint in the sky. A Scarab.

"Jack!" Charlotte screamed. She began jumping up and down, waving her arms. "Jack! We're here!"

"Helm of Athene," Linnet gasped. She joined in Charlotte's frantic shouting.

The Scarab continued its descent. Its propellers cleared away some of the smoke. Jack's face became clear in the cockpit. He waved, and Charlotte began to cry.

33.

Two Weeks Later

CHARLOTTE SAT ON the edge of the bed, holding her father's hand.

His eyelids flickered, then opened. "Lottie."

"I didn't mean to wake you," Charlotte said.

Charles Marshall smiled at his daughter. "I sleep far too much as it is."

"The doctors say that's the only way you'll recover," Charlotte told him. "And you can't rush the healing process."

"The doctors always have plenty to say." He smirked. "Their verbosity notwithstanding, I am grateful for the attention."

"Good."

When her father propped himself up on his elbows,

Charlotte adjusted his pillows so he could sit upright comfortably.

"Tell me what's happening in the world."

Charlotte sighed. So much was happening. All the time. "Ash says the Resistance delegates have almost reached an agreement with the French," she told him. "They won't get everything they hoped for, but he says the leadership seems happy with the terms."

"Not an independent nation, then." Charles raised one brow.

Charlotte nodded. "A territorial province. But with the autonomy to set up its own government and elect its officials."

"That doesn't sound too bad."

"I think it will work," Charlotte said. "Ash is certainly enthusiastic."

"Your brother is on the verge of becoming a political," her father said with wry smile. "He's a natural leader. Your mother has told me he's made quite the impression on both the Resistance leadership and the French dignitaries."

Charlotte tilted her head, asking hesitantly, "How are things with you and Mother?"

"You don't have to be afraid of asking me about your mother," Charles told her. "I think you understand that it's a complicated situation."

Giving her father's hand a squeeze, Charlotte said, "I just want you to be well again. And to be happy."

Charlotte had seen her mother break down when Charles Marshall was carried off a transport ship after the liberation of the Crucible. Admiral Winter had been true to his word: Charlotte's father had been found in a medical ward that served the prison, receiving treatment for his illness. But even now that her husband was recovering from his ordeal, Caroline couldn't be in his presence without a haunted cast creeping over her features. Charles had forgiven his wife, but Caroline had yet to forgive herself. Charlotte didn't know if her parents would ever reconcile, or even if they should.

Charlotte leaned down and kissed her father's cheek.

"Is that a good-bye?" he teased. "We've barely spoken, and I'm already boring you away."

With a laugh, Charlotte said, "Don't be silly. I have a prior engagement."

"That sounds quite important," her father said.

This time Charlotte's smile was bittersweet. "It is."

The Garden quadrant was redolent of jasmine and dogwood. Birds flitted overhead and darted in and out of the flowering shrubs in an endless game of hide-and-seek. That afternoon Io's body had been committed to the earth. It had taken a good deal of negotiation to gain permission to bury Io in the city gardens. But when Lord Ott entered the fray on behalf of Birch's petition, a significant amount of bureaucratic nonsense had been handily set aside.

Both of the Otts were present at the service. As were Linnet and, to Charlotte's surprise, Jean-Baptiste

Lachance. Charlotte joined Jack, Ash, and Meg at the graveside. Scoff and Pip stood together while Birch read one of his aunt's favorite poems. Like so many things Io was fond of, it was strange.

> *No up nor down*
> *No right nor wrong*
> *Life is no more*
> *Than a favorite song*
> *Tra la la la*
> *Tra la la la*

When Birch finished the reading, Pip set a dozen mechanical butterflies to flight. She'd crafted each of them herself.

At the end of the service, Charlotte fell into step with Linnet. With arms linked, they meandered through the garden.

"Is *Sang d'Acier* at port for business or pleasure?" Charlotte asked.

Linnet laughed. "I believe he would answer that he refuses to do business without pleasure."

"That sounds about right."

"He's about to undertake a major voyage," Linnet said. "The *Perseus* will sail around the southern tip of the Americas to reach a place called California."

"By Athene," Charlotte said. "That will be an adventure."

"Indeed." Linnet's voice was soft.

Charlotte stopped, turning to face her friend. "You're going with him, aren't you?"

A blush crept into Linnet's cheeks. "Yes. I'm afraid I have finally surrendered to my pirate."

"This is no surrender," Charlotte said with a laugh. "You know that, and Lachance had better know it too if he plans to keep you."

Mischief flashed in Linnet's eyes. "You know me too well, kitten."

"Only what you've taught me," Charlotte replied.

"Would you like those lessons to continue?" Linnet asked, her gaze intent.

Charlotte frowned.

Linnet leaned close, whispering in a conspiratorial tone, "Come with us."

Charlotte laughed again. "You want me to be a pirate?"

"That's just a name," Linnet shrugged. "It means nothing. I'm inviting you to see the world."

"Does Lachance know about this invitation?" Charlotte asked.

"It was a condition of my agreeing to join him," Linnet replied. "That's an awfully long time to be aboard a ship without my dearest friend."

"Oh, Linnet." Charlotte hugged the other girl.

"It's just the truth," Linnet said with a smile. "And it wasn't a hard bargain to drive. Lachance is quite fond of you."

Charlotte's spirit had leapt at the notion of such an incredible adventure, but accepting Linnet's invitation wouldn't be without its costs.

"When must I give you an answer?" Charlotte asked.

"We sail in a week."

34.

LATER THAT EVENING as Charlotte sat gazing out her window at the lazy flow of the Mississippi, a knock sounded at her door. Smiling to herself and feeling her skin warm, Charlotte answered the door.

"Ashley!" Charlotte blurted out in surprise.

With a knowing smile, Ash said, "You were expecting Jack."

Charlotte averted her eyes. "I don't know what you're talking about."

"No need to dodge the question, Lottie," Ash told her. "You have my approval."

"How magnanimous of you, dear brother." Charlotte laughed. "Please come in."

She returned to her chair near the window, gesturing for Ash to sit in its nearby partner.

"You must have something to tell me," Charlotte said. "Given the surprise visit."

"Quite a lot to tell you, actually," Ash replied. "We reached terms today. I thought it would be in poor taste to bring it up at the memorial, but I very much wanted to tell you myself. Things will move quickly now."

"How exciting," Charlotte said, giving her brother a warm smile.

"They're saying Jefferson will return from France to lead the new government." He was breathless with excitement. "A new beginning, Lottie. It's incredible. All we'd hoped for."

"You want to be part of it." Charlotte admired the vivaciousness in her brother's voice. "I'm happy for you."

Ash's smile was full of bright hope, and Charlotte was sorry to see that fade as he waited for her to join in an enthusiasm she couldn't share.

"You don't," he said.

"No." Even though she'd known the answer, Charlotte was surprised to hear herself say it.

But she knew why.

Every night before she drifted into sleep, images filled her mind. The scene that had unfolded as Jack piloted the Scarab away from New York. The world was in flames, and it fell to the earth in pieces. Jack's mother screaming while Charlotte held her tightly, to keep her from harming herself. The sky that had been home to the Floating City had been emptied. That glory of Britannia lay strewn across the island of Manhattan, a ruin of smoke and fire.

She would never forget that sight, and to stay in this place, to join this new province, would be to forever tether her to that destruction.

"Then what will you do?" Ash sighed. "Go west? Or north on the Mississippi to join the river trade?"

"I'll let you know when I've decided."

Ash drew a long breath. "Would it make a difference if I told you I'm going to ask Meg to marry me?"

"That's wonderful!"

"Do you think she'll say yes?" he asked. She heard true fear in the question. Charlotte wondered if Ash would ever get over Meg's decision to join the Temple, leaving him behind.

"She will say yes," Charlotte told him.

"And?"

"And what?" Charlotte parroted.

"Will it make a difference?" Ash asked.

"No," Charlotte admitted with a bit of regret. "But it makes me very happy."

Sadness flitted over Ashley's face, but he smiled. "Thank you."

He cleared his throat, looking out the window.

For a moment, Charlotte thought he was resentful of her words, but then her brow furrowed. "There's something else, isn't there?"

"There is," Ash said. "It's about the prisoners."

Charlotte stiffened. "You mean it's about Coe."

"Yes." He met Charlotte's gaze. "They're moving the highest ranking prisoners to the Crucible."

With a scowl, Charlotte said, "The Crucible should have been destroyed."

Ash didn't argue.

"After they've been transferred," he went on, "they'll be sentenced. Those sentences will be carried out swiftly."

"I gave him my word, Ash," Charlotte said quietly. "We promised his life in exchange for information."

"The leadership has decided you and the others didn't have the authority to make that judgment," Ash said.

"Mother asked you to tell me, didn't she?" Charlotte gave him a jaded smile. "To ease the blow."

"He's the greatest of traitors." Ashley didn't answer her question. He didn't need to. "He cannot be suffered to live."

There was no sense in arguing.

"I understand," Charlotte told Ash.

"I know you're disappointed, Lottie," Ash said. "And I'm truly sorry for that."

"It's not your fault," Charlotte said, meaning it, but her mind had moved on to other things.

Much later, though, she was still gazing out her window when another knock sounded at her door.

"You're very late." Charlotte greeted Jack, who was leaning in the door frame.

"And I'm horribly sorry about it," Jack said. "May I come in, or am I banished?"

Charlotte laughed and pulled him into her room.

Later still, when Charlotte was folded in Jack's arms, she said. "Ash was here this evening."

"How is old Ash?" Jack asked. "He's so busy being important I barely see him."

"He's well," Charlotte said. "He's happy with the terms they've reached with the French."

"Good for him." Jack leaned over to kiss her ear.

"Are you happy with the terms?" She turned in his arms so she could look at him.

"To be honest, I'm not that concerned about it," Jack replied. "I hope that doesn't disappoint you."

"It doesn't," Charlotte said. "How do you feel about building a new government?"

Jack answered with a grin. "It all sounds rather tedious, doesn't it?"

"I suppose it does." Charlotte began to smile. "So tell me this: how do you feel about piracy?"

35.

WHEN CHARLOTTE AWOKE the next morning, her heart had made its decision. Six days would be enough time to make what arrangements were necessary, to say her good-byes. But before she could give Linnet her answer, Charlotte needed to speak with one more person.

In addition to her quarters in the Daedalus Tower, Aunt Io had kept a more spacious and more comfortable house in the Garden quadrant of New Orleans. Upon her passing, that house had become Birch's. He'd made it his residence, and he'd invited Pip, Scoff, and Grave to live there as well if they so wished. Each of them accepted his offer.

At first, Charlotte had found it odd to be in the same city as Grave but to see him with less and less frequency. She missed his odd company sometimes, but she was encouraged to see him building a life of his own.

When Charlotte knocked on their door that morning, Pip answered. "Charlotte!" Pip's braids were no longer green, but a deep violet.

"Good morning, Pip. Is Grave here?" Charlotte asked. "There's something I need to speak with him about."

"He's in his room."

After exchanging a few more pleasantries with Pip, Charlotte climbed the stairs to the second floor of the house. She gave a few light raps on Grave's door.

"Hello, Charlotte." Grave smiled at her.

"May I come in?"

"Yes." He moved aside so Charlotte could enter.

Grave's room was almost empty. He had a bed, though he didn't need to sleep, as well as a desk and a chair. Charlotte opted to stand.

"I have some news, Grave," Charlotte began. And she told him about Linnet's invitation and her decision to accept it. She was about to offer him a place aboard the ship, when Grave interrupted her.

"I want to stay with Birch, Pip, and Scoff," he said.

"You do?" Charlotte blurted out, taken aback by the firmness of his declaration.

"They can help me understand who I am, to find my place in this world. And I want to help Birch continue Aunt Io's work."

"If you ask me to stay, I will," Charlotte said. "I won't leave you here."

Grave shook his head. "You should go. You'll be happy with Linnet."

He paused, then asked, "Is Jack going?"

"Yes," Charlotte replied. "His mother is being well cared for here, so he doesn't feel obligated to stay."

She didn't add that Lady Winter's mind had been so addled by laudanum and the trauma of witnessing the Floating City's destruction that she no longer recognized her son. When they'd returned to New Orleans Jack had been wracked by guilt, blaming himself for his mother's condition. Linnet had been the one to persuade Jack otherwise. With Lord and Lady Ott's assistance, an apartment overlooking the gardens and a full-time caretaker had been arranged for Jack's mother. When Jack saw her now, he said she seemed at peace.

"Good." Grave smiled at Charlotte. "Jack makes you happy, too."

When she didn't respond, Grave asked, "Are you angry?"

"No," Charlotte said quickly. "I'm not angry, Grave. Not at all."

Surprised? Yes. But Charlotte couldn't even claim to be perplexed by Grave's choice. In many ways it was a relief, but not in the selfish way that meant Grave's staying absolved Charlotte's sense of responsibility for him. No. Her relief came from the knowledge that by exerting this autonomy, he was demonstrating his capacity to truly be part of the world, not subject to it or to any one person. It was choice itself that set Grave free.

But it wasn't as though he hadn't made choices before, she reminded herself. He'd chosen loyalty to Charlotte.

He'd fought for her, beside her, been subjected to torment because of her. Grave had made so many choices, all for Charlotte's benefit.

As much as Charlotte had felt responsible for Grave, he'd taken responsibility for her.

And now whatever symbiosis had existed between them was complete.

The time to part ways had arrived.

"I wish you well, Grave." Charlotte took his hands in hers. "Always."

"I wish you well, Charlotte," Grave said. He smiled in a way she'd never seen. A smile that touched his eyes and revealed part of his soul. Grave might never be fully human, but he'd become something close. Someone who made the world better for being in it.

With that thought, Charlotte's heart twisted at what she was about to ask of him.

"Grave, there's one more thing. A favor I need your help with."

"I'll help you, Charlotte," Grave said.

"Let me tell you what it is before you agree," Charlotte cautioned. "It might be too much."

"Nothing you ask of me will ever be too much."

36

AWN HAD BARELY kissed the horizon when Charlotte, Jack, and Grave walked to the far edge of the Quay.

Jack leaned close to Charlotte and said in a low voice, "Are you sure you want to do this?"

"Yes," she said. "And as I've told you before, you don't need to be here."

"And as I've told you before, I'm not letting you do this without me," Jack said.

Despite her forceful demeanor, Charlotte was relieved to hear him say it again. By the time the sun shone its full light on New Orleans, Charlotte and Jack would be aboard the *Perseus*, sailing into a new life. And this unpleasant, but necessary task would be behind them.

New Orleans's stockade had been erected in the Quay long ago, and no one could quite recall why that decision had been made. Obviously none of the quadrants fancied the idea of playing host to a prison, but mostly the city's residents joked that the location of the stockade guaranteed a short trip for the criminal element of the Quay to their cells. Like most of the structures in this part of the city, the stockade was dank. The guards posted on duty looked miserable and showed no interest in their work, which Charlotte was pleased to note, considering her aims.

The guards did straighten up when Jack presented his credentials. The younger Winter had become the source of grand tales, outlandish rumors, and wide-ranging speculation. Not only was he related to the blackguard Coe Winter, may he forever rot in Hades, but he had also shot down the most enemy aircraft during the siege of New Orleans only to undertake a secret rescue mission to the Floating City immediately thereafter.

Because of this, Jack's name could be very useful. As it was now.

"There are times you need to look a traitor in the eye," Jack was saying to the enraptured guards. "When I stare into my brother's face, I see the dark shadow of what I might have become."

One of the guards shivered.

"You're a good man, Lieutenant Winter," the other guard said. "A good man."

Once that rapport had been established, Jack had no trouble getting the guards to unlock Coe's cell for an unscheduled brotherly visit.

Coe sat on a pile of moldy straw. Heavy irons circled his wrists, chaining him to wall. His skin was sickly pale, and his cheeks hollowed. He didn't look up as they entered, but when Jack pulled the door shut with a clang, Coe lifted his head. When he recognized his visitors, his eyes brightened for a moment, but just as quickly, he slumped against the wall in resignation.

Jack kept watch at the door while Grave and Charlotte approached the prisoner.

"Come to see justice done?" His laugh was a croak.

"You could say that," Charlotte replied.

Coe's gaze moved to Grave. In the darkness, the boy's pale amber eyes took on an unearthly gleam.

"Will you tear me open as I had done to you?" Coe asked. "I suppose that's only fair. Though I'd much prefer it if you'd just break my neck."

"I promised to spare your life," Charlotte said. "And I'm going to keep my word."

Coe put on a rueful smile. "Do you think this is a way to torture me?"

"I have no interest in your torment," she said. "I'm here to clear my conscience."

Coe stared at her. He leaned forward as he grasped that she meant her words.

"Why would you free me?"

"I've already told you."

"They'll want *you* swinging from the Hanging Tree when they find me gone," Coe told her, shaking his head. "You'll be the traitor who dies in my stead."

"I'm no traitor." Charlotte nodded to Grave, who went forward and began to break the iron bonds. "Too much blood has been spilled. Nothing would be enough to slake the thirst of this beast of a war. No matter how many voices clamor to the contrary, your death would mean nothing. Sparing your life does. As I said, I'm keeping my word."

Coe stared at Grave and Charlotte in disbelief even as he rubbed his chafed wrists.

Charlotte had acted according to her conscience. Later that day Grave would deliver a letter to her mother in which Charlotte explained her actions and made it clear that Grave acted only according to her wishes; he was not to blame for Coe's escape.

Grave went to the back of the cell, where a single barred window sat high in the wall. He reached up and grabbed the bars. With one hard tug, the iron bars and their frame came free from the wall.

Coe scrambled to his feet. He approached the gateway to his freedom warily and looked up at the window, then back at Charlotte. "It's too high."

"Grave will help you."

Coe turned to Grave, who nodded.

Coe passed a hand over his eyes, as if trying to wake from a dream. But when he blinked at the dim interior of the cell, nothing had changed. "Why don't you hate me?" he asked Grave.

"Hate has no purpose," Grave said simply. Then he cupped his hands, so he could boost the prisoner up.

"I should thank you," Coe said to Charlotte.

She didn't answer.

He put one foot into Grave's hands. Grave easily lifted

him to the opening in the wall. Without a backward glance, Coe wriggled through the window and was gone.

Grave returned to Charlotte's side, frowning in the way he always did when he was worried about her. "It's done. Are you all right?"

"Yes, Grave." She smiled at him. "Everything is all right."

Epilogue

HARLOTTE LEANED AGAINST the rail, gazing at the lush jade forests of the coast. They would take the small boats ashore in an hour, more or less. Pirate time, Charlotte had learned, was an approximation. She quite liked that. Whenever they happened to get around to dragging the boats onto the beach, Charlotte would be introduced to yet another new place and quite possibly new people who would broaden her understanding of the world. Every small piece of that infinite puzzle was a gift.

"Daydreaming again?" Jack stood behind Charlotte, wrapping his arms around her and resting his chin on her shoulder. "Don't let the captain see you lazing about. He'll make you swab the deck."

"You do realize that you're the only person Lachance ever makes swab the deck," Charlotte replied.

"That can't be true."

"It is."

"Charlotte, Jack!" Linnet waved to them from the fore of the ship. "Stop lazing about and come help me ready the boats!"

"I told you so," Jack said to Charlotte.

"That is Linnet, not the captain," Charlotte said. "And readying the boats is not swabbing the deck."

"Unimportant details." Jack waved a dismissive hand.

Though she had yet to develop sea legs, Charlotte had decided she preferred the buffeting of the waves to that of the winds in the sky. She wouldn't have minded at all if she never again set foot in an aircraft. Breezes full of salt and sea never failed to enliven her senses, prompting dreams of adventure, of all that was possible. Endless blue in ever-changing shades. Infinite mystery. Boundless joy.